CW00543021

Beyond the Field

Ada, Volume 2

Morgan Nash

Published by Morgan Nash, 2023.

BEYOND THE FIELD

First edition. December 15, 2023.

Copyright © 2023 Morgan Nash.

ISBN: 979-8223784258

Written by Morgan Nash.

In loving memory of my dear sister FC,

Your spirit continues to shine bright in our hearts. Your presence in our lives was a gift, and the love and warmth you shared with all of us continue to inspire and guide us every day.

Though you left this world too soon, your memory lives on in the hearts of your two wonderful sons, who carry your legacy with grace and strength. They are a testament to the love and care you gave as their mother.

As I pen down these words, I know you are watching over us, smiling with the same kindness that defined you in life. You are missed beyond words, and your memory will forever be cherished.

With all my love,

MN

Chapter One

T he sun dipped low behind the horizon, casting a warm, golden glow over the small town of Ada. As the last rays of light faded, the football stadium came to life, its brilliant lights illuminating the field like a beacon in the encroaching twilight. I could feel the anticipation and excitement in the air, and it sent shivers down my spine as I stood at the edge of the stands.

"Come on, Jordy," Ana tugged at my arm, her eyes wide with excitement, "we don't wanna miss Ethan's big moment!"

I allowed myself to be pulled along by my little sister, feeling my heart rate quicken as we took our seats among the sea of people clad in Ada Cougars' colors. My hands were clammy, and I wiped them on my jeans, trying to slow my breathing and focus on the task at hand: cheering for my boyfriend, Ethan, as he played his first game of the season – the storied Battle of The Cats.

"Deep breaths, Jordan," I whispered to myself, watching as Ethan and the rest of the team stormed onto the field, their cleats digging into the grass, sending up a spray of earth in their wake. He looked so confident out there, every inch the star quarterback he was known to be. I couldn't help but admire the way his golden hair caught the stadium lights, his muscular build visible even from where I sat. But beneath that strong exterior, I knew he felt immense pressure to live up to his late father's legacy.

As the game began, the crowd erupted around me, cheers, boos, and jeers blended into a deafening roar. The scent of popcorn and hot dogs wafted through the air, mingling with the earthy aroma of freshly cut grass. I leaned forward in my seat, my eyes locked on Ethan as he moved with grace and agility across the field, his arm arcing through the air as he launched a perfect spiral.

"Go, Ethan!" I yelled, my voice barely audible above the din. But in my heart, my thoughts were a whirlwind of emotions: pride, love, and concern all swirled together. As much as I wanted to see him succeed on the field, I couldn't help but worry about the toll that football – and the town's obsession with it – was taking on our relationship.

"Jordy, are you even watching?" Ana asked, her eyes wide as she waved a foam finger in front of my face. "That was an amazing pass!"

"Of course, I am," I said, forcing a smile. But my mind was elsewhere, lost in memories of lazy summer days spent sketching in the park while Ethan was cooped up at practice or away at football camp. Moments that felt like stolen glimpses of the life we could have if things were different, if the weight of expectation wasn't looming so heavily over us both.

"Look!" Ana cried out suddenly, snapping me back to the present. "Ethan's going for the touchdown!"

My heart leapt into my throat as I jumped out of my seat and watched him sprint down the field, his movements fluid and powerful. It was like witnessing poetry in motion, and for that moment, all my worries melted away, replaced by pure, unadulterated joy.

But as the stadium lights cast long shadows on the field, the cheers of the crowd echoing in my ears, I knew that our story was far from over. And as the game hung in the balance, I couldn't shake the feeling that something big was about to happen – something that would change everything.

Sitting back down in the bleachers, I could feel the excitement buzzing all around me. The stadium was packed with people from both Ada and Ardmore, their faces painted in a mix of school colors, red and black for the Cougars and blue and gold for the Tigers. The rhythmic pounding of drums and the blaring of horns from the marching band matched the beat of my anxious heart.

"Battle of the Cats, ugh." I muttered to myself, listening to the crowd chant and cheer for their respective teams. From where I sat, the Ada Cougars looked strong, each player carved from muscle and determination. But across the field, the Ardmore Tigers were just as fierce, their eyes hungry for victory. The tension was thick in the air, only adding to the weight of anticipation on my chest. This game was more than just a football match; it was a battle for pride, legacy, and the hearts of two towns that lived and breathed this rivalry.

As the star quarterback, Ethan bore the brunt of that pressure. With every snap of the ball, I could see his father's legacy etched into the lines of his face, his broad shoulders carrying the hopes and dreams of an entire community. He moved with grace and power, a well-oiled machine built for speed and precision. His blond hair, slightly longer than he usually wore it, stuck to his forehead with sweat, and his warm brown eyes sparkled with intensity whenever he glanced in my direction.

I couldn't help but admire him, not just for the way he played, but also for the person he was trying so hard to become. It wasn't easy living in the shadow of a legend, especially one who had been taken from us too soon. But Ethan was determined to honor his father's memory, to find his own path through the storm of expectations that swirled around him like a tornado.

"Come on, Ethan! You got this!" I shouted, my voice joining the well of support that echoed through the stadium. My palms were slick with sweat, my heart pounding like a drum as I watched him weave through the sea of bodies on the field.

"Man, he's really giving it his all," remarked someone beside me, and I nodded in agreement. There was something mesmerizing about the way Ethan moved, a kind of grace that defied gravity itself.

"Yeah," I replied, my eyes never leaving him. "He's incredible, isn't he?"

As the clock ticked down on the second quarter bringing on halftime and the second half, the tension between the two teams only intensified. Every yard gained felt like a victory, each tackle a small battle won on the road to glory. And though I knew there could be only one winner, I couldn't shake the feeling that, no matter the outcome, this night would be etched into our memories for years to come – a reminder of the moments when dreams and reality collided, when love and longing danced together on a field bathed in moonlight and the roar of a thousand voices.

I decided to stretch my legs during halftime and wandered down to the concession stand. The bleachers vibrated above me, a living entity pulsing with the energy of the crowd. Everyone chatted while waiting for the teams to emerge from the halftime break, their voices melding into an electric hum that buzzed in my ears.

"Hey, Jordan!" Ana nudged me from my reverie, her eyes wide with excitement as she leaned closer. "Do you think we have a chance at winning? I mean, the Ardmore Tigers are pretty good."

"Of course, we do," I replied, trying to sound more confident than I felt. "Ethan's been working really hard. We've got this." Inside, though, I couldn't help but worry about the outcome. The pressure on Ethan was enormous, and I knew it weighed heavily on him.

"Man, Ethan has been amazing in the first half!" my friend Lucas exclaimed, a grin stretching across his face as he pointed toward the field. "He's like a freakin' gazelle out there!"

I smiled, feeling a warmth spread through my chest at the thought of Ethan gracefully dodging opponents. "Yeah, he's amazing.?"

"Totally!" Ana chimed in, her enthusiasm infectious. "He's going to lead us to victory!"

As the teams came out of the tunnel, and the game resumed, the stadium seemed to pulse with anticipation. The cheers grew louder, more intense, and I found myself lost in sensory overload. My heart raced in time with the pounding footsteps on the field, and the cool night air sent a shiver down my spine.

"Come on, Cougars!" shouted someone behind me, and I joined in the rallying cry. "Let's go, Ethan!"

"Did you see that play?" Lucas marveled, clapping me on the back. "Your boyfriend is unstoppable!"

"Thanks," I said, my cheeks flushing with pride and love for Ethan. "He really is something, isn't he?"

"Definitely," Ana agreed, her eyes never leaving the field. "You two make a great team."

"Thanks, sis." My heart swelled as I glanced at her, grateful for her support.

As the final minutes of the third quarter ticked away, I found myself holding my breath, each play feeling like a dance between victory and defeat. My pulse raced, my stomach twisted in knots, and I knew that this was more than just a game. It was a testament to our resilience, our strength, and our love – a tangible reminder of the power we held within our hearts.

"Jordan, are you okay?" Lucas asked, concern etched on his face as he peered at me. "You look kind of pale."

"I'm fine," I assured him, forcing a smile. "Just a little nervous."

"Hey, whatever happens, it's been one hell of a game," Ana reminded me, her hand resting reassuringly on my shoulder. "And no matter what, we're proud of Ethan and the rest of the team."

"Yeah," I whispered, my voice barely audible above the roar of the crowd. "I'm proud of him, too." I said as I tracked him on the field.

Ethan's eyes locked onto his target, and I knew that spark in his warm brown eyes meant he was about to make a move. He dropped back, scanning the field for an opening as the offensive line held back the Ardmore Tigers. The muscles in his legs tensed, ready to spring into action, and I found myself holding my breath, waiting for the moment he'd let the ball fly.

"Come on, Ethan," I whispered under my breath, clenching my fists tightly. "You got this."

With a sudden burst of speed, Ethan sprinted to the side, evading a tackle with grace and agility that left me in awe. His arm drew back, and then the football soared through the air, cutting a perfect path towards its intended receiver. As the ball landed securely in the wide receiver's hands, the crowd erupted into cheers, and my heart swelled with pride.

"Your boy is killing it out there!" Lucas shouted over the noise, giving me a friendly nudge.

I grinned, unable to take my eyes off Ethan as he jogged back to the huddle, focused and determined. "He always does."

The game continued, each play feeling like both an eternity and a heartbeat. As Ethan led the Cougars down the field, my thoughts drifted to the hours we'd spent together off the field – the stolen moments when it was just us, no expectations or pressure. I wondered if it was selfish of me to crave more of those moments when I knew how much this game meant to him.

"Jordan?" Ana's voice snapped me back to reality, her concerned gaze meeting mine. "You okay?"

"Yeah," I replied, forcing a smile. "Just thinking."

"About what?" she asked gently, her dark eyes searching mine.

"About...how much this means to Ethan," I admitted, watching as he called the next play, his voice strong and confident. "I want him to succeed, you know? But sometimes I worry about what it's doing to us."

"Hey," Ana said, placing a comforting hand on my arm. "You two are stronger than any game or championship. Just remember that."

As the final seconds of the quarter ticked away, I couldn't help but feel the weight of those words. My love for Ethan was fierce, unwavering – but so was his drive to win, to carry on his father's legacy. And as the crowd roared with anticipation, their eyes fixed on the field, my heart lay suspended between hope and fear, caught in the delicate balance between dreams and reality.

The tension in the stadium was palpable as the fourth quarter started. Everyone's eyes were glued to the field, including mine, following Ethan as he expertly maneuvered through the opposing team's defense. The score was too close for comfort, and I could practically feel the nerves radiating from the Ada Cougars' side of the bleachers.

"Come on, Ethan!" I shouted, clenching my fists tightly. "You got this!"

"Fourth down," Ana murmured beside me, her voice strained with anxiety. "They have to make this play."

As Ethan huddled with his teammates, I couldn't help but let my mind wander back to earlier that summer when he'd been away at football camp. I remember the long hours spent alone in my room, pouring my heart into my art while aching for his touch. It had been tough, but I knew how important it was for him to hone his skills, to become the best player he could be.

"Hey! Torres! You really think your boyfriend can pull this off?" A voice called out from behind us, causing my cheeks to flush with a mixture of embarrassment and anger.

"Shut up, Mike!" I shot back, without turning around. My focus remained on Ethan, watching as he wiped the sweat from his brow and nodded to his teammates with determination etched across his face.

"Ready, set, hike!" Ethan barked, as the ball was snapped into his hands. Time seemed to slow down as he scanned the field for an open receiver, the Ardmore Tigers closing in fast.

"Throw it!" I yelled, my heart pounding in my chest.

In that instant, memories of our shared experiences outside of football flashed before my eyes – the late-night conversations, the laughter, the whispered words of love, and the passionate kisses. Those moments were what kept us connected, despite the demands of the game and the pressure to live up to expectations.

Just as the opposing team's linebacker lunged for Ethan, he released the ball with a powerful throw. The stadium held its collective breath as we watched it sail through the air, spiraling towards its intended target.

"Come on, come on," I muttered under my breath, clenching my eyes shut as I silently prayed for a miracle.

"Did he catch it?" Ana asked, gripping my arm tightly, her voice barely audible above the deafening roar of the crowd.

I opened my eyes just in time to see one of our receivers leap into the air, his fingertips brushing against the ball before it slipped through his grasp and fell to the ground.

"No," I whispered, disappointment and dread settling in the pit of my stomach. "He didn't."

"Time's up," Ana murmured, her eyes filled with tears as she glanced at the scoreboard. "We lost."

"Hey," I said softly, placing a reassuring hand on her shoulder. "There's still a whole season ahead of us." But even as the words left my lips, I knew that the loss weighed heavily on Ethan's shoulders – and on mine as well.

As the stadium began to empty and the players trudged off the field, their heads hung low in defeat, I couldn't help but feel a sense of foreboding settle over me like a heavy cloak. What did this loss mean for Ethan? For us?

"Jordan?" Ana nudged me gently, her eyes searching mine for some semblance of reassurance.

"Let's go find Ethan," I said, forcing a smile onto my face even though my heart felt like it was breaking. "He needs us."

But as we made our way down the bleachers and towards the locker room, I couldn't shake the nagging feeling that something had changed – that the future we'd once imagined together was slipping through our fingers like sand through an hourglass. And I couldn't help but wonder if this was the beginning of the end.

Ethan walked out of the locker room with a dejected look on his face. My heart broke as I watched him walk towards me. I knew he had given this game his all, and the loss must have been crushing for him.

"Hey," I said softly, wrapping my arms around him. "You did great out there."

Ethan leaned into my embrace, his head resting against my shoulder. "I let everyone down," he muttered, his voice thick with emotion.

"You didn't let anyone down," I replied firmly. "You played your heart out, and that's all anyone could ask for."

Ethan pulled back, his eyes locking with mine. "What about you?" he asked, his voice barely above a whisper. "Did I let you down, too?"

"No," I replied, shaking my head. "You could never let me down."

Ethan leaned in, his lips meeting mine in a tender kiss. It was a small gesture, but it meant everything to me in that moment. And as we walked hand in hand out of the stadium, I knew that our love would be strong enough to weather any storm – even the crushing defeat of this game. .

The walk back to the car was quiet, the only sound being the shuffling of our feet on the pavement. I kept replaying the game in my mind, trying to find a moment where things could have gone differently. But the truth was, they had given it their all, and it just wasn't enough.

"Jordan," Ethan's voice broke through my thoughts, his hand finding mine as we walked. "I'm exhausted."

"I know, baby," I said, squeezing his hand. "Let's go home and rest."

As we got into the car and started driving, the silence between us was heavy. I knew that Ethan was still processing the loss, and I didn't want to push him to talk about it before he was ready.

As we pulled up to his house, Ethan let out a sigh. "I don't know what to do," he said, his voice filled with despair. "I feel like everything I've worked for is just slipping away."

I turned to him, taking his face in my hands. "You are so much more than just football, Ethan," I said firmly. "You are kind, and loving, and strong. And I know that you will find your way, no matter what happens on the field."

Ethan looked at me, his eyes searching mine for some kind of answer. "I just...I don't know if I can keep doing this," he said, his voice trembling. "The pressure, the expectations...it's all just so much."

I wrapped my arms around him, holding him close. "You don't have to do anything you don't want to, Ethan," I said softly. "I love you, no matter what."

Ethan leaned into my embrace, his body shaking with sobs. "I love you too," he whispered. "I just wish I knew what to do."

We stayed like that for a long time, holding each other close and offering each other comfort.

Chapter Two

The art room was a sanctuary of creativity, vibrant, free, and unfettered.. Canvases stood like soldiers against the walls, their surfaces adorned with a myriad of colors and ideas. Shelves overflowed with paint tubes and brushes, as if they were begging to be used. The scent of turpentine hung heavy in the air, mingling with the faint aroma of drying clay.

I stood before the mural, my heart swelling with an unspoken ache as I dipped my paintbrush into a pool of cerulean blue. The grand canvas before me held the whispers of my soul, painted in hues of sorrow and longing. It captured the turmoil of the summer, when the world had crumbled beneath my feet and left me gasping for air.

As I carefully traced the outline of a figure, memories of that fateful season washed over me. The sun-drenched days spent sketching by the lake, the evening breeze carrying echoes of laughter and secrets shared. And the loneliness of spending my days and nights without Ethan.

I had thrown myself into my art, desperate for an outlet to express the unhappiness that threatened to consume me. The mural had taken shape, born from the raw emotions that coursed through my veins. Each stroke of the brush was a tear shed, a silent scream, a plea for understanding. And as the mural grew, so did the weight of my heart.

"Jordan," a gentle voice called out, breaking me from my state of rumination. I turned to see Emily, her dark curls framing a warm smile that seemed to chase away the shadows.

"Hey, Em," I replied, forcing my lips to curve upwards as I stepped back from the mural. I watched her eyes scan the scene before her, taking in the vivid colors and haunting imagery.

"Wow," she breathed, her gaze lingering on the figure I'd just painted. "This is... incredible. I can feel the emotion radiating off of it."

"Thanks," I murmured, my fingers tightening around the paintbrush. The words felt hollow, as if they couldn't quite capture the depth of what I was trying to convey.

"Look, I need some inspiration for my next shoot. Mind if I snap a few shots of the artist at work?" she asked, her eyes flicking up to the mural.

"Only if you promise not to make me look too tragic," I joked, returning her smile. We shared a love of art that went beyond our individual mediums, a connection forged over late-night critiques and hours spent together in the art room.

"Deal," Emily agreed, raising her camera to her eye. As she snapped away, I turned back to my mural, my brush dancing across the canvas.

As we stood there, the art room came alive around us. The hum of conversation and laughter swirled through the air, a melody of shared passion. Paint splatters adorned the floor like abstract constellations, and sketches lay scattered about like discarded dreams.

I continued working on the mural, my eyes tracing the lines and shapes that formed a tapestry of grief. With each brushstroke, I felt a piece of myself bleed onto the canvas. And though I knew the journey was far from over, I couldn't help but feel a flicker of hope ignite within me.

For in that moment, surrounded by color, love and longing, I realized that perhaps – just perhaps – my art could be the key to healing the wounds etched upon my soul.

During the chaos that was the art room, I found solace. The room was a symphony of colors, textures, and emotions, each one vying for attention. Paints and brushes were scattered across every surface and canvases lined the walls, their surfaces adorned with the vivid dreams and aspirations of my peers. Amidst this maelstrom of creativity, I lost myself in the world of my mural.

In the background, I could sense the watchful gaze of Ms. Hernandez, our art teacher. She was a woman of few words, but her presence carried a quiet authority that demanded respect. With her graying hair pulled back in a tight bun and her glasses perched on the edge of her nose, she observed us with a discerning eye. She was a source of gentle guidance and support, always there to offer a kind word or helpful suggestion when we needed it most.

"Your use of color is quite striking, Jordan," Ms. Hernandez commented as she approached Emily and me. "But don't be afraid to push your boundaries. Sometimes, that's where the true magic lies."

"Thank you, Ms. Hernandez," I replied, my heart swelling with gratitude for her mentorship. "I'll keep that in mind."

As I picked up my brush to paint again, I felt a renewed sense of purpose. With my friends by my side and my passion for art burning brightly within me, I knew that I could overcome any obstacle that stood in my way. And though the road ahead was uncertain, one thing was clear: this journey was only just beginning.

I STOOD STARING AT the mural that had become my very heart and soul, I couldn't help but feel a pang of frustration. I could see the emotions I was trying to express so clearly in my mind but capturing them on canvas felt like trying to hold water in my hands. Every time I thought I'd found the perfect shade or stroke, it would slip through my fingers, leaving me grasping at air.

"Ugh, why won't you just cooperate?" I muttered under my breath, my knuckles turning white as I clenched my paintbrush. The canvas taunted me, daring me to try again and fail once more.

"Hey, Jordan, don't be too hard on yourself," Emily said softly, her voice pulling me from my thoughts. "You've got this. Just take a deep breath and trust your instincts."

I sighed, nodding my head even though I wasn't sure I believed her. The art room buzzed around us. The soft scratch of charcoal against paper melded with the gentle swish of brushes, creating a symphony of artistic expression that both comforted and challenged me.

The walls were adorned with splatters of paint, a testament to the passion and determination of those who had come before us. Sketches lay strewn across tables and easels, each one a window into another artist's soul.

"Jordan, did you hear about the new art exhibit coming to town?" Emily asked, trying to divert my attention from the mural for a moment.

"Uh-huh," I mumbled, my focus still locked onto the stubborn canvas.

"Maybe we should go check it out together," she suggested, her tone hopeful. "It might give you some inspiration."

"Maybe," I replied, not wanting to commit to anything right now.

"Look, I know you're frustrated," Emily said, her voice gentle but firm. "But remember, the best art comes from the heart. You just need to trust yourself, and the painting will follow."

I looked at her, searching for the confidence she seemed to have in me. And deep down, I knew she was right. It wasn't about technique or skill; it was about baring my soul and letting the world see who I was.

"Thanks, Emily," I whispered, feeling a small spark of determination ignite within me. "I'll keep trying."

"Good," she smiled, patting me on the shoulder before returning to her own work.

With renewed vigor, I turned back to my mural, determined to wrestle my emotions onto the canvas. It would be a battle, but one I was ready to fight. And as I dipped my brush into the paint once more, I felt the first stirrings of victory in my heart.

The scent of paint and turpentine filled my nostrils, a comforting reminder of the creative space I inhabited. My eyes scanned the mural before me, taking in each stroke of color as it melded together to form a cohesive image. I felt the weight of my brush in my hand, the bristles saturated with vibrant hues.

"Jordan," Emily's voice broke through my concentration, her tone full of excitement. "Look at this photograph I just developed. I think it could really help you with your mural."

I turned toward her, my curiosity piqued. She held up a glossy black-and-white print, showcasing a somber scene of an empty football field under a stormy sky. The contrast between the darkness and light was striking, mirroring the turmoil raging within me.

"Wow, that's amazing, Emily," I admitted, my awe genuine. "You managed to capture so much emotion in a single shot."

"Thanks! But I thought it might inspire you too. Look at how the shadows play across the field, creating this sense of tension and longing. You could incorporate something like that into your mural?" she suggested, her dark eyes sparkling with enthusiasm.

A sudden burst of inspiration hit me like a bolt of lightning. Emily was right; I could use the same interplay of light and shadow to enhance the emotional impact of my art. Emboldened by her suggestion, I returned my focus to the mural and began to add layers of depth and texture to the canvas.

"Emily, have you ever thought about what you want to do in the future? You know, within the art world?" I asked, my brush gliding effortlessly across the surface.

"Sometimes," she admitted, looking thoughtful. "I'd love to be a professional photographer, maybe even work for a magazine or travel the world capturing moments like these. What about you?"

"Me? I don't know," I sighed, my fingers trembling slightly as emotion threatened to overtake me. "All I've ever wanted is to create art that speaks to people, that helps them understand themselves and the world around them."

"Then that's what you'll do," she said with conviction. "You're already doing it, Jordan. You just need to keep pushing yourself, keep exploring new ideas and techniques. The sky's the limit for us."

"Thanks, Emily," I whispered, the corners of my mouth turning up in a grateful smile. "I'm glad we're in this together."

"Me too," she agreed, her own smile warm and genuine.

As I continued to work on the mural, Emily's words echoed in my mind, giving me the strength and determination I needed to push through my doubts and fears. And as the day wore on, the shadows on the canvas seemed to come alive, reflecting not only my emotions but also my dreams and aspirations for the future.

Near the end of the day, as I stood back to examine the mural, my fingers stained with paint and my heart pounding with a mix of excitement and apprehension, I felt a presence behind me. Turning around, I saw Ms. Hernandez, our art teacher, approaching Emily and me with a kind smile on her face.

"Jordan, Emily," she said softly, her dark eyes taking in the details of the mural with an experienced gaze. "I've been watching your progress, and I must say, you two have really captured something special here."

I couldn't help but feel a swell of pride at her words, yet my hands still shook, unsure of whether my emotions had truly found their way onto the canvas.

"Thank you, Ms. Hernandez," Emily replied, her voice filled with gratitude. "We've been trying to create something that speaks to both Jordan's experiences and the overall theme of loss and growth."

Ms. Hernandez nodded, her attention focused on the swirling colors that represented my inner turmoil and grief. "You've done an excellent job of conveying those feelings, Jordan," she said, turning to face me. "But I can sense that there's still something holding you back, something you're struggling to express."

I hesitated, unsure of how to put my thoughts into words. It felt like there was a wall within me, one that was preventing me from fully unleashing my emotions and laying them bare for all to see. But then I remembered Emily's suggestion, her encouragement to keep pushing myself, and I knew what needed to be done.

"Ms. Hernandez, I think I need to explore new techniques, maybe even venture into unfamiliar territory," I confessed, my voice shaking but determined. "I want to break through this barrier and create art that truly resonates with people."

She smiled warmly, her approval evident in her eyes. "That's a wonderful goal, Jordan. And I believe you have the talent and determination to achieve it. Remember, art is about pushing boundaries, constantly evolving, and growing. It's a journey that never ends."

"Thank you," I murmured, feeling a renewed sense of purpose.

As we continued to work on the mural, the dynamic between Emily, Ms. Hernandez, and me felt like a harmonious dance. Our shared passion for art created an environment that was both nurturing and challenging, one that allowed us to explore our talents and grow as artists.

Emily snapped photos of our progress, her camera clicking softly as she captured each new detail we added. Ms. Hernandez offered gentle guidance, her insights helping us refine our techniques and delve deeper into our emotions.

And as I stood before the mural, brush in hand, my heart full of longing and love for the craft that had become such an integral part of my life, I realized that this moment, surrounded by those who understood and supported my dreams, was one I would carry with me forever.

The brush trembled in my hand as I carefully added another stroke to the mural, the deep blues and fiery reds intertwining like the threads of a tapestry. I stepped back, squinting at the massive canvas before me, trying to make sense of the chaos that had taken over my thoughts.

"Hey Jordan, what's this part supposed to be?" Emily asked, pointing to a section where swirling colors seemed to clash against each other in a heated battle.

I hesitated, gathering my words before speaking. "It's... it's like the turmoil inside me, you know? All these emotions fighting for control. Losing my dad, falling in love with Ethan, finding my place in this world... It's all so overwhelming."

Emily nodded, her eyes scanning the mural with newfound understanding. "I can see it now. It's like the colors are emotions, battling for dominance. But there's beauty in the chaos too, like life itself."

"Exactly," I breathed out, grateful for her insight. "But sometimes I just wish I could find some peace within the storm, to quiet the noise and just... be."

"Maybe that's what you need to show in your art too," Emily suggested gently. "Find that small moment of calm in the midst of the chaos."

I stared at the mural, feeling both inspired and daunted by the idea. My grip on the paintbrush tightened, determination flooding through me as I began to work with renewed focus. I searched for the balance between chaos and tranquility, my brushstrokes growing more confident with each passing moment.

"Remember what Ms. Hernandez said," Emily reminded me, her voice full of encouragement. "It's about pushing boundaries and evolving. You've got this, Jordan."

"Thanks, Em," I responded, my heart swelling with gratitude for her support. "You always know how to help me find my way."

As I continued to work on the mural, my determination and resilience were tested with every stroke. The challenge of capturing my emotions on canvas was a constant battle, but I refused to let it defeat me. I would find that balance, that moment of peace in the chaos, and share it with the world through my art.

The hours passed, our laughter and conversation filling the art room as we worked side by side. And though the journey was far from over, as I stood there, paint-splattered and exhausted, I knew that I was one step closer to finding the harmony I so desperately sought. And I couldn't have done it without Emily and Ms. Hernandez by my side.

The sun dipped below the horizon, casting long shadows across the art room as I took a step back to assess my progress. I wiped the sweat from my brow with the back of my hand, leaving a streak of paint in its wake. My mural was slowly coming together, but it wasn't there just yet.

"Jordan," Emily said, her eyes scanning my artwork, "this is incredible. But you know, sometimes less is more."

I pondered her words, staring at the canvas that represented so much of me - my past, my present, and my future. The colors swirled together, both clashing and complementing each other, reflecting the turmoil within me.

"Maybe you're right, Em," I admitted, my voice barely audible above the hum of our shared thoughts. "But it's hard to find that balance, you know?"

"Of course, I do," she replied, giving my shoulder a reassuring squeeze. "But that's what makes this journey so rewarding - facing those challenges head-on and discovering your true potential."

As I leaned against the wall, my mind wandered to the path that lay ahead. My artistic journey had only just begun, and I knew there would be countless challenges to face. The world of art was vast and unyielding, filled with both beauty and pain. It was up to me to navigate that world, to push past my limits and find my place among the stars.

"Jordan, you okay?" Emily asked, snapping me out of my reverie.

"Yeah, I'm good," I reassured her with a small smile. "Just thinking about everything we've got ahead of us. It's exciting and terrifying all at once."

"Hey, that's what makes life worth living, right?" She grinned, her eyes sparkling with mischief. "Besides, we've got each other's backs. We'll face whatever comes our way together."

"Thanks, Em," I murmured, feeling a warmth spread through my chest at her unwavering support.

As I returned to my mural, I couldn't help but marvel at how far I'd come. My art had become an extension of my soul - a means to express the emotions that had been locked away for so long. Through the colors and shapes, I was able to share my story with the world, revealing both my strengths and vulnerabilities.

And as I added another stroke of paint, I knew that this journey was only just beginning. The road ahead might be filled with uncertainty, but one thing was for sure - no matter what obstacles I faced, I would continue to grow and evolve as an artist, and as a person.

The scent of oil paints and turpentine lingered in the air, a symphony of colors swirling around me as I dipped my brush into a deep, rich shade of blue. The canvas before me seemed to breathe with life, pulsating like a heartbeat beneath my fingertips as I lost myself in the dance of creation.

"Looks like you're really getting into it, man," Emily remarked, her voice lilting like a playful melody as she joined my side. Her eyes danced across the mural, taking in the vibrant hues and bold strokes that poured from my soul like a river of unspoken emotions.

"Thanks, Em," I replied in a whisper, as if speaking too loudly might shatter the fragile balance between reality and the world of color that enveloped me. "It's like...I can't even explain it. It's just flowing out of me, you know?"

"Like a river of dreams," she mused, her fingers tracing the curve of a crimson wave that rolled across the canvas. "And it's beautiful, Jordan. Really."

Her words filled me with a warmth that spread through my veins like molten gold, igniting a fire within me that fueled my brushstrokes. The canvas was both an open sky and a tempestuous ocean, a place where my dreams could soar, and my fears could be drowned beneath the relentless tide of creation.

"Hey, what do you think about adding some yellow here?" Emily suggested, gesturing to a corner of the mural that was calling out for a burst of sunlight. "You know, like a ray of hope breaking through the storm?"

"Great idea, Em," I agreed, my heart swelling with gratitude for her keen insights. Together, we painted a brilliant streak of gold that pierced the darkness like a beacon, guiding us towards a future yet unknown.

"Where do you think this journey will take us, Jordan?" Emily asked, her voice tinged with a wistful longing that mirrored my own.

"I don't know," I admitted, my eyes locked on the canvas as I searched for answers in the swirling tempest of color and emotion. "But wherever it leads, I'd love to get there pretty soon."

"Wouldn't we all?" she questioned, an infectious grin lighting up her face like a thousand suns.

We shared a laugh, the sound echoing off the walls of the art room like a joyous melody. The hours passed in a blur of color and movement, the canvas before us slowly transforming into a masterpiece that captured the essence of our souls.

I nodded, feeling a sense of peace settle over me like a warm blanket. The road ahead might be uncertain, but I knew that with Emily as my friend, I could face anything.

As we packed up our supplies and prepared to leave the art room behind, I felt a sense of accomplishment wash over me. My journey as an artist had only just begun, but I knew that every stroke of the brush, every drop of paint, would bring me closer to my true self.

And as I stepped out into the autumn air, I couldn't wait to find Ethan and face the world that was waiting for us- full of color and possibility, just waiting to be explored.

Chapter Three

The racket of laughter, excited chatter, and the occasional slamming locker filled the bustling school hallway. It was an orchestra of teenage energy that I found both invigorating and intimidating. The hum of fluorescent lights overhead mingled with the vibrant school banners lining the walls, creating a diversity of color and movement.

"Man, we gotta step it up," Ethan said, his voice cutting through the noise as he shook his head. "Losing to the Ardmore Lions was bad enough. We can't let it happen again."

I leaned against my locker, watching Ethan's face as Mason and Tyler nodded in agreement. His warm brown eyes sparkled with determination, and I felt a familiar surge of pride for my boyfriend – the star quarterback who carried the weight of our town's football legacy on his shoulders. But beneath the pride, there was also an undercurrent of worry for him.

"Definitely," Mason chimed in, his bright green eyes glinting with mischief. "Next game, we'll show them what we're made of."

"Damn right," Tyler agreed, his hazel eyes narrowing as if focusing on an invisible opponent. "There's no way we're letting them walk all over us again."

As their conversation unfolded, I tried to engage, but my mind kept drifting back to my sketchbook tucked away in my backpack. Each page contained a piece of me – dreams, fears, longings – all etched onto paper in charcoal and ink. While they talked strategy and plays, I couldn't help but wonder how my own life would play out; whether I'd be able to pursue my passion for art while still being the supportive boyfriend Ethan needed.

"Jordy," Ethan called, snapping me back to the present. "You okay?"

"Of course," I replied, forcing a smile past the knot of uncertainty in my chest. "You guys are unstoppable."

"Damn right we are," Tyler grinned, clapping Ethan on the shoulder.

As they continued their conversation, I allowed myself to be swept up in the moment. The hallway swirled around me like a storm, and I found solace in knowing that no matter what the future held, I would face it with my friends by my side.

Just as the first bell rang, the hallway erupted with students pouring through the hallways and into classrooms like water from a broken dam, filling the air with a palpable energy that was overwhelming. Amidst the chaos, I found myself wedged between Ethan, Mason, and Tyler, their voices blending as they dissected every detail of last weekend's football game.

"Man, that loss still stings," Mason said, shaking his head. "I can't believe we let those Ardmore Lions slip through our fingers like that."

"We'll make up for it in the next game," Ethan assured him, clenching his fists determinedly. "We're not going down without a fight."

"Hey guys!" Bella's voice cut through the din, her bright eyes sparkling with enthusiasm as she joined our circle. She slipped her arm around Mason's waist, resting her head on his shoulder. "What are we talking about?"

"Football, what else?" Tyler replied, rolling his eyes playfully.

"Ugh, you boys and your sports," Bella teased, sticking her tongue out at him before turning to me. "How about you, Jordan? Are you as obsessed with this stuff as they are?"

I chuckled, rubbing the back of my neck. "Not exactly. I'm more into art, as you know."

"Ah, that's right! The talented artist of the group," she said, giving me an encouraging smile. "Don't worry, Jordy. We love you even if you're not all about touchdowns and tackles."

"Thanks, Bella," I said, feeling a warmth spread through me at her words. It was nice to be reminded that I belonged, even if my passions lay elsewhere.

"Besides," Ethan added, slinging an arm around my shoulders, "we need someone to capture our glorious moments on the field, right?"

"Absolutely," I rolled my eyes, capturing my boyfriend's hand.

"Alright guys, let's get moving," Mason said, giving Bella a quick peck on the cheek. "We don't want to be late for class."

As we navigated the bustling hallway, I couldn't help but marvel at the ease with which we all interacted. Despite our differences and varied interests, we were a tight group that went beyond the typical high school cliques. And as we laughed and teased one another, I felt a sense of belonging that I knew would stay with me long after we walked across the graduation stage.

As I walked toward my first period class with Ethan by my side, the din of lockers slamming and the hurried footsteps of students rushing to their classes filled the air, adding to the sense of movement and activity in the hallway. I was momentarily distracted by the chaos around me, but my thoughts quickly returned to Ethan.

"Hey, you ready for history?" Tyler asked, snapping me out of my reverie.

"Uh, yeah," I responded, trying to regain focus.

As we walked together, I couldn't help but feel a pang of worry for Ethan. His football ambitions weighed heavily on his mind, and I knew it was eating away at him. He had confided in me that he was scared he wouldn't win another state championship, and I could see the fear lurking behind his warm brown eyes.

"Man, I really hope we can pull off a win next game," Ethan said, his voice thick with anxiety.

"Of course you will," I reassured him, giving his hand a gentle squeeze. "You guys are unstoppable."

Ethan smiled weakly, but I could tell he wasn't entirely convinced. The pressure of living up to his late father's legacy and the expectations of our football-obsessed town was immense, and I worried that it might become too much for him to bear.

"Thanks, Jordy," he murmured, leaning in to give me a brief, tender kiss.

"Anytime," I whispered, feeling a bittersweet mixture of love and concern wash over me.

As we continued down the hall, the vibrant energy of our surroundings heightened the intensity of my emotions. The sounds of laughter and excited chatter mingled with the scent of teenage hormones and stale cafeteria food, creating a sensory overload that only served to amplify my internal turmoil.

"Alright, let's do this," Mason said, clapping his hands together as we reached our classroom door. "Time to face the music."

"Good luck, guys," Bella chimed in, giving us all an encouraging smile.

"Thanks," we chorused, steeling ourselves for the challenges that awaited us both in and out of the classroom.

I took one last look at Ethan before stepping inside, my heart aching with a mixture of love, longing, and worry. I knew that our journey together was far from over, and as I faced the uncertainty of what lay ahead, I couldn't help but wonder if our love would be enough to conquer the obstacles that threatened to tear us apart.

First period drug on forever.

Mr. Johnson's monotone voice droned on and on, drilling facts and figures into our heads as if our lives depended on it. I glanced over at Mason, who was slumped in his seat, his eyes half-closed in boredom. It was obvious that his mind was elsewhere, lost in the world of football and the pressure to win.

As the minutes ticked by, I found myself growing more and more restless. The walls of the classroom were closing in on me, suffocating me with their dullness and monotony. I longed to escape, to run free and create something beautiful, something that would capture the essence of life and love and all the things that made it worth living.

Just when I thought I couldn't take it any longer, the bell rang, signaling the end of class. I practically bolted out of my seat, eager to put as much distance as possible between me and the prison of the classroom.

"Hey, Jordy," Mason called out, grabbing my arm. "You okay?"

"Yeah, I'm fine," I replied, trying to keep the desperation out of my voice. "Just ready to get out of here."

"Me too," Mason agreed, his eyes brightening with anticipation. "Let's go grab some lunch and find the group."

We made our way to the cafeteria, the chatter and laughter of our fellow students filling the air. As we stood in line, waiting for our turn to order, I couldn't help but marvel at the variety of people around us. There were jocks and nerds, cheerleaders and drama geeks, all united by the common goal of surviving high school.

"Hey guys, over here!" Tyler called out, waving us over to a table where Bella and Ethan were already seated.

As we settled into our seats, the conversation turned to the upcoming football game. Ethan practically vibrating with nervous energy, his eyes darting around the table as he tried to gauge our reactions.

"I don't know about you guys, but I'm feeling good about this game," Tyler said, his voice brimming with confidence. "We've got this in the bag."

"I hope you're right," Ethan muttered, his fingers drumming anxiously on the table.

Bella leaned over, placing a comforting hand on his arm. "Hey, you've got this. We all believe in you."

Ethan gave her a grateful smile, his face softening with emotion. "Thanks, Bella. I don't know what I'd do without you guys."

We all laughed, the tension in the air dissipating as we returned to our usual banter and teasing. It was moments like these, surrounded by the people I loved, that made high school bearable.

As we finished our lunch and prepared to head to our next class, Ethan pulled me aside. "Hey, I was thinking...do you want to come to practice with me after school? I could use some extra support."

"I'd love to but I have an appointment," I said, my heart swelling with love for him. "I can't miss it."

Ethan's face fell and he mumbled something under his breath. "It's okay," he said, masking his disappointment with a forced smile. "I understand."

"I'll make it up to you, I promise," I said, giving him a kiss on the cheek. "I'll be cheering you on from the sidelines in spirit."

Ethan's smile returned, his eyes shining with love and appreciation. "Thanks, Jordy. You're the best."

As we parted ways, I couldn't help but feel a twinge of guilt. I knew that Ethan needed my support now more than ever, and the thought of letting him down filled me with a sense of dread. But I also knew that I had other obligations, other responsibilities that needed my attention. I had a session today with my therapist, and I couldn't miss it.

The cacophony of lockers slamming and sneakers squeaking against the linoleum floor faded as I turned the corner, leaving Ethan and the others behind. Vibrant school banners lined the walls, a testament to Ada High's proud athletic history. The myriad of colors seemed to dance before my eyes, but as I made my way to my next class, my mind was consumed with thoughts of Ethan and the pressures he faced. I wondered if our love would be enough to sustain us through the challenges that lay ahead, or if we were destined to fall victim to the same forces that had torn so many high school sweethearts apart.

Only time would tell, I thought, as I took my seat and prepared to face the next round of mind-numbing lectures and tedious assignments. But no matter what the future held, one thing was certain: I would always love Ethan, with all my heart and soul.

"Hey, Jordan!" Olivia said as she took her seat. "Ready for Mr. Thompson's pop quiz?"

"Ugh, don't remind me," I groaned, forcing a smile. My mind couldn't help but drift back to Ethan.

"Everything okay? You seem a little...distracted," Olivia asked, her brow furrowed with concern.

"Ah, it's just...Ethan, you know?" I said, stifling a sigh. "I want to be there for him, but sometimes it feels like everyone in this town is watching us, waiting for him to mess up."

"Hey, listen," Olivia placed a comforting hand on my shoulder. "You're amazing, and so is Ethan. Together, you guys can handle anything that comes your way. Don't let what other people think get in the way of your relationship."

"Thanks, Olivia," I replied genuinely, grateful for her kind words. "It's just hard, you know? Football means everything here, and I don't want to be the reason he loses focus."

"Jordan, if there's one thing I know about you, it's that you're always there for the people you care about," she said, her voice firm. "You've got this. Now, let's go ace that quiz!"

As we settled in for Calculus, I took a deep breath and tried to push my doubts aside. Olivia was right – I had to be there for Ethan, no matter how tough things got. And I also had to be there for myself and my mental health. If we could just hold onto each other just maybe, we'd find a way to navigate the rough waters together.

"Alright," I said under my breath and gripping my pencil. "Let's go."

The bell rang, I stepped into the hallway filled with laughter, gossip, and the screech of sneakers on linoleum. I took a moment to soak in the sights around me – the vibrant school banners hanging from the ceiling, their colors a declaration of pride; the posters advertising various clubs, plastered on every available surface; and the ever-present throngs of students, each one trying to squeeze in as much socializing as possible before the next class began.

"Ethan! Jordan, wait up!" A chorus of high-pitched voices interrupted my thoughts. As I turned, I saw a group of giggling girls approach Ethan, who was walking beside me. They seemed oblivious to my presence, their eyes fixed on him with unbridled adoration.

"Hey, Ethan," one of them said, batting her eyelashes. "Great game last night, even though we didn't win. You were amazing out there."

"Thanks, Sarah," he replied, his tone polite but distant. I could tell that he was growing tired of the constant attention. Still, he gave them a warm smile, which only seemed to make their infatuation grow stronger.

"Um, so, do you think you'll be able to make it to our next cheer practice?" another girl asked, twirling a strand of her hair around her finger. "We've been working on some new moves, and we'd love your feedback."

"Sure, I'll try to stop by," Ethan said, shifting his backpack from one shoulder to the other. "I can't promise anything, though. Practice has been kicking my ass lately."

"Totally understand," she gushed, her face flushed with excitement. "Just let us know if you can make it. We'll be waiting."

As they walked away, still tittering amongst themselves, I felt a pang of annoyance at being so easily dismissed. It wasn't as if I was invisible, but to them, I might as well have been. I looked at Ethan, searching for some sign that he felt the same way, but his face remained impassive.

"Does it ever bother you?" I asked quietly, my voice barely audible over the din of the hallway. "All these people fawning over you, like you're some kind of god?"

He sighed. "Sometimes. But it's just part of the deal, you know? Football is everything in this town. If I want to play, I have to accept the attention that comes with it."

I nodded, understanding but still unsettled by the weight of being the star quarterback's boyfriend. As we continued down the hall, I took note of the familiar faces around me – classmates who had grown up alongside me, each of us molded by the same pressures and desires that defined our small corner of the world.

"Hey, Jordan," Mason called out, slapping me on the back as he fell into step beside us. "Ready for art class today? I heard we're working with pastels."

"Definitely," I smiled, grateful for the distraction from my thoughts. I was the teacher's aid in the beginning art class once a week and Mason had taken it this year. "I can't wait to see what you've got."

"Great," he said, grinning. "Just don't be too hard on me if it doesn't come naturally. We can't all be prodigies like you.."

As we laughed together, I felt a sense of kinship with my friends that went beyond simply sharing a class or a school. These were the people who knew me best, who understood the complex web of emotions and ambitions that drove me to create, to love, and to dream. And even as the world shifted beneath our feet, threatening to pull us apart, I knew that I could rely on them to help me find my footing once more.

"Hey, Ethan!" a girl from his chemistry class called out, her voice breathy and sweet as she sidled up to him. "Can you help me with my homework tonight? I'm just so lost."

"Sure thing," Ethan replied with an easy smile, the kind that made everyone feel like they were his best friend. But then he glanced at me and winked, a conspiratorial glint in his eye that only I could see. "Just don't tell Jordan. He gets jealous when I tutor other people."

"Very funny, Ethan," I said, trying not to let the hurt show in my voice. I schooled my face and watched the girl lollop away from us. This was a daily thing between us – how girls fawned over him while I faded into the background, just another face in the crowd. Deep down, it stung and it made all of my insecurities prickle. I knew I could never compete with Ethan's charm or popularity, and it felt like I would never be good enough for him.

"Relax, babe," Ethan whispered, leaning in close so that our cheeks brushed together. "You know you're the only one for me."

"Ugh, you two are so gross," Bella teased, rolling her eyes as we walked to class. "Save it for after school, will you?"

"Sorry, Bella," I said, laughing despite myself. "We'll try to keep our affection to a minimum."

"Good," she replied, smirking. "I've got enough distractions as it is."

As we turned the corner, I found myself lost in thought once more. The hallway buzzed with activity, students hurrying to their classes as snippets of conversation floated through the air. The energy was infectious, a heady mix of excitement and anticipation for the challenges and conflicts that lay ahead. But beneath the surface, I couldn't shake the nagging feeling that something wasn't quite right.

It was as if I was standing on the edge of a precipice, the ground shifting beneath my feet as I struggled to find my balance.

"Earth to Jordan," Mason said, snapping his fingers in front of my face. "You're zoning out again."

"Sorry," I mumbled, forcing myself to focus on the here and now. "Just got a lot on my mind, I guess."

"Hey, we all do," Tyler chimed in, clapping me on the shoulder. "But that's what friends are for, right? To help each other through the tough times."

"Definitely," I agreed, feeling a warm surge of gratitude for the people who had become my second family. "And speaking of tough times, we've got art class next. Wish Mason luck." I joked look around the group.

"Good luck, Mason!" Bella called out as we went our separate ways, her voice fading into the din of the bustling hallway. Mason groaned as he watched her walk away.

I couldn't help but smile at them, even as I struggled to shake the lingering sense of depression that hung over my head like a storm cloud, threatening to burst at any moment.

Helping out with the lower level art students was fun and the class passed by very quickly. After the class ended, I walked down the school hallway, feeling the familiar energy of students rushing to their classes. The hum of laughter and excited chatter filled the air, alongside the occasional locker slamming shut.

"Hey, Jordan!" called out Alex, one of my newer friends. He waved as he approached me, his artistic energy almost palpable. "Are you almost done with your mural?"

"Almost," I grinned, glad for his presence. His unique perspective on art had helped me grow as an artist, and our friendship had been a lifeline through some of my darker moments.

"Great! Let's get to it then," Alex said, leading the way. We wove through the crowded hallway, dodging backpacks and elbows with practiced ease. Before I entered the art room I saw Tyler, Mason, and Ethan heading down the hall to the locker room.

"Yo, Jordy!" Tyler shouted from across the hall, snapping me out of my thoughts. He jogged over, Mason and Ethan following closely behind. "You coming to watch us practice today? We're getting prepped to crush those McAlester Buffaloes." He said earnestly smacking my shoulder.

"Jordan can't come today. He has another appointment." Ethan replied quietly, his voice strained.

"Ah that sucks," Mason chimed in, his own grin infectious. "Will we see you after?"

"No. I need to catch up on school work, so my mom will just take me home." I said.

Tyler grinned widely, "Oooohhh that sounds like a boys night! We can take Ethan out and corrupt him without his boyfriend judging us." He laughed nudging Mason.

"Good luck with that," I teased, nudging Ethan gently. "Maybe you should go out with the boys."

"Hey now, don't encourage them," Bella scolded playfully, looping her arm through mine.

"True," I admitted, sharing a smile with her. We continued walking together, the sounds of the busy hallway surrounding us.

"Jordan, you'll come by tonight, right?" Ethan asked, his tone quiet and worried. "You're gonna have dinner with me?"

"I don't know," I replied, trying to sound more upbeat than I felt. "It's just...I'm a bit behind in my classes, you know? And I'm really needing a catch up night."

"I could come by yours," Ethan sighed, running a hand through his blond hair. Our eyes met, and for a moment, we shared an understanding that went beyond words.

I knew if Ethan came to my house tonight I wouldn't catch up on a single class. But I nodded anyway, not wanting to hurt his feelings.

After saying my goodbyes to the boys, I headed back to the art room. Inside, the walls were covered with vibrant paint and sketches, Alex already hard at work on his own project. He gave me a wave as I walked in, and then went back to mixing colors on his canvas.

I got to work on my mural right away. The hours flew by as I worked diligently on the mural. With every new brushstroke and dab of color, I felt more connected to the painting—my thoughts and emotions coming through in each line and swirl.

Finally, after what felt like ages, the mural was finished. It had taken me days of dedication and passion—and it showed in every single detail. I stepped back from the wall and smiled proudly at my creation—it was beautiful, just as I'd imagined it would be.

Emily snapped a few pictures before we cleaned up our supplies and headed out for school pick up together. As we walked down the hallway arm-in-arm she asked me about Ethan again—but this time something about her tone made me pause before answering her question.

"What is it, Em?" I asked, narrowing my eyes at her. I had known her long enough to pick up on any signs of trouble.

"It's nothing, Jordan," Emily replied, shaking her head. But I could tell she was lying.

"Come on," I insisted, stopping in the middle of the hallway. "What's going on?"

Emily hesitated for a moment before finally speaking. "I just don't think Ethan is good for you," she said, her voice barely above a whisper. "He's obsessed with football and this state championship, and you're always sacrificing your own happiness for his."

I felt a jolt of anger and defensiveness surge through me at her words. "That's not true," I snapped. "Ethan loves me and I love him. He's supportive of my art and my dreams."

"Is he?" Emily challenged, her eyes searching mine. "Or are you just telling yourself that because you don't want to face the truth?"

I opened my mouth to reply, but no words came out. She had hit a nerve, and I wasn't sure how to respond.

Emily sighed, her voice softening. "I just want you to be happy, Jordan. And from what I've seen, I don't think Ethan can give you that."

I didn't know what to say, so I just nodded and we continued walking in silence. But her words stayed with me, gnawing at the back of my mind like a persistent itch. Was I really sacrificing my own happiness for Ethan's? Was he as obsessed with football and his own dreams as Emily claimed? And most importantly, was our relationship as good as I thought it was?

I met my mom in front of the school. She was going to take me to my therapist appointment, and I was grateful for the distraction from my thoughts. On the drive over, I tried to push Emily's words out of my head, but they kept coming back, making me doubt my relationship with Ethan.

When we finally arrived at the therapist's office, I took a deep breath and squared my shoulders. I was determined to make the most of this session, and hopefully come out with some clarity on my relationship with Ethan.

I walked into the therapist's office with a sense of determination. I was ready to face my fears and doubts head-on, and I was determined to come out with a better understanding on how to make my relationship with Ethan healthier and happier.

The therapist asked a lot of questions, and I tried my best to answer them honestly. I talked about my feelings of loneliness and insecurity, and how I often felt like I was sacrificing my own happiness for Ethan's.

By the end of the session, I felt like a huge weight had been lifted off my shoulders. I had come to terms with the fact that my relationship with Ethan was not perfect, and that I needed to take more time for myself. I knew that I needed to make my own happiness a priority, and that I could no longer put my own dreams on the backburner.

I left the therapist's office feeling more confident and ready to take on the world. My mom drove me home, and I couldn't help but smile as I looked out the window. The future looked brighter now, and I was ready to take on any challenge that came my way.

Chapter Four

The moment I stepped into my room after therapy, I felt like a dam had burst inside me. It was as if everything I'd held back all these years came flooding out, filling me with determination and purpose. My fingers danced across the keyboard as I searched for information on the upcoming art exhibition in town. This wasn't just about signing up to attend; it was an affirmation of who I was and what I wanted to achieve.

My heart thudded with anticipation as my cursor hovered over the RSVP button, a feeling that could only be compared to standing at the edge of a cliff, ready to take a leap of faith. I clicked, and a tingling sensation washed over me, and I was filled with a giddiness I hadn't felt in a long time.

The doorbell chimed, pulling me back to reality. Ethan stood there, his broad smile matched by the warmth in his eyes. The sight of him always filled my chest with a sense of contentment, like coming home after a long day.

"Hey, babe," he greeted, stepping inside. "How was therapy?"

"Good," I said, feeling a swell of excitement rise within me. "I found out about this amazing art exhibition happening soon, and I signed up to attend!"

"Really? That's awesome, Jordan!" Ethan's enthusiasm was contagious, and I couldn't help but grin in response. "When is it?"

"Thanks, Ethan. It's on Thursday and Friday." I said quietly.

He nodded and our eyes locked "Are you going both nights?" He asked and I could see the challenge in his eyes.

"Yeah. I think it's important." I said confidently.

"You know that's when we're playing McAlester, right?" He asked.

My heart sank as Ethan reminded me of the game. I had forgotten all about it in my excitement for the art exhibition. For Ethan, the game was a big deal. I had promised to be there to cheer him on, but the thought of missing the art exhibition filled me with a sense of dread.

"I know," I said, trying to keep the disappointment out of my voice. "But this is something I really want to do."

Ethan's expression softened, and he stepped closer to me, his hand reaching for mine. "I understand, Jordan. And I support you. But I also need you there, cheering me on. It means a lot to me." He said leaning into me.

I pulled back from his embrace and looked into his eyes, and I knew he was right. He had always been there for me, supporting me in everything I did. And now it was my turn to do the same for him.

"You're right," I said, squeezing his hand. "I'll make it work. I'll go on Thursday to the art exhibition and I won't miss the game on Friday, okay?" Ethan's face lit up at my words, and he pulled me close, his lips meeting mine in a passionate kiss. As we separated, he looked at me with an intensity that made my heart race.

"Jordan, there's something I want to tell you," he said, his voice low and urgent.

I felt a flutter in my stomach, knowing that whatever he was going to say was going to be important. "What is it?"

"I love you," he said, his eyes never leaving mine. "I've loved you since the moment I met you." Tears welled up in my eyes as his words sank in, and I felt a warmth spreading through my chest.

"I love you too, Ethan," I said, my voice choked with emotion. "I've loved you for so long, and I want to be with you forever."

He pulled me close once again, holding me tightly as we swayed to some imaginary music. In that moment, nothing else mattered except the two of us, wrapped up in each other's embrace.

As we pulled away from each other, Ethan's eyes sparkled with mischief, and I knew that he had something up his sleeve. "You know, Jordan," he said, a grin spreading across his face. "I think we could make that art exhibition a little more interesting."

I raised an eyebrow, intrigued by what he meant. "What do you mean?"

He leaned in, his lips brushing against my ear. "I could come to the exhibition after practice on Thursday night." He said waggling his eyebrows.

I laughed. "Ethan, you're incorrigible!" I said, shaking my head in amusement. "But I like the way you think."

"Of course you do," he said with a wink. "I'm irresistible."

I rolled my eyes but couldn't help the smile that spread across my face. Ethan always knew how to make me laugh and forget about my worries. And in that moment, I was grateful for him and the love we shared.

"Come on," he said, taking my hand. "Let's get some food. I'm starving."

As we sat down for dinner, our conversation continued to flow effortlessly, punctuated by laughter and playful banter. We talked about everything from football practice to our shared dreams and aspirations. We didn't need grand gestures or declarations of love; it was in these simple moments that the strength of our connection truly shone.

Dinner came and went in a whirlwind, each bite of the home-cooked meal fading into insignificance beneath the weight of our shared connection. I could feel the unspoken words that hung between us, as if they were tangible threads weaving around our intertwined fingers. My family's laughter filled the air, their voices mingling with the warm aroma of garlic and spices.

"Jordan, honey, tell us more about this art exhibition you're going to," Mom asked, her eyes sparkling with curiosity.

"Sure, it's a showcase of local artists, and there are some pretty well-known names attending," I explained, feeling a surge of excitement at the prospect of being among such creative individuals.

My sister smiled, her eyes shining with interest. "That sounds amazing. You could take me with you?" she asked, and I could see the hope in her eyes.

"I don't know, Ana," I said, happy to have someone to share the experience with. "I think Ethan will come along on Thursday and on Friday I'll go to the game."

Ethan looked at me, his expression filled with pride and admiration. "It's going to be great, Jordan," he said, his voice filled with confidence.

I smiled back at him, feeling grateful for his unwavering support. "I agree."

After dinner Ethan and I went back to my room and I gathered my books to start tackling Calculus and History. I was so far behind. I settled on my bed and spread my things out, while Ethan sat below on the floor.

As the evening wore on, the glow of twilight slowly seeped through the curtains, casting the room in shades of indigo. Ethan's came and sat behind me on the bed, leaning over my shoulder and tugging at my waist.

"Ethan!" I chided, "I've got to focus on this."

He nuzzled his lips into my neck below my ear and began to kiss as he squeezed me into him. "But Jordan, I can help," he said, his voice soft and low in my ear.

I sighed and tried to ignore the sensations flooding my body. "No, you can't," I said firmly, my mind already racing ahead to all the tasks I had to finish.

But Ethan continued his gentle kisses, and I soon found myself melting into his embrace. I put my pencil down and turned around to face him, my heart already racing at the sight of his face.

He leaned in and captured my lips with his own, and I felt the world around us fade away as I gave in to the moment. All my worries melted away, and I was left with a feeling of pure contentment.

This was the feeling I wanted to keep forever.

Ethan and I stayed in that moment for what felt like an eternity, before I finally broke away and looked into his eyes. "I thought you wanted to help me with my work," I said, my voice soft and teasing.

Ethan smiled, his gaze never leaving mine. "I did," he said, his voice filled with emotion. "I'm trying to help right now." Ethan pulled me closer and prodded my lips with his tongue. I let out a soft gasp as I felt his warmth course through my body. His hand moved to the back of my neck, pulling me even deeper into him. His kiss intensified with every passing second, until I felt completely submerged in his embrace.

When he finally broke away, I opened my eyes and found myself gazing up at him, lost in the depths of his gaze. He brushed his thumb across my cheek, sending shivers down my spine as I leaned into him.

"I think it's time to get back to work," he said softly.

I smiled and nodded in agreement before reluctantly pulling away from him and resuming my studies on the bed. Ethan sat silently behind me, keeping a watchful eye over me while I worked through Calculus problems and History essays.

He never once interrupted or distracted me; instead, he offered encouraging words and offered advice when needed. It was reassuring to know that even if things got tough, Ethan would still be there for me.

I finished up my last paragraph for my history essay and turned to look at Ethan, he had fallen asleep. I put my books away and began to take my clothes off, getting ready to sleep. I smiled as I looked at him, his face peaceful in his slumber.

I kissed him softly on the forehead and whispered, "Ethan let's get under the covers." He moan and stirred quietly. His eyes fluttering open.

"What time is it?" He asked, his voice thick with sleep.

"It's late. But I'm all caught up and maybe you can stay the night?" I asked pulling my pants down.

He nodded, wiping his face and sitting up. "Let me text my mom and let her know that I'm sleeping over." He said pulling his phone out of his pocket. Ethan sent the text to his mom and stood up from the bed. He pulled his shirt off and I couldn't help but stare at his muscular body. He noticed my gaze and smiled, beginning to unbutton his pants.

My body reacted as he pulled his pants down and I noticed his boxers were half open giving me a glimpse of his manhood. He smiled and caught me looking, his eyes smoldering with heat.

"Jordan," he said with a smirk, "come here."

I could feel my heart racing as I shuffled towards him. I felt so vulnerable in that moment, as he reached out and pulled me into his arms. We kissed deeply, our tongues exploring each other with urgency. His hands traveled down my body, and I felt my skin tingle with electricity.

We broke away and looked into each other's eyes, the intensity of the moment palpable. I didn't want the moment to end, and I could feel the same desire mirrored in his gaze.

"Ethan," I said, my voice filled with emotion. "Let's get in bed."

He smiled, and nodded, and pulled his boxers off. I did the same and lifted the blankets and climbed under. Ethan climbed under the blanket and used his knees to push my thighs apart as he settled between my legs and put his hands under my lower back lifting my hips to pull me tight against him. I felt his stomach on my hard cock and his own pressing against my bottom as he kissed me deeply.

I broke the kiss and looked into his eyes, which were simmering with passion. I knew the answer, but I asked him anyway, "Do you want me?" I said with a small smile wiggling my butt on his dick.

He groaned and leaned into me whispering my mouth, "Fuck, yes." His eyes lingered on mine, a question. I nodded. He put his hand to his mouth and spit to use as lube. I nodded again, this time spitting on my own hand and using it for my hole. He guided himself inside me and I gasped as I felt him fill me up.

He started to move slowly at first, his thrusts gentle and slow. I moaned and moved in time with him, my head spinning as I felt his every thrust. We moved together, our hips in perfect rhythm as we sought out that sweet spot. I couldn't take my eyes off his perfect abs and chest and he thrust into me, every muscle straining.

Soon, our movements became more urgent and we both felt the edge of pleasure nearing. I clung to him, my nails dug into his back as I felt my orgasm building. Ethan increased his thrusts and I cried out in pleasure as I felt my orgasm wash over me. I heard Ethan moan as he followed me into bliss.

We lay panting in each other's arms, our bodies still intertwined with sweat. I felt so content and safe in his arms and as I drifted off to sleep.

THE NEXT MORNING WE got ready for school and our day ahead. School went by in a blur and I couldn't wait for the evening and going to the exhibition. I felt on edge and panicky all day thinking about the exhibition.

When end of school finally arrived, my anticipation bubbled like a crescendoing melody. I stood before the entrance of the art gallery, feeling as if I were on the edge of a precipice, ready to take flight. As I stepped inside, I was greeted by a kaleidoscope of colors, vibrant and diverse art pieces adorning the walls, each one a window into the artist's soul.

I couldn't help but feel a profound sense of awe in this sanctuary of creativity, knowing that I was surrounded by individuals who had dared to dream, just as I was beginning to do. Time seemed to slow as I wandered through the gallery, my eyes drinking in every brushstroke, every intricate detail. And in that moment, I knew I was exactly where I was meant to be.

I meandered through the gallery, each piece of art tugging at my soul like a siren's call, pulling me deeper into this world I'd only dared to dream about. The air was alive with murmurs of appreciation and admiration, punctuated by the clink of glasses and soft laughter.

Amidst the eclectic crowd, one figure stood out: Alex Reynolds. His presence was magnetic, drawing me closer as if caught in his orbit. His confident demeanor and effortless charm were evident in the way he engaged with others, his laughter like a melody in the air.

"Jordan! You made it!" Alex exclaimed, turning toward me with a warm smile that lit up the room. He looked stunning in a tailored blazer and dark jeans, an outfit that perfectly matched his unique blend of sophistication and playfulness.

"Hey, Alex," I greeted him, my voice betraying a hint of nerves. "This is really something, isn't it?"

"Isn't it just?" He gestured at the surrounding art with a graceful sweep of his hand. "There's so much talent here. It's inspiring."

Our conversation flowed effortlessly, centered on the art that surrounded us. I found myself entranced, not just by Alex's words but by the way he moved, the graceful gestures that punctuated his speech. Inside, I felt a strange swirl of emotions, a longing that dared not speak its name.

"Have you seen this piece over here?" Alex asked, tugging gently at my arm as he led me to a painting that captured the essence of a stormy sea. We stood side by side, our shoulders touching, as we gazed at the tempestuous waves.

"Wow," I breathed, unable to tear my eyes from the canvas. "The artist really managed to capture the raw power of the ocean, didn't they?"

"Definitely," Alex agreed, his eyes shining with appreciation. "It's a reminder of how small we are in the grand scheme of things, don't you think?"

"Absolutely," I murmured, my mind lost in thought. As I stood there with Alex, I couldn't help but wonder if this was what I'd been searching for – someone who could understand and appreciate my passion for art, who could challenge me to see the world through new eyes.

"Jordan?" Alex said softly, his hand on my arm bringing me back to the present.

"Sorry, I got lost in thought for a moment," I admitted, feeling my cheeks flush.

"No need to apologize," he reassured me, his smile never wavering. "That's what great art is supposed to do, after all."

As we continued to explore the exhibition, I couldn't shake the feeling that something significant was happening. With each stolen glance and shared insight, the connection between us grew stronger, the pull of our mutual passion drawing me closer to Alex like gravity.

But as much as I longed to surrender to the allure of this newfound connection, I couldn't ignore the love and loyalty that anchored me to Ethan. And so, I found myself caught between two worlds, my heart torn between the familiar comfort of home and the intoxicating promise of uncharted territory.

During my conversation with Alex, a distinguished figure caught my eye. Malcolm Foster, an accomplished artist I had long admired, was making his way towards us. My heart raced, my palms growing clammy as he approached. His attire was impeccable, a harmonious blend of artistic flair and sophistication.

"Jordan Torres?" Malcolm extended a hand, his voice rich and commanding. "I've heard about your work."

My stomach fluttered, and I took his hand, feeling the firm grip of someone who knew their way around a canvas. "Yes, that's me," I managed to say, my voice betraying my nerves.

"Your passion for art is evident," Malcolm observed, his eyes meeting mine with a keen curiosity. "Tell me about your process and inspirations."

My mind swirled with images of late-night sketches and half-finished canvases, but as I investigated Malcolm's encouraging gaze, my thoughts began to crystallize. "Well, my art is... it's like a language, you know? A way to express emotions and experiences words can't always capture."

Malcolm nodded, urging me on. "And what do you draw inspiration from?"

"From life, I guess," I said, feeling bolder with each word. "From the people around me, the places I've been, and the dreams I have. I'm inspired by the world's beauty and its struggles, too."

"Ah, the human experience." Malcolm smiled warmly, his eyes reflecting genuine interest. "There's no better muse than life itself."

"Exactly!" My voice grew more confident, fueled by the connection we were building. "Sometimes it feels like my art is the only way I can truly be myself, you know? It's the one place where I can break free from expectations and just... be."

"Bravo, Jordan." Malcolm clapped a hand on my shoulder, his approval sending a thrill down my spine. "You have the heart of an artist. Never lose sight of that."

"Thank you," I whispered, feeling a mixture of awe and gratitude wash over me.

As our conversation continued, I couldn't help but be drawn into the world of possibilities Malcolm painted with his words. Here was someone who understood my passion, my longing to create, and my desire to explore the depths of human emotion.

In those moments, as we exchanged ideas and shared our dreams, I felt as if I were standing on the edge of a great precipice, ready to leap into the unknown. And for the first time in my life, I didn't hesitate.

The soft jazz music playing in the background was like a lover's caress, its gentle notes whispering sweet nothings into the ears of everyone present. Each melody wrapped itself around the guests, infusing the gallery with an aura of sophistication and creative energy that seemed to vibrate through the air. As I stood there, surrounded by the breathtaking artwork, I couldn't help but feel as if I were floating on a cloud of inspiration, my heart soaring higher with each passing moment.

"Jordan," Malcolm said, drawing me out of my reverie. "I want you to meet someone. Come." He led me toward a small group of people, their laughter a welcome melody amidst the hum of conversation.

"Everyone, this is Jordan Torres, a talented artist I've had the pleasure of speaking with tonight." Malcolm introduced me with such warmth that I felt a blush creep up my cheeks. The group welcomed me with nods and smiles, and for a moment, I allowed myself to bask in their acceptance.

But just as I was beginning to lose myself in this new world, a familiar figure appeared at the edge of my vision. Ethan had arrived at the gallery, his tall frame standing out among the crowd. He hesitated near the entrance, his warm brown eyes scanning the room until they found me. I could see curiosity in his gaze, mixed with something else—perhaps insecurity?—as he took in the unfamiliar surroundings.

"Excuse me," I murmured to the group, my chest tightening with a sudden surge of longing. My heart belonged here, in this world of art and beauty, but it also belonged to Ethan, who had supported me through thick and thin. I needed to bridge the gap between these two parts of my life, to show Ethan that he could be a part of this world, too.

"Hey," I greeted him softly as I approached, my hand instinctively reaching for his. "You made it."

"Of course," Ethan replied, his voice tinged with the slightest hint of uncertainty. "Practice went a little long" He glanced around at the magnificent artwork that filled the gallery, his eyes wide with wonder. "This place is incredible, Jordan."

"Isn't it?" My heart swelled with pride as I led him through the gallery, eager to share my passion with him. It reminded me of camp when I had given him tour of the courtyard and all the sculptures, including my own. We paused before each piece, our fingers entwined as I explained the artist's vision and inspiration.

"Wow," Ethan breathed, his gaze locked on a particularly striking painting. "I never realized how much emotion could be captured in a single image." He turned to face me, his eyes shining with newfound understanding. "I can see why you're so drawn to this world, Jordan. It's... powerful."

"Thank you for being here, Ethan," I whispered, my voice thick with emotion. "This means everything to me."

"Always," he promised, pressing a tender kiss to my forehead.

I led him to another piece that I had seen with Alex earlier. I stood before the painting with Ethan, surrounded by the vivid colors

and haunting images that clung to the canvas. As Ethan looked at
the art. I thought about Alex and Malcolm and looked around to see
where they were.

As my eyes flickered between them and Ethan, I felt the weight
of my uncertainty settling upon me like an anchor. It was a strange
sensation, caught between two worlds that both seemed so alluring
and so daunting. My fingers absentmindedly traced patterns on my
palm, and I shifted my weight from one foot to the other, seeking
solace in the familiar motion.

"Hey, Jordan." Ethan's voice broke through my reverie as he
approached me, his determination evident in every step. "I don't
really get this, what is the artist saying here?"

I took a deep breath, my eyes lingering on the painting as I
tried to gather my thoughts. "I think it's about... loss," I said slowly,
my voice barely above a whisper. "The artist is trying to capture the
feeling of emptiness, of something missing. But at the same time,
there's this beauty to it, you know? The colors and the shapes and
the way they all come together... it's like a reminder that even in the
darkest moments, there's still something worth holding onto."

Ethan nodded thoughtfully, his eyes following my gaze. "I can
see that," he murmured, his hand finding mine again. "It's like...
everything is connected, in a way."

"Yes." I breathed out the word, feeling a sense of awe wash over
me. It was as if Ethan had summed up everything I'd been feeling,
everything that had been inside me the last few months. "That's
exactly it."

We stood there for a moment longer, lost in the painting's
depths, until Alex appeared at my elbow. "Jordan, I'm glad to see
you're enjoying the artwork," he said, his eyes crinkling with warmth.

"I am," I replied, a sense of gratitude flooding through me. "How
about you?"

"Oh my god I'm loving it." Alex gaze flickered between Ethan and me, his expression unreadable. "Hey Ethan?"

Ethan snapped out of his reverie looking between me and Alex. His eyes narrowed.

"Hey," Ethan said, his tone guarded. "What's up?"

"I was just wondering if you were enjoying yourself. It's a little different that what you're usually into I'm sure." Alex said smoothly, his eyes flickering with something that made my stomach lurch.

"Eh, I'm enjoying it," Ethan said, casting an incredulous look in my direction. "How do you know what I'm usually into? Do I know you? Who the fuck are you?" He challenged aggressively.

"Oh, um, I go to our school. I'm in Jordan's Art and Sculpture class." Alex's voice was silky smooth, but there was a hint of something dark lurking in his eyes. "So yeah, you probably don't know me, since you're a football god and all. I just wouldn't expect you to like an art exhibition."

Ethan nodded and sneered. "Yeah, well, maybe I have more depth than you think. Don't judge a book by its cover, right?"

"Right." Alex's voice was too smooth, too composed. "I just didn't want you to feel out of place, that's all." He said putting his hands out in front of him. "Of course, of course. I'm sorry, I didn't mean to offend. It's just... Jordan and I have been friends for a while, and I know how much this means to him."

"Okay, okay, guys." I stepped between them, my hands held up in a placating gesture. "Let's just take a deep breath and enjoy the art, okay? There's no need to get worked up."

But the tension lingered, thick and palpable, and I couldn't shake the feeling that something had shifted between the three of us. It was like a web of secrets and insecurities had woven itself around me, trapping me in its sticky tendrils. And as much as I tried to shake it off, I knew that it was only a matter of time before it consumed me whole.

Alex turned to me then, his eyes flickering with something that made my skin tingle. "Jordan, I wanted to talk to you about something. Do you have a minute?"

"Sure," I said, aware of Ethan's eyes on me as Alex led me away from him. "What's up?"

"It's about your art," Alex said, his voice low and secretive. "I've been thinking about it a lot lately, and... well, I have some ideas I think could really take it to the next level. If you're interested, that is."

"Really?" My heart quickened with excitement. Alex was an experienced artist, and if he thought he could help me improve, then I was all ears. "What kind of ideas?"

"Well, let's just say I have some connections in the art world. People who could get your work seen by the right people, you know? And I have some ideas for collaborations, too. I think we could create something really amazing together, Jordan."

I was practically vibrating with excitement by this point, my mind racing with possibilities. "That sounds incredible, Alex," I said, my voice breathless. "I would love to hear more about it."

"Good." Alex's eyes glinted with something that made me feel both exhilarated and uneasy

As soon as he was out of earshot, Ethan turned to me, his expression wary. "What was that about?" he asked.

"He wanted to talk about maybe doing a collab." I said, shaking my head. "And maybe getting my art before some people that could help me break into the gallery scene."

"I don't trust him," Ethan spat, his grip on my hand tightening. "I don't really want you talking to him."

I pulled my hand away from Ethan's grip and stepped back, feeling a sense of frustration welling up inside me. "What, you don't trust me to make my own decisions?" I asked, my voice rising with each word. "Alex is offering me an amazing opportunity, and you're just trying to hold me back because you're jealous."

"Jealous?" Ethan's eyes widened in disbelief. "I'm not jealous, Jordan. I just don't want you to get hurt. You don't know what kind of person he is, what kind of things he's involved in."

"And you do?" I challenged. "You barely know him, Ethan. You're just making assumptions based on nothing."

"I'm not making assumptions," Ethan said, his voice low and dangerous. "I have a feeling about him, Jordan. And I don't want you getting involved with someone who could hurt you."

I took a step forward, my anger bubbling over. "I can take care of myself, Ethan," I said, my voice trembling with emotion. "I don't need you trying to protect me like I'm some kind of fragile flower. And I don't need you telling me who I can and can't talk to."

Ethan looked taken aback by my outburst, his eyes flickering with something that I couldn't quite read. "Jordan, I'm sorry," he said, his voice softening. "I just... I care about you, okay? And I don't want anything to happen to you."

I let out a sigh, feeling some of the tension in my body dissipating. "I know you do, Ethan," I said, my voice gentle now. "And I appreciate that. But I need to make my own choices, even if they're not the ones you would make. Can you understand that?"

Ethan nodded slowly, his eyes still fixed on me. "Yeah, I understand," he said, his voice hoarse. "I'll try to be more supportive. I just... I don't want to lose you, Jordan."

"You won't," I said, stepping forward and wrapping my arms around him. "I'm not going anywhere. And besides, it's not like I'm going to run off and elope with Alex or anything." I laughed, trying to lighten the mood.

Ethan chuckled too, his arms encircling me tightly. "Well, you better not," he said, his voice low. "Because if you do, I might have to challenge him to a football game or something."

I grinned up at him, feeling a sense of warmth spreading through me. "I don't think Alex would stand a chance," I said, teasingly. "You're way too much of a tough guy for him."

Ethan rolled his eyes, but I could see the hint of a smile on his lips. "Yeah, well, just keep that in mind," he said, his hand tracing circles on my back. "I'm not going to let anyone mess with you, Jordan. Not if I can help it."

I leaned into him, feeling a sense of contentment settling over me. "Thanks, let's go look at some more art." I said pulling his hand to another area of the gallery.

We came to the center piece and Ethan let go of an audible gasp. "Wow. This is... Wow." He stumbled.

"Y-yeah," I stammered, trying to push the tension of our last few moments aside. "It really is." I said relaxing as I looked at the painting.

"Tell me about this," Ethan said, his voice filled with genuine interest. He gestured towards the painting, the colors swirling together in a mesmerizing dance. "Who painted this?"

"Her name is Mariana Santos," I replied, feeling a spark of confidence ignite within me. "She uses bold strokes and vibrant colors to express her emotions. Each piece tells a story, you know? Like a glimpse into her soul."

"Wow," Ethan murmured, his eyes locked on the painting as he took in every detail. "I never realized how much emotion could be captured in a single image." He turned to face me, his gaze searching mine. There was a hint of curiosity there, tinged with insecurity. "I can see why you're so drawn to this, Jordan. I can totally see you exhibiting like this in the future"

"Thank you for being here, Ethan," I whispered, my voice thick with emotion. "And I hope I get to do something like this someday."

"Always," he promised, pressing a tender kiss to my forehead. "And you will, I know it."

We continued exploring the gallery together, hand in hand, and I knew that we would find a way to navigate this new chapter in our lives—together.

As the night wore on, I found myself torn between my desire to delve deeper into the art world and my loyalty to Ethan. I wanted to share this passion with him, but I also understood that the unfamiliarity of it all might be overwhelming. It was a delicate balance, and I couldn't help but feel the weight of that responsibility resting heavily upon my shoulders.

On one hand, I was entranced by the art surrounding me, each piece igniting a fire within me that I couldn't ignore. But on the other hand, there was Ethan – my rock, my constant, the one person who understood me like no one else ever could.

"Jordan, are you okay?" Ethan's voice broke through my thoughts, his brow furrowed with concern. I turned to face him, my eyes searching for the words that were lodged in my throat.

"Y-yeah," I stammered, trying to put on a brave front. "It's just... this is my dream, and I don't want to lose you in it."

Ethan smiled gently, reaching out to squeeze my hand. "You won't lose me. I'm right here, ready to learn about all of this with you."

The hum of conversation and the scent of oil paint mingled in the air as I stood there, my heart pounding with a mixture of excitement and uncertainty. My gaze lingered on a particular painting, its bold colors and intricate brushstrokes telling a story that spoke to me on a visceral level. I could feel the artist's passion seeping through the canvas, their creative fire igniting something within me.

"Jordan," Malcolm's deep voice broke through my reverie, his eyes shining with approval. "You have an incredible talent for capturing the essence of life with your art." He leaned in closer, his words carrying the weight of experience. "I want you to put together a portfolio and submit it for consideration to be exhibited."

My heart skipped a beat as Malcolm's words sunk in. Me, exhibiting my art in a gallery? It was a dream I had held onto for years, but I had always been too afraid to pursue it. But now, with Malcolm's encouragement, I felt a surge of confidence building within me.

"Thank you," I said, my voice barely above a whisper. "I'll do it. I'll put together a portfolio and submit it."

Malcolm smiled, his eyes crinkling at the corners. "I knew you had it in you, Jordan. And I can't wait to see what you come up with."

I felt a sense of pride swelling within me as I turned to face Ethan, my eyes shining with excitement. "Did you hear that? Malcolm wants me to put together a portfolio!"

Ethan's face lit up with a smile, his hand squeezing mine. "That's amazing, Jordan! I'm so proud of you."

I could hear the genuine happiness in his voice, and it sent a wave of warmth through me. "Thank you," I said, leaning in to press a kiss to his cheek. "I couldn't have done it without you."

We stayed at the gallery for a while longer, soaking in the atmosphere and admiring the artwork. As we made our way back to Ethan's car, I felt a sense of contentment settle over me. It was a feeling that I had been searching for, a sense of belonging that I had been craving for so long. And now, with Ethan by my side and my art finally being recognized, I knew that I had found it.

Chapter Five

The late afternoon sun cast long, golden shadows across my garage as I stood amidst the creative chaos that had become my sanctuary. Paint-splattered floors, canvases in various stages of completion, and an array of brushes all sang a harmony of inspiration that only I could hear. My fingers were stained with colors that mirrored my thoughts, each hue a memory or emotion that I'd poured onto the canvas.

As I dipped my brush into a pool of vibrant red, the door creaked open, and Alex Reynolds stepped into the room. The moment he entered, it felt like the air crackled with electricity, and I couldn't help but feel a shiver run down my spine. He was one of those people who just "got" me, and our connection was undeniable from the moment we first met at school.

"Hey, Jordan," he said, his voice filled with warmth and familiarity. "Mind if I join you?"

"Of course not," I replied, trying to sound casual while my heart raced in my chest. I gestured towards an empty stool near one of my unfinished pieces. "Have a seat."

Alex made his way through the clutter, pausing for a moment to admire a half-finished painting that leaned against the wall. His eyes traced the lines and curves I'd carefully drawn, and I found myself holding my breath, waiting for his verdict. When he finally looked up, his eyes were shining with appreciation.

"Wow, this is incredible," he murmured, running a hand through his messy curls. "You've really captured something special here."

I felt a flush creep up my neck, and I ducked my head to hide my embarrassment. "Thanks," I mumbled, focusing on the canvas in front of me. My hands trembled as I tried to steady the brush.

"Seriously, though," Alex continued, taking a seat on the stool, "the way you use color and light is just... breathtaking."

As much as I wanted to believe his words, doubt gnawed at the edges of my confidence. The more recognition my art received, the more I struggled to balance my passion with my personal life. My relationship with Ethan was a fragile thing, much like the pastel chalks that lay scattered across my work table. I feared that one wrong move, one moment of selfish ambition, could shatter us both.

"Jordan," Alex said, a gentle note of concern in his voice. "Is everything okay?"

I blinked back the haze of my thoughts, forcing a smile onto my face. "Yeah, I'm fine," I lied, hoping he couldn't see through my facade. "Just lost in my own world, I guess."

"Hey, it happens to the best of us," he reassured me, his eyes warm and understanding. "That's the life of an artist, right?"

I chuckled softly, though the laughter felt hollow in my chest. "Yeah," I agreed, dipping my brush into a new shade of blue. "That's the life of an artist."

Staring at the canvas, I felt a chill run down my spine. I was being torn in two directions: one by my art and another by my heart. Each pulling me further and further away from each other, with no path to unite them. Alex stood beside me, his presence a reminder of the tension that I had in my life.

The sun had begun its descent, casting an orange hue across the room, but it wasn't enough to comfort me. The light streaming through the window illuminated the paint-splattered garage as I stood there, brush in hand, lost in thought as I surveyed the chaos of my creations. The air was thick with the potent aroma of oil paint and turpentine.

"Hey, Jordan," Alex said, sensing my mood and letting his lips curl up in an easy grin. "What are you thinking about?"

"I don't know. Everything," I replied, trying to keep my voice steady. "Just...trying to find answers, inspiration, anything, I guess."

"May I?" he asked, gesturing toward my paint brush.

"Sure," I said, handing him the brush and stepping aside to give him a better look.

Alex studied the piece for a moment before speaking again. He then moved the brush against the canvas adding to my painting in a way that took my breath away. The strokes were confident and deliberate, each one adding depth and dimension to the piece. I watched in awe as he worked, marveling at the way his movements seemed to flow effortlessly from his fingertips. It was as if he had a deep understanding of the piece, of what it needed to come to life.

As he finished, he stepped back and smiled, looking at me with a glimmer in his eye. "There," he said. "I think it's complete."

I stared at the painting, taking in the changes he had made. The colors were bolder, the lines more defined. The piece had an energy that it had been missing before. It was as if Alex had breathed a new life into it, and it was now something entirely different, something even more beautiful.

"Wow," I breathed, feeling a sense of pride and appreciation welling up inside of me. "Thank you, Alex. You're amazing."

He grinned, his eyes warm and sincere. "No, you are. You've got a gift, Jordan. Don't ever forget that."

I nodded, taking in his words and letting them sit with me. It was a reminder that I needed, a reminder of why I created, of what my art meant to me. And as I looked into his eyes, I realized that it was same for him. He had added a piece of his soul to my work, infusing my painting with reflections of his feelings. His strokes stood in juxtaposition to the things that I had been struggling with, of the things that I had been feeling. He was confident and brash and he knew exactly what he wanted to express with his art.

"I like the way you captured the movement here. It's so fluid, like you can almost feel the energy flowing through the painting." He said turning back to the painting.

"Thanks," I said, feeling a flush rise in my cheeks. "I've been experimenting with different techniques lately."

"Seems like it's paying off," Alex remarked, his eyes still on the canvas. "You know, I've been working on something too. I'd love to get your thoughts on it sometime."

"Of course," I agreed, my curiosity piqued. "I'd be happy to help."

As our conversation flowed, we moved from piece to piece, discussing our latest projects and artistic visions. We spoke freely, voices animated and full of passion, but beneath the surface, I could sense a tension building, an unspoken desire that threatened to consume us both.

"Your work has always intrigued me, Jordan," Alex confessed, his gaze locking onto mine. "There's something about the way you blend colors and textures – it's almost hypnotic."

"Thank you," I stammered, taken aback by the intensity of his words. "I – I try to let my emotions guide me, you know? To let the colors speak for themselves."

"Isn't that what art is all about?" Alex mused, moving closer to me. "Telling a story through color and form, allowing our deepest feelings to take shape on the canvas?"

"Exactly," I breathed, my heart racing as our eyes met once more. The heat between us was undeniable, growing stronger with each passing moment.

"Jordan, I –" Alex hesitated, his face inches from mine. "I've always admired your talent, your dedication to your craft."

"Alex," I whispered, feeling a shiver run down my spine. "I – I feel the same way about you. Your work...it's like nothing I've ever seen before."

For a long moment, we stood there, caught in the electric current that crackled between us, both of us lost in the raw intensity of our connection. And although neither of us dared to voice it, the unspoken longing that simmered just beneath the surface threatened to spill over and change everything.

He nodded and turned from me, stepping away with a regretful expression on his face. "I'm sorry," he murmured. "I forget myself sometimes. You're just really amazing Jordan. And your art is so captivating." The sunlight filtering through the paint-splattered windows cast a warm glow on Alex's face as he looked at other pieces in the room.

"Your use of light in this piece is just mesmerizing, Jordan," Alex said, his eyes tracing the lines of one of my summer pieces. "I can't help but feel drawn into the scene."

"Thanks, man," I replied, trying to keep my voice steady despite the growing tension between us. My thoughts raced, plagued by the reminder of my argument with Ethan and his distrust of Alex. The guilt and uncertainty weighed heavy on my heart, like wet clay waiting to be molded. I wished I could let go of these feelings and find some semblance of balance, but they clung to me like stubborn stains on my favorite shirt.

"Jordan, don't sell yourself short," Alex continued, bringing me back to the present moment. "You have an incredible gift, and I'm not just saying that because I'm your friend. Malcolm inviting you to put together a portfolio is a testament of that."

"I know," I murmured, forcing a smile onto my lips even though it felt as genuine as a knockoff designer bag. "I appreciate your support, really."

"Of course," he said, stepping closer and placing a hand on my shoulder. The warmth of his touch sent shivers down my spine, and I couldn't help but be reminded of the undeniable chemistry between us. "You know, if you ever need someone to talk to about all this, I'm here for you."

"Thanks," I whispered, my voice barely audible as our eyes locked once more, the air crackling with tension. In that moment, it felt like we were teetering on the edge of something monumental, something that could change everything.

"Jordan, I -" Alex hesitated, his fingers lightly squeezing my shoulder. "I just want you to know that I believe in you and your talent, no matter where this journey takes you."

"Thank you, Alex" I replied softly, feeling a mix of gratitude and longing wash over me. As much as I wanted to explore the connection between us, I knew I had to find a way to balance the different facets of my life before they threatened to tear me apart completely.

I felt a warmth spread throughout me as Alex's hand rested on my shoulder. Even though I was scared to admit it, I couldn't deny the magnetic connection between us. We had so much in common, united by our love for art that was both consuming and exhilarating.

"Sometimes, I worry that I'm not good enough," I admitted, opening to him about one of my deepest insecurities. "I mean, I love creating art, but what if I never reach the level of success everyone expects from me?"

"Jordan, you're extremely talented," Alex reassured me, his hazel eyes filled with sincerity. "But I get it. I feel the same way sometimes. Like, what if all this effort and sacrifice we put into our art is all for nothing?"

"Exactly." I nodded, relieved to know that I wasn't alone in my fears. It was comforting to find someone who understood the pressure I felt, someone who could see past the facades we often put up to hide our vulnerabilities.

"Hey," he said softly, his fingers gently brushing a stray curl away from my face. The touch was innocent, but it sent a shiver down my spine. "I get it. You're not alone in feeling this way. And besides, I've seen your work, and it's amazing."

"Thank you," I responded, my voice wavering slightly. The flirtatious undertone in our conversation was impossible to ignore any longer, and I found myself drowning in the depths of his gaze, feeling the heat rise to my cheeks.

"Is it getting hot in here, or is it just me?" Alex joked, fanning himself dramatically before letting out a light-hearted chuckle.

"Must be the creative energy in the room," I replied, playing along with his teasing while trying to keep my own feelings at bay. But deep down, I knew it had more to do with the undeniable chemistry between us than anything else.

"Speaking of creative energy," he said, shifting his weight closer to mine and our eyes meeting for what felt like the hundredth time that night. "I've been thinking about a collaboration. Our styles would mesh well together, don't you think?"

I nodded in agreement, feeling a thrill at the prospect of working alongside someone who understood me on such a profound level. But there was more to it than that – the idea of spending more time with Alex sent my heart racing, filling me with a mixture of excitement and trepidation.

"I think we should create a painting together," he continued, his voice low and inviting. "You can paint the dark and I'll paint the light."

My breath caught in my throat as I imagined us standing side-by-side, exploring our creative sides while falling further for each other in the process. It felt like a dream too good to be true, yet here it was right in front of me.

"Alright," I agreed cautiously, not wanting to seem too eager despite how badly I wanted this partnership to work out.

"Great!" Alex said with enthusiasm before adding quietly: "Just promise me one thing."

"What's that?" I asked curiously.

He looked deep into my eyes and smiled softly before saying: "Promise you won't break my heart."

My cheeks flushed at his words, both from embarrassment and from an indescribable emotion that overwhelmed me whenever we were together. Taking a deep breath to steady myself, I nodded and replied: "I promise."

As we continued to discuss our artistic visions for the collaboration, our body language grew more intimate. We leaned in closer, our fingers occasionally brushing against each other as we gestured excitedly, each touch sending a spark of electricity through me. Though I knew I should be focusing on our conversation, I found myself lost in his presence, captivated his eyes lit up when he spoke about his art.

"Jordan?" Alex's voice cut through the haze of my thoughts, causing me to blink and refocus on him.

"Sorry, I just... got a little lost in thought, I guess," I confessed, giving him a sheepish smile.

"Maybe we should take a break from all this art talk, huh?" he suggested, his eyes twinkling with mischief. "We don't want to burn out before we even get started."

"Sounds like a plan," I agreed, grateful for the reprieve but equally aware that I was walking a fine line between following my heart and staying true to my commitments. As much as I longed to explore the connection between Alex and me, I couldn't help but wonder what consequences might lie ahead if I allowed myself to fall any deeper.

But as we stood there during our creative chaos, the world around us faded away, leaving just the two of us and the electric energy that pulsed between us. The room felt charged with an energy that was palpable, and I found myself drawn to Alex like a moth to a flame.

I broke the silence and asked, "Do you want a coke or something?"

Alex's eyes lit up with amusement, and he grinned at me. "Sure, a coke sounds great. Thanks, Jordan."

I nodded and made my way to the mini-fridge, feeling a mix of relief and disappointment. Part of me had hoped that Alex would make a move, that we could explore the undeniable attraction between us. But another part of me knew that it was better to keep things professional, at least for now.

As I grabbed two cans of coke, I took a deep breath and reminded myself of my priorities. I had worked hard to get to this point in my career, and I couldn't risk jeopardizing it all for a fleeting romance. But at the same time, I couldn't help but wonder what might happen if I allowed myself to take a chance on love.

I returned to Alex, handing him a can of coke and settling back into our conversation. Though we kept things light, the tension between us was palpable, a living, breathing thing that refused to be ignored. As we continued to work, I found myself struggling to keep my focus where it belonged, constantly drawn back to the pull of Alex's gaze.

"Have you ever tried painting with your non-dominant hand?" Alex asked suddenly, his eyes fixated on one of my incomplete works.

"Can't say I have," I replied, intrigued by the suggestion. "Why do you ask?"

"Sometimes it helps to break free from the constraints our own habits put on us," he explained, his voice filled with the excitement of discovery. "It might be worth a shot."

"Alright," I agreed hesitantly, picking up a brush with my left hand as Alex watched intently. His nearness sent my heart racing, and I could feel the heat rising in my cheeks.

"Here, let me show you," he offered, stepping closer and guiding my hand gently. Our fingers intertwined as he helped me make a few bold strokes on the canvas, causing my breath to hitch at the unexpected intimacy. The line between collaboration and attraction seemed to blur with each passing moment.

"See? It's not so bad, is it?" Alex grinned, his eyes meeting mine for a heartbeat before returning to the canvas.

"Actually, it's kind of liberating," I admitted, continuing to experiment under his watchful gaze. My thoughts churned with uncertainty, torn between the exhilaration of exploring this new connection with Alex and the guilt of potentially betraying Ethan's trust.

"Hey, Jordan," Alex said softly, breaking through my internal turmoil. "You don't have to figure everything out right now. Just... allow yourself to be in the moment."

"Thanks, Alex," I whispered back, grateful for his understanding and the sense of freedom he seemed to instill in me. Together, we continued to push the boundaries of our artistic connection, challenging each other to reach new heights while the ghosts of my unfinished works stood witness to our blossoming relationship.

The sun dipped low in the sky, casting warm shadows that danced across the paint-splattered studio floor. Alex and I stood side by side, our brushes moving in sync as we added the finishing touches to our collaborative piece. The air between us crackled with an electric energy, unspoken words lingering just beneath the surface.

"Jordan, can I ask you something?" Alex's voice, barely above a whisper, drew me out of my reverie.

"Of course," I replied, pausing mid-stroke to meet his gaze.

"Do you ever feel like you're meant for more than this? More than what people see or expect from you?" His eyes were filled with a quiet intensity, mirroring the vulnerability laid bare on the canvas before us.

I hesitated, surprised by the depth of his question. A part of me longed to escape the confines of societal expectations, to chase after the dreams that burned within me – dreams that included my art and the connection I shared with Alex. But another part of me was anchored by my love for Ethan, the boy who had been my rock through so much heartache and loss.

"I... sometimes, yeah," I confessed, glancing away from Alex's probing stare. "But it's hard, you know? It's like I'm constantly being pulled in different directions, and I don't want to disappoint anyone."

"Especially Ethan, right?" Alex's voice held a note of understanding, but also something else – a hint of longing that made my heart ache.

"Exactly," I sighed. "He means the world to me, and I don't want to hurt him. But at the same time, I can't help but wonder if there's more out there for me." My thoughts drifted to the football games I'd attended with Ethan, cheering him on from the sidelines as he chased his own dreams. It seemed unfair that I couldn't fully pursue mine without feeling like I was betraying him.

"Jordan, you deserve to follow your heart, wherever it leads you," Alex said softly, his fingertips brushing against mine as he handed me a clean brush. "Life is too short to live within the confines of other people's expectations."

His words resonated within me, but they also sparked a fierce internal battle. My love for Ethan warred with my desire to explore the depths of my art and the connection I felt with Alex – a connection that threatened to consume me if I let it.

"Thank you, Alex," I whispered, my voice thick with emotion. "But I... I don't know what to do."

A tense silence settled over us, punctuated only by the faint rustling of paintbrushes against canvas. The weight of our unspoken feelings seemed to hang in the air, a palpable force that left me breathless and uncertain.

"Take your time, Jordan," Alex murmured, his hand coming to rest on my shoulder in a gesture of support. "No matter what you decide, I'll be here for you."

As the sun dipped below the horizon, casting the studio into darkness, I stood at the crossroads of my future – torn between the familiar comfort of my life with Ethan and the intoxicating allure of the unknown.

Chapter Six

The sun was slowly dipping in the sky as I nervously handed my battered leather portfolio over to Professor Malcolm Foster. He leafed through it with an appraising eye, scrutinizing every page like a father would observe his own offspring. My heart beat ferociously, and I felt a bead of sweat trickle down my forehead.

"Jordan," he murmured after a few moments, his voice calm yet compassionate. "You have a prodigious talent, son. Your artistry is nothing short of extraordinary."

"Thank you, Professor," I stammered, exhaling in relief. It was one thing for people near and dear to me to recognize my creativity, but it meant so much more coming from someone of Malcolm's caliber who had made it big in the art industry.

"I have an offer for you," he began, snapping the portfolio shut. "Would you be interested in meeting Marcus Harris? He has a prestigious gallery downtown."

"Marcus Harris?" I asked in disbelief, my stomach flipping with anticipation. His name resonated success and reputation throughout the art world. "Absolutely!"

"Excellent," he said warmly with a smile on his face. "I'll set up an appointment for you tomorrow then. All you need is your portfolio and try being yourself."

"Thank you so much Professor Foster," I gushed, unable to express how appreciative I was for this chance.

"Remember Jordan," he warned me sagely, his gaze intense, "the realm of art can be quite ruthless and cruel at times. Stay true to yourself and your craft no matter what."

I firmly nodded in agreement as I left his office, my head spinning with the opportunities that lay ahead.

The next day, I arrived at the Marcus Harris Art Gallery, clutching my portfolio tightly. My palms were sweaty, and my heart pounded in my chest as I stepped inside. The gallery's pristine white walls and meticulously arranged art pieces immediately struck me. It was a world away from the chaotic, colorful studio where I spent most of my days.

"Ah, Mr. Torres," a smooth voice greeted me, and I turned to see Marcus Harris himself. He was even more handsome in person, with striking features and an air of sophistication that made me feel small. "Professor Foster told me wonderful things about you."

"Thank you for agreeing to meet with me, Mr. Harris," I said, my voice barely above a whisper.

"Please," he grinned, gesturing for me to follow him further into the gallery. "Call me Marcus. Now, let's see what you've got."

As we walked, the sound of wine glasses clinking and murmured conversations filled the air. I couldn't help but wonder if I truly belonged here – in this world of opulence and refinement. But as I handed my portfolio to Marcus, I knew I had to try. This could be the opportunity of a lifetime, and I wasn't about to let it slip through my fingers.

As he looked over my portfolio I looked around his gallery, it loomed before me like a dream, its sterile white walls and meticulously arranged art pieces drawing me in despite the fear that gnawed at my insides. It was as if I had stepped into another world, where every brushstroke held a secret waiting to be discovered. The faint sound of wine glasses clinking and hushed conversations

brought me back to reality, reminding me that this was no dream –
it was an opportunity that could change my life forever.

"Jordan, I've been looking forward to meeting you. Malcolm's
told me all about your talent." He said still studying my portfolio.

"Thanks, Mr. Harris," I managed to say, feeling the weight of the
world on me. "I appreciate you taking the time to see my work."

"Please, call me Marcus," he insisted, looking into my eyes and
flashing a charming smile that made my heart race. "Now, let's get
through this portfolio and have a look around?"

As Marcus flipped through the pages of my artwork, I couldn't
help but feel exposed. Each piece was a part of me, a glimpse into the
deepest corners of my soul. And here I was, handing them over to a
man who held the key to my future in his hands.

"Your work is incredible, Jordan," Marcus said, admiration
shining in his eyes. "But there's one thing missing – exposure. You
need to be seen by the right people, and I can make that happen for
you."

His words stirred a whirlwind of emotions within me –
excitement, hope, and a nagging sense of doubt. This was everything
I'd ever wanted, but the price I would have to pay weighed heavily on
my conscience. Would I have to compromise my artistic integrity to
succeed in this world?

"Think about it," Marcus continued, his voice dripping with
promise. "I can take your career to heights you never imagined. All
you have to do is say yes."

My eyes scanned the gallery, taking in the breathtaking beauty of
the art pieces that adorned the walls. They were all so polished, so
perfect – and I couldn't help but wonder if my own creations would
lose their raw authenticity if I agreed to Marcus' terms.

"Can I think about it?" I asked, my voice wavering with
uncertainty. The sound of wine glasses clinking seemed to grow
louder, as if they were trying to drown out my doubts.

"Of course," Marcus replied, his smile never faltering. "Take all the time you need."

As he walked away, leaving me alone with my thoughts, I knew that I had a decision to make. Would I choose the path of fame and success, or would I stay true to myself and my art? The answer lay somewhere amidst the hushed conversations and the haunting beauty of the paintings that surrounded me, waiting for me to find it.

As I stood there, the pristine gallery mocked the chaos of my emotions. The crisp white walls and the perfectly arranged art pieces were a stark contrast to the turmoil that raged within me. My desire for recognition battled against my fear of compromising my artistic voice, and I felt torn between two worlds.

"Are you alright?" Marcus asked, his smooth voice cutting through my thoughts like a knife.

I looked over at him and forced a smile. "Yeah, just taking it all in."

"Good," he said, his eyes sparkling with interest. "Now, about my offer. I must be honest – there are certain conditions attached to it. But I truly believe that together, we can take your career to new heights."

"Conditions?" I echoed, feeling a knot tighten in my stomach. "What kind of conditions?"

"Nothing too drastic," Marcus assured me, his voice softening. "Just some minor adjustments to your style, perhaps. We need to cater to the tastes of our clientele, after all."

I stared at him, my heart pounding in my chest. Was this what success looked like? Sacrificing my artistic integrity for the sake of fitting into someone else's mold?

"Look, Jordan," Marcus said, placing a hand on my shoulder. "I know this might seem overwhelming, but trust me – the rewards will be worth it. Just think about it, okay?"

"Okay," I murmured, my mind racing as I tried to weigh the potential benefits and drawbacks of accepting his offer.

"Take your time," he said, giving me a reassuring pat on the back before walking away.

I wandered through the gallery, my footsteps echoing softly across the polished marble floors. Each piece of art seemed to call out to me, beckoning me closer with their vibrant colors, intricate details, and haunting beauty. And yet, amidst the elegance and opulence, I couldn't help but feel a sense of unease.

My eyes were drawn to a particular painting – one that captured the essence of my internal struggle. It depicted a figure standing at the crossroads, their face etched with uncertainty as they gazed into the unknown.

"Quite a powerful piece, isn't it?" Marcus' voice startled me.

"Y-yes," I stammered, feeling my cheeks flush with embarrassment. "It really speaks to me."

"Art has a way of doing that," he said, his tone gentle and understanding. "Listen, Jordan, I know my offer might seem daunting, but I truly believe in your talent. And sometimes, in order to grow, we have to take risks."

I nodded, my mind a whirlwind of conflicting emotions. But as I stared at the painting, I couldn't help but wonder – was I willing to risk everything for the sake of success? Or would I choose to remain true to myself, even if it meant missing out on the recognition I so desperately craved?

"Think about it," Marcus said softly, leaving me alone once more with my thoughts and the haunting beauty of the art around me.

As I stood in front of the artwork, I took a deep breath and tried to explain my worries to Marcus. "I'm not sure if I want to compromise my artistic vision," I said, looking him in the eye. "It feels like it would be too much of a challenge for me to know where to start."

"Jordan, I understand your concerns," Marcus said, his voice persuasive. "But think about all the doors that could open for you if you accept my offer. Opportunities like this don't come around often."

I shifted uncomfortably, feeling the weight of his words settle on my chest. He was right – opportunities like this were rare, especially for someone like me. But at what cost? My fingers traced the edge of a nearby sculpture, its cool marble a stark contrast to the warmth of my skin.

"Your art speaks volumes," Marcus continued, his tone softening. "You have an incredible gift, and you deserve to be recognized for it. But sometimes, we have to make sacrifices in order to reach our full potential."

I glanced around the gallery, taking in the hushed conversations of the patrons and the quiet clink of wine glasses. The atmosphere felt heavy with expectation, and I couldn't help but overhear snippets of chatter about my own work. There were gasps of admiration, but also whispers of critique - words that stung, even though I knew they came from a place of honest appraisal.

"Marcus, I..." My voice wavered, betraying the storm of emotions brewing beneath the surface. "I'm not even sure I know what I would be sacrificing. It's a difficult choice."

"Life is full of difficult choices," he replied, a knowing smile playing on his lips. "But that's what makes us who we are. And in the end, you have to decide what's more important to you – staying true to yourself or seizing the chance to share your talent with the world."

I took a deep breath, my heart thundering in my chest like the beat of a drum. All around me, the art seemed to pulse with life, each piece a testament to the dreams and sacrifices of its creator. And as I listened to the murmur of voices and the hum of anticipation, I knew what I had to do.

"Alright," I said, my voice firm despite the anxious flutter in my stomach. "I'll do it. I'll take the offer."

The moment the words left my lips, I felt an odd mix of elation and dread. Had I made the right choice? Would this decision bring me closer to my dreams, or would it cost me everything I held dear?

As I moved through the gallery, taking in the eloquent expressions of fellow artists, I couldn't shake the feeling that my path had been forever altered. But whether that change led to triumph or heartache remained to be seen.

My steps echoed softly against the pristine white floor as I wandered deeper into the gallery, my heart heavy with the decision I had just made. The weight of my ambition clashed with a newfound trepidation, and I couldn't help but wonder if fame would come at the cost of my artistic soul.

"Is it worth it?" I whispered to myself, my voice barely audible amidst the hushed conversations around me. "Can I really stay true to myself and still reach for the stars?"

As I stood there, lost in the depths of that my thoughts, I knew that no matter what happened, I couldn't let my dreams go. And with a newfound sense of resolve, I vowed to do anything to become the artist I dreamed of.

As I stood, mesmerized by the painting that seemed to dive into the depths of my soul, I felt a presence beside me. I glanced over and met the gaze of an older woman, her eyes shining with wisdom and experience. Her name was Isabella Sanchez, as I would soon learn. She wore her age gracefully, like a masterpiece adorned with the finest brushstrokes. Smiling warmly, she approached me.

"Beautiful piece, isn't it?" she asked in a voice that carried the melody of a thousand stories.

"Y-yeah," I stammered, caught off guard by her sudden appearance. "It's like...it knows me."

"Ah, yes," Isabella nodded knowingly. "Art has a way of speaking' to our souls, revealing' the struggles we often hide from the world."

I studied the painting again, my heart tightening with every stroke that danced across the canvas. It was as if the artist had captured the essence of my internal battle – the tension between ambition and authenticity.

"Tell me," Isabella said gently, "what is it you fear most about following' your dreams?"

I hesitated, unsure if I should confide in this stranger. But there was something about her, a sense of understanding that resonated within me. And so, I shared my thoughts, pouring out my fears like spilled paint on a blank canvas.

"Sometimes," I admitted, "I worry that chasing fame might change me. That it'll turn my art into something' hollow, just to please the masses."

Isabella listened intently, her eyes never leaving mine. When I finished, she exhaled slowly, her breath carrying a lifetime of experience.

"Many artists grapple with that same fear," she told me softly. "But remember, Jordan, at the end of the day, it's up to you to decide what path to take. You have the power to stay true to yourself and your craft."

"Thank you," I whispered, touched by her words. They felt like a gentle breeze on a sweltering summer day, soothing my troubled thoughts.

"Always remember," Isabella added with a knowing smile, "no matter how far you go or how high you rise, never lose sight of who you are. Your art is an extension of your soul, and as long as it remains pure, it'll continue to touch the hearts of those who experience it."

"Thank you," I repeated, my voice cracking with emotion. Her wisdom was a beacon, guiding me through the stormy seas of doubt and fear.

As Isabella walked away, leaving me to ponder her words, I realized that no matter what challenges lay ahead, I would remain anchored to my truth. And as I stood before that painting – a reflection of my own struggles – I knew that I had found the strength I needed to forge my own path, wherever it may lead.

Isabella's words echoed in my mind, like the distant notes of a familiar melody. I moved through the gallery, my eyes drawn to the eloquent expressions of fellow artists. Each piece seemed to capture the emotions swirling within me – longing, love, and an insatiable hunger to be seen and understood.

A painting of two football players caught my attention, their bodies entwined in a passionate embrace beneath the field lights. It reminded me of Ethan and the love we shared, which had blossomed amidst the societal expectations that threatened to keep us apart.

"Powerful piece, isn't it?" a voice said from behind me.

I turned to see an older woman, her eyes filled with the same longing that tugged at my heartstrings. "Yeah," I replied, my gaze lingering on the painting. "It reminds me of someone I love."

"Ah, love – the most powerful force in the universe," she mused with a wistful smile. "May you always hold onto it, no matter where life takes you."

"Thank you," I whispered, feeling a pang of longing for Ethan's comforting embrace. As I continued to explore the gallery, my thoughts drifted to the uncertain future that awaited me. I knew that my journey was only just beginning, and that the road ahead would be fraught with challenges. But with every brushstroke, every line and curve, I would remain true to myself and my art, navigating the path between ambition and authenticity.

And as I stepped into the unknown, I carried with me the love and wisdom of those who had touched my soul – their voices a guiding light in the darkest of nights.

Chapter Seven

The smell of oil, paint and turpentine filled the air as I stood beside Alex at our easels. He was a whirlwind of color, his brush sweeping across the canvas with confident strokes that captured the essence of the scene before us. It was mesmerizing to watch him work, the way he seemed to dance between the palette and the canvas, each stroke a bold declaration of his artistic vision.

"Hey, Jordan," he said, not even looking up from his painting. "You ever paint outdoors? There's something about the way the light changes that really brings a piece to life."

"Sometimes," I replied, watching the way his golden hair fell over his eyes as he leaned in closer to his work. "I usually stick to the studio, but maybe I should try it more often."

"Definitely," he grinned, flicking a stray brushstroke of blue onto the edge of my canvas. "Happy accidents, right?"

"Right," I laughed, stealing another glance at Alex as he dipped his brush into the swirling colors on his palette. Our styles were so different, yet somehow they seemed to merge effortlessly on the canvas. His free-spirited approach challenged me to push my own boundaries, to take risks I might have shied away from otherwise.

As we worked side by side, I couldn't help but feel a growing tension between us. It was a magnetic pull, an inexplicable force that made my heart race and my breath catch whenever our brushes accidentally touched. I wanted to reach out, to trace the curve of his cheekbone or the slope of his strong shoulders, but I held back, focusing instead on the image taking shape before me.

"Can I make a suggestion?" he asked, stepping back from his easel to study my progress.

"Sure," I nodded, eager for any insight that might help me tap into the wellspring of creativity that flowed so freely from Alex's brush.

"Try holding your brush like this," he demonstrated, adjusting the angle of his hand ever so slightly. "It'll give you a little more control over the finer details."

"Thanks," I said, trying out his technique and marveling at the difference it made in my work. "You're really good at this, you know?"

"Practice makes perfect," he shrugged, a hint of red creeping into his cheeks. "But you've got a real talent, Jordan. Don't ever doubt that."

As the afternoon sunlight streamed through the windows, casting a warm glow over our shoulders, I allowed myself to get lost in the rhythm of our brushes, the easy banter that flowed between us, and the irresistible pull of the connection that was growing stronger with every stolen glance. It was exhilarating, terrifying, and utterly unforgettable. And for one brief, shining moment, it felt as if time itself had stopped, leaving just the two of us, our art, and the unspoken promise of something more.

Sunlight dappled the art room floor, casting shadows that danced alongside the hum of creativity. Ms. Hernandez paced between rows of easels, her watchful gaze landing on each student in turn. When her eyes met mine, I quickly averted my gaze, focusing back on the canvas before me. Beside me, Alex's brush moved effortlessly across his own canvas. The colors seemed to melt together, a visual symphony that mirrored the growing connection between us.

"Hey, Jordan," Alex whispered, leaning towards me with an impish grin. "What do you think of adding a little more blue to your sky? It'll contrast nicely with the oranges and yellows."

I glanced at his suggestion, then back at him. "You sure? I don't want to overdo it."

"Trust me," he said, playfully nudging my shoulder. "Sometimes, taking risks pays off."

Ms. Hernandez approached us, her eyes shifting from one canvas to another. She lingered for a moment, sensing the shift in our dynamic. Her lips curved into a knowing smile as she continued down the row.

"Alright," I conceded, picking up the cerulean hue. As I added the color, I couldn't help but steal another glance at Alex. His eyes were focused on his work, but a subtle smile played on his lips. I found myself wondering what he was thinking, what lay beyond those deep emerald eyes.

"Wow, look at that," Alex teased, drawing me out of my reverie. "You really are a risk-taker, huh?"

"Only when I'm inspired," I retorted, smirking as I dabbed my brush into a pool of green paint.

"Speaking of inspiration," he said, his voice lowering to a conspiratorial whisper, "I've noticed you have a thing for football motifs. Is there something you're not telling me?"

My face flushed as I tried to find the right words. "Well, it's just... football has always been a part of my life. My dad was a huge fan, and I guess it sort of rubbed off on me."

"Ah, I see," Alex nodded, his gaze softening. "It's like a connection to your past, then."

"Something like that," I agreed, feeling both exposed and grateful for his understanding.

As our brushes continued to dance across the canvases, the air around us seemed to hum with energy. We were two artists, bound by shared passion and unspoken longing, navigating the delicate balance between societal expectations and the call of our hearts. And in that moment, surrounded by the colors and scents of creation, I couldn't help but feel that we were on the cusp of something truly beautiful.

A streak of sunlight spilled through the window, casting a warm glow on our intertwined shadows as they danced across the floor. The air was thick with the scent of oil paints and turpentine, punctuated by the soft rustle of brushes against canvas. I could feel my pulse quickening, each beat mirroring the steady rhythm of my brushstrokes.

"Hey, check this out," Alex said, nudging me gently with his elbow. "What do you think of these colors?"

I glanced over at his canvas, my breath catching in my throat as I took in the vibrant hues that seemed to leap off the page. They were bold, daring choices - a reflection of the artist himself. "I love it," I murmured, my voice barely audible above the hum of the fluorescent lights overhead. "It's amazing."

"Thanks," he replied, grinning as he dipped his brush into a pool of scarlet paint. "I was going for something a little different, you know? Pushing the boundaries."

As we continued to work side by side, our brushes occasionally touched, sending a jolt of electricity coursing through my veins. My heart raced, pounding out a staccato beat that echoed in my ears. Every touch felt like a secret shared between us, their meanings hidden beneath layers of paint and unspoken desire.

"Jordan," Alex whispered, leaning in closer until I could feel the warmth of his breath against my cheek. "Do you ever wonder what it would be like to just... let go? To break free from all the rules and expectations that bind us?"

His words resonated deep within me, stirring up long-buried feelings and desires. "All the time," I admitted, my voice trembling with emotion. "But it's not always easy, is it?"

"No, it's not," he agreed, his gaze never leaving mine. "But sometimes, I think it's worth the risk."

The atmosphere in the art room became charged with sexual energy, as if our very thoughts had infused the space around us with an electric current. The air crackled with anticipation, each brushstroke a silent declaration of longing and connection.

"Maybe you're right," I whispered, my eyes locked on his. "Maybe it is worth the risk."

And as our brushes continued to weave their magic across the canvas, I couldn't help but wonder what lay beyond the confines of that small, sun-drenched room - and if, perhaps, we were destined to find out together.

The sunlight filtering through the dusty windows lent a dreamlike quality to the art room, casting our easels in a warm glow. As Alex and I continued to paint side by side, our artistic collaboration began to take on a life of its own. I was amazed at how our styles seemed to merge on the canvas, as if two streams of consciousness had converged into one.

"Hey, try this," Alex suggested, handing me a palette knife. "Scrape it gently across the surface. It'll create an interesting texture."

I hesitated for a moment before following his lead, my hand trembling slightly as I guided the blade over the wet paint. To my surprise, the effect was mesmerizing, like waves crashing against the shore or leaves rustling in the wind.

"Wow," I breathed, my eyes widening with wonder. "That's incredible. Thank you."

Alex grinned, a mischievous glint in his eyes. "No problem. We're all about breaking boundaries here, right?"

I smiled back, feeling a strange sense of camaraderie with this boy who understood me on a level that few others did. As we continued to work, sharing ideas and techniques, I felt something within me begin to shift. It was as if I was being pushed to explore new artistic territories, to break free from the confines of my comfort zone.

"Have you ever tried mixing different mediums?" Alex asked, his voice soft and lilting. "Like incorporating ink or charcoal into your paintings?"

"I've thought about it," I admitted, my heart pounding in my chest. "But I've never really had the courage to try."

"Then let's do it together," he suggested, his eyes shining with excitement. "Who knows what we might create?"

As we experimented with new materials and techniques, I felt a burgeoning sense of freedom. The world around us seemed to fade away, leaving only the canvas and the connection that pulsed between us. It was as if we were explorers charting unmapped territory, discovering hidden truths about ourselves and each other.

"Jordan," Alex murmured, his voice barely audible over the soft swish of our brushes. "Do you ever feel like there's something more out there, just waiting for us to find it?"

"Sometimes," I confessed, my chest aching with longing. "But then reality comes crashing down, and I remember that there are rules and expectations we have to follow."

"Maybe," he said softly, his eyes locked on mine. "Or maybe, sometimes, we need to break those rules in order to truly find ourselves."

As we continued painting, my thoughts swirled like the colors on our canvas - a heady mix of hope, fear, and desire. And though I couldn't be certain what lay ahead, I knew that, together, Alex and I had the power to create something truly extraordinary.

The brushstrokes on the canvas danced like a visual symphony, each stroke a note in harmony with our voices. As we spoke, I felt a connection deepening between us, our words weaving together like the colors on our shared masterpiece.

"Wow, Jordan, it's like your brush has come alive," Alex said, admiration evident in his tone.

"Thanks," I murmured, feeling a warmth surge through me at his words.

As we painted, our conversation ebbed and flowed, our voices intermingling with the soft rustle of brushes against canvas. Our words were half-whispered confessions, dreams, and fears, borne aloft by the gentle rhythm of our movements.

"What do you think happens when we let go of all those expectations, Jordan? All those rules that society imposes on us?" Alex asked, his voice tinged with a wistful longing.

"Freedom, perhaps," I mused, my heart swelling with the possibilities. "But also uncertainty. It's a double-edged sword."

"Isn't that what makes life worth living, though?" Alex pressed, his eyes searching mine. "The risk, the thrill of chasing after what truly moves us?"

"Maybe," I admitted, my heart pounding in my chest. "But it can be terrifying too."

"Only if we face it alone," Alex said softly, his gaze never leaving mine.

Time seemed to stand still as we lost ourselves in the creative process, the room around us fading into a blur of color and sound. The connection between us grew stronger with each passing moment, an invisible thread that bound us together, transcending the boundaries of our art.

I couldn't help but wonder if this was what it truly meant to be free – not just from society's rules, but from the limitations we placed on ourselves. As the final brushstrokes settled onto the canvas, I knew that whatever lay ahead, Alex and I had created something special, a testament to the power of love, friendship, and the pursuit of one's own truth.

The soft hum of conversation that filled the art room seemed to fade into the background as we continued to work, our brushes dancing across the canvas in a flurry of color and movement. I could feel the eyes of our classmates on us, their curiosity piqued by the undeniable chemistry that crackled between Alex and me.

"Hey, Jordan," one of the other students called out, her voice pulling me back to reality. "What are you guys working on? It looks amazing."

"Thanks," I replied with a grin, my heart swelling with pride. "We're just... exploring something new together, I guess. Trying to push ourselves beyond our usual boundaries."

"Sounds fun," she said, her eyes darting between me and Alex before returning to her own easel. "Keep up the good work."

I could see the others exchanging glances with each other, their whispers barely audible over the rhythmic strokes of our brushes. It was as if they knew, on some level, that what was unfolding between Alex and me was more than just a simple collaboration. It was a journey of self-discovery, a shared experience that transcended the realm of art and touched upon something deeper, something infinitely more profound.

"Isn't it strange," Alex mused, his voice barely audible amidst the subdued chatter, "how sometimes, when you least expect it, someone comes into your life and changes everything?"

"Life has a way of surprising us," I agreed, my gaze flickering to meet his for a moment before returning to our masterpiece. "But maybe that's part of the beauty of it all – the unpredictability, the endless possibilities."

"True," he said, his fingers brushing against mine as we reached for the same shade of blue, sending a shiver down my spine. "And sometimes, those surprises make you question everything you thought you knew about yourself."

"Like what you really want in life," I whispered, my heart aching with a longing I couldn't quite put into words.

"Exactly," he murmured, his eyes locking onto mine once more. "And who you're meant to share it with."

The sun had begun to dip below the horizon, casting a warm, golden glow over the room as we finally stepped back from our canvases, our breaths catching in our throats at the sight that greeted us. Our collaborative masterpiece had taken shape before our very eyes – a breathtaking fusion of our individual styles and techniques, a visual representation of the connection that had blossomed between us.

"Wow," I breathed, my hand reaching out to touch the still-wet paint, as if to reassure myself that it was real. "We did it."

"Together," Alex echoed softly, his fingers intertwining with mine as we stood side by side, gazing upon the fruits of our labor. "Together, we created something truly extraordinary."

As the day ended, I couldn't help but feel a sense of wistful nostalgia for the moments that had led us to this point – the laughter, the tears, the endless nights spent dreaming of a world beyond the confines of our small town. But most of all, I felt grateful for the unexpected gift that life had bestowed upon me: the chance to explore the depths of my own heart, hand in hand with someone who understood me like no one else ever could.

Chapter Eight

The familiar scent of Ethan's bedroom wrapped around me like a warm embrace. Soft, golden light spilled from the desk lamp onto his worn football posters and trophies that lined the shelves. The room felt cozy and intimate, each carefully chosen item a testament to his passions and memories.

"Man, this year has been insane," Ethan said, running a hand through his slightly long blond hair. He flopped down on the bed, his muscular body sinking into the plush mattress, and patted the space next to him.

I settled beside him, our bodies naturally gravitating towards each other. "Tell me about it," I replied, my fingers tracing the pattern of the quilt beneath us. "At least we've had some good times, though."

"Definitely," he agreed, his warm brown eyes meeting mine. Our conversations always flowed effortlessly.

"Remember when I tried to teach you to paint?" I asked, grinning at the thought of Ethan covered in more paint than the canvas.

"Hey, I wasn't that bad!" he protested, but the smile tugging at his lips betrayed his amusement. "And what about the time I taught you how to throw a perfect spiral?"

"Okay, I'll admit that was pretty fun," I conceded, remembering the feel of the football in my hands and the thrill of watching it sail through the air.

Ethan pulled me closer, his arm wrapping around my waist as we continued reminiscing. The sense of comfort and familiarity that enveloped us only deepened the connection we'd forged over the years. As we talked, I couldn't help but think about how lucky I was to have found someone who understood me so completely, despite our seemingly opposite interests. In those moments, with our hearts beating in unison, it felt as if nothing could ever tear us apart.

The milky light of dusk filtered through the blinds, casting golden stripes across Ethan's bedroom. The soft glow illuminated his football trophies lined up on the shelves, while the scent of recently blown-out candles hung in the air. A sense of warmth and coziness enveloped us as we lay on his bed, our fingers intertwined.

"So, have you thought about which college you want to go to?" I asked tentatively, breaking the comfortable silence between us.

Ethan sighed, running his free hand through his slightly mussed hair. "I don't know, Jordan. There are so many options, and all of them come with their own set of challenges."

"Tell me about it," I said, my mind drifting to my own dreams of attending art school. "But no matter where we end up, at least we'll both be pursuing what we're passionate about, right?"

"Right," he agreed hesitantly, a shadow crossing his face. "It's just... sometimes I worry that our different paths might pull us apart, you know? Football is such a huge part of my life, and I know how important your art is to you."

I could feel the tension building between us as we both acknowledged the elephant in the room. The thought of losing each other weighed heavily on our hearts, filling the air with a bittersweet heaviness.

"Hey," I said softly, brushing a stray lock of hair from his forehead. "We've made it this far, haven't we? We can work through anything, as long as we do it together."

Ethan's eyes met mine, his warm brown gaze filled with love and uncertainty. "I want to believe that, Jordan. But what if our dreams take us to opposite ends of the country? Or what if football consumes so much of my time that I can't be there for you like I want to be?"

His words echoed my own unspoken fears, and a lump formed in my throat. "Ethan, the truth is, I don't have all the answers. But I do know that we're stronger together than we are apart. And when two people love each other as much as we do, they find a way to make it work."

The air in the room seemed to shift, becoming charged with emotion. I could feel the warmth of Ethan's breath against my cheek, our heartbeats pounding in sync as we lay there, lost in thought.

"Jordan," he whispered, his voice cracking with vulnerability. "I'm scared."

"Me too," I admitted, swallowing hard against the tears threatening to spill over. "But we can face whatever comes our way, as long as we hold on to each other."

In that moment, surrounded by the soft glow of fading sunlight and the intimate closeness of our bodies, it felt like everything might just be okay. We had each other, and for now, that was enough.

"Remember when we met at summer camp?" I asked, a smile playing at the corner of my lips as I recalled the memory. "You were on the practice field and I was there on the sidelines, sketching away."

Ethan chuckled, his chest shaking beneath my hand. "I'll never forget that day. You were so focused on your drawing that you didn't even notice me running straight toward you."

My face flushed at the memory, but I couldn't help grinning. "Well, I certainly noticed when you crashed into me. My sketchbook went flying, and I thought my heart was going to leap out of my chest."

"Mine too," he admitted, turning to face me, the golden light making his brown eyes shimmer. "But it was worth it because that's how we met."

Our gazes locked, and I felt the familiar flutter in my stomach whenever I looked into Ethan's eyes. I traced my thumb along his jawline, marveling at the strong lines and angles of his face. The weight of our shared fears seemed to lift for a moment, replaced by the warmth of our connection. As if drawn by an invisible force, our lips met in a tender, unhurried kiss.

"Jordan," Ethan whispered when we finally broke apart, his breath ghosting across my lips. "No matter what happens, promise me that we won't let our dreams tear us apart."

My chest tightened at his words, but I managed to nod. "I promise."

"Good," he murmured, his voice thick with emotion. Then, as if to seal our vow, he leaned in for another kiss, this one deeper and more urgent than before.

As our bodies pressed closer, the heat between us flared, fueled by the intensity of our feelings. Our hands roamed each other's skin, seeking out every curve and contour, driven by a desire to be as close as possible.

"God, I love you," Ethan breathed against my neck, his words sending shivers down my spine. "I'm so afraid of losing you."

"I'm scared too," I confessed, feeling the tremble in my own voice. "But I believe in us, Ethan. We'll find a way to make this work."

I cuddled into his body, breathing in his scent. Lost in thought, I stared at the ceiling as I laid in the crook of his arm. The lines and curves of his face danced above my sight line. My fingertips traced the soft skin of his upper arm, lingering on the delicate hair of his armpit.

"That tickles, Jordan," Ethan said softly, turning his body and capturing my lips. "You're so gorgeous." He said nipping at my bottom lip.

"Thanks," I replied, feeling the warmth of his praise wash over me. But even as a smile tugged at my lips, I could sense a shadow falling over our conversation like a dark cloud.

"Jordan, I want to be honest with you," Ethan began hesitantly, rolling over on top of me. He nudged my legs apart and settled between them propped above my chest and looking into my eyes. "I'm worried about how your art career might impact us. You know how important football is to me, and I don't want either of our dreams to suffer because we're trying to make this relationship work."

His words cut through me like a knife, leaving me breathless with pain. I knew that he was right - our paths were diverging, and it was only a matter of time before we faced the harsh reality of our situation. But I couldn't help the frustration that bubbled up within me, a fierce desire to prove that I could have both love and art, no matter the obstacles.

"Shouldn't we at least try?" I asked, my voice strained with emotion. "I know it won't be easy, but I refuse to give up without a fight. Don't you think our love is worth that?"

Ethan sighed heavily, his brown eyes filled with a mix of love and concern. "Of course it's worth it, Jordan. But I also don't want us to hold each other back. College scouts are already looking at me, and I can't afford any distractions if I'm going to get a scholarship. And your art... it deserves every chance to thrive."

"Football has been your life for as long as I've known you," I said quietly, my fingers tightening around my sketchbook. "I don't want to be the one who holds you back from achieving everything you're capable of. But my art is just as important to me, Ethan. It's who I am."

"I know, Jordan," he replied, his voice thick with emotion. He reached over and grabbed my hand, intertwining our fingers. "And I don't want to stand in the way of your dreams either. Maybe we can find a way to make it work... somehow."

His eyes were locked on mine, and I could see the determination burning in them. He was as afraid of losing me as I was of losing him. Despite our fears and the challenges we faced, neither of us was willing to let go of what we shared. Meeting his eyes and holding my gaze was like looking into a mirror that reflected our hearts.

"Let's promise each other," I whispered, putting my hand behind his neck and pulling his forehead to mine. "No matter what happens, we'll always fight for our dreams and our love."

With a nod and a determined look in his eyes, Ethan agreed, sealing our vow with a quick kiss.

As I looked into Ethan's eyes, the intensity of our connection seemed to deepen. Our hands still intertwined, his thumb gently brushed over my knuckles, sending shivers down my spine. I couldn't help but become lost in his warm brown gaze.

"Can I kiss you?" he asked softly, his voice barely audible as if he was afraid to break the fragile moment we shared.

"Please," I whispered, leaning in ever so slightly.

Our lips met, and it felt as though everything else had fallen away. The world outside his bedroom ceased to exist, leaving only us and the love that bound us together. It was a gentle kiss at first, tentative, as if we were exploring new territory. But as the passion built between us, the kiss became more urgent, more desperate.

I could feel the heat radiating from his body, and I longed to be even closer. My free hand reached up to tangle in his blond hair, pulling him towards me until there was no space left between us. His arms wrapped around me, holding me firmly against his solid chest. The feeling of his strong heartbeat against my own was exhilarating, making my pulse race in response.

Ethan broke away, gasping for breath, his eyes filled with desire. "Jordan," he murmured, his voice thick with emotion. "I—"

"Shh," I hushed him, pressing a finger to his lips. We didn't need words right now; our bodies would do the talking.

His hands roamed over my back, tracing the contours of my muscles before settling on my hips. I could feel the tension in them, the silent plea for reassurance that we were both okay, that this was what we both wanted. In response, I leaned in and captured his lips once more, pouring all my love and longing into the kiss.

The sound of our ragged breathing filled the room, punctuated by the occasional soft moan or sigh. I felt as though I was floating, lost in a sea of sensations, unable to tell where my body ended and Ethan's began. The intensity threatened to consume me, but I welcomed it, allowing myself to be swept away by the passion we shared.

Finally, we broke apart, both of us panting and breathless. Ethan rested his forehead against mine, our eyes meeting in silent understanding.

"I love you, Jordan," he whispered, his voice filled with emotion. "And I'll do whatever it takes to make this work."

"Me too," I replied, feeling my own tears spilling down my cheeks. "I promise, Ethan. No matter what, I'll never give up on us."

"Are you okay?" he asked quietly, his thumb gently brushing away a bead of sweat from my brow. His voice trembled with uncertainty, revealing the fragile nature of our emotions.

"More than okay," I whispered back, a small smile tugging at my lips despite the turmoil within me. "Let's not worry about what happens when we leave this room and face the world outside."

Ethan's expression mirrored my own, his eyes clouded with concern. He hesitated for a moment, before pulling me closer, pressing our bodies together as if to shield us from any harm that might come our way.

"Okay," he said, his voice barely audible, as though confessing his fears could make them more real. "I could stay here with you forever."

I nodded, feeling the comforting warmth of his body against mine. We were two halves of a whole, our love a beacon shining through the darkness of doubt. In that instant, I knew I had to trust in our connection, even as we ventured into uncharted territory.

"Let's forget about the world for a little longer, Ethan," I murmured, my hands moving to his hips, slowly pulling him towards me. "Let's just be here, together."

He acquiesced, allowing me to pull us up, until we stood naked before each other, baring not just our bodies, but our souls as well. Our eyes met again, an unspoken understanding passing between us. This was our sanctuary, a place where we could escape the pressure of expectations and simply be ourselves.

"Against the desk," Ethan suggested, his voice husky with desire. I glanced at the sturdy piece of furniture, littered with football trophies and his books – symbols of the passions that drove him.

I complied, leaning back against the cool surface as Ethan's strong hands gripped my thighs, lifting and positioning me onto the edge of the desk. His fingertips trailed along my inner thighs, sending shivers up my spine, before finding their way to my hips. As he entered me, I let out a gasp, feeling a mixture of pleasure and vulnerability wash over me.

Ethan moved with purpose, each thrust a declaration of. Our bodies intertwined, moving in sync as our moans and heavy breathing filled the air. The intensity heightened, and I clung to him, seeking solace in the strength of his arms.

"Jordan... I love you," he whispered into my ear, his breath hot on my skin.

"I love you too, Ethan," I replied, our voices barely audible above the cacophony of emotions that surrounded us.

As we reached our peak, the world beyond our bedroom walls seemed to fade away, replaced by the overwhelming sense of unity we shared. In that moment, I knew we had something worth fighting for – a love that would carry us through the uncertain waters of the future. And though the challenges ahead were daunting, together we would navigate them, hearts entwined and spirits unbreakable.

The air around us grew still, a quiet calm settling over the room as our breaths began to slow. Ethan's strong arms enveloped me, pulling me close in a tender embrace. My heart swelled with love and gratitude at the depth of our connection.

"Jordan," he said, his voice soft and vulnerable, "You know I'll always support your dreams, right?"

I nodded, my throat tight with emotion. "I know, Ethan. And I'll do everything I can to be there for you too."

We held each other for a moment longer, the weight of our fears and uncertainties suspended in the space between us. But even as we clung to one another, I couldn't help but feel the shadow of our conflicting dreams looming over us.

Slowly disentangling ourselves from our intimate embrace, we began to pick up the scattered clothes that littered the floor. As I reached down to grab my shirt, my hand brushed against an old picture frame that had fallen during our passionate encounter.

"Shit," I muttered, picking up the broken frame. The glass had shattered into jagged pieces, the once-pristine image of a younger Ethan and me, grinning widely after a pee-wee football game, now marred by cracks.

"Let me help you clean that up," Ethan offered, reaching for the shards. Our hands met during the wreckage, fingers brushing against each other as we both paused, our eyes locking onto one another.

"Be careful," I whispered, my voice trembling slightly as I became acutely aware of the fragility of the moment – a metaphor for the precariousness of our own relationship.

Ethan nodded, his warm brown eyes searching mine for reassurance. "We'll figure it out, Jordan," he said softly, determination etched in his features. "No matter what happens, we'll find a way to make it work."

I smiled at him, the love I felt for this incredible man radiating from deep within me. As we carefully gathered the broken pieces of glass, I couldn't help but think about how our love, like the shattered picture frame, was fragile and vulnerable, yet somehow still beautiful in its imperfection.

We knew there were obstacles ahead, challenges that would test our bond and force us to confront our deepest fears. But as we stood there, side by side in the dim light of Ethan's bedroom, I believed with all my heart that we could overcome anything – together.

Chapter Nine

The noise of voices and laughter filled the high school cafeteria like a symphony, punctuated by the clinking of trays and silverware. The scent of pizza and french fries hung in the air, mingling with the anticipation of the weekend's upcoming football game. I sat there, feeling the energy around me, each face telling its own story.

Ethan slid into the seat next to me, his warm smile lighting up my world. My heart swelled with affection for him, knowing that our love defied stereotypes and expectations. His blond hair, slightly longer than usual, framed his face perfectly, accentuating those captivating brown eyes that sparkled with intensity. He was the star quarterback, the epitome of what it meant to be popular in this small town, but beneath that confident exterior was a vulnerability that only I had been privileged enough to witness.

"Hey, Jordan," Ethan said, his voice as smooth as honey. "How's your day been so far?"

"Pretty good," I replied, brushing my short, curly hair out of my eyes. "I just finished up an art project in class. You know, the one I've been working on for weeks."

"Ah, the masterpiece," he teased, nudging me playfully. "Can't wait to see it."

We exchanged smiles, our conversation flowing effortlessly between topics – from the mundane details of our classes to our shared memories of laughter and tears. As we spoke, I couldn't help but marvel at the way our relationship had blossomed in spite of the challenges we faced. We were both haunted by the loss of a parent, and yet we found solace in each other's arms, healing the wounds that life had inflicted upon us.

A part of me still struggled with balancing my passion for art and my commitment to Ethan. I knew how important football was to him, how he bore the weight of his late father's legacy on his broad shoulders. And though I yearned to support him, there were times when my own dreams demanded my attention – when the canvas beckoned me to pour my heart and soul into every stroke of the brush.

"Hey," Ethan said, snapping me out of my reverie. "You've been miles away for a minute. What's up?"

"Nothing," I assured him, smiling weakly. "Just thinking about the future, I guess."

His eyes softened with understanding. "It's tough, isn't it? Balancing what we want and what's expected of us."

"Tell me about it," I sighed. "But I wouldn't trade what we have for anything."

"Me neither," he agreed, reaching over to squeeze my hand. "Hey, did you catch that insane pass I made during practice yesterday?" Ethan asked between bites of his turkey sandwich. His eyes were alive with excitement, and I couldn't help but smile at his enthusiasm.

"Of course, I was there," I replied, sharing in his joy. "You looked unstoppable."

As we continued talking about football and our plans for the weekend, a sudden shift in the air caught my attention. I glanced up to see Alex Reynolds sauntering toward our table, his dark curls bouncing with each step. A knowing grin played at the corners of his lips as he locked eyes with me.

"Hey, Jordan. Can I talk to you about our art project?" Alex asked, sliding into the seat beside me without waiting for an invitation. His arm brushed against mine, the warmth of his touch lingering even after he pulled away.

"Sure, what's up?" I responded, trying to ignore the prickling anxiety that crept up my spine.

"Your latest sketch is amazing, but I think we can push it further. We can meet up after school to brainstorm some ideas?" Alex suggested, his voice low and inviting.

I could feel Ethan's gaze burning into me as he observed the interaction between Alex and me. The weight of his stare bore down on my shoulders, heavy with unspoken questions and concerns. I turned to him, searching for reassurance in his warm brown eyes, but they had taken on a colder hue.

"Actually, I've got plans with Ethan tonight," I said, hoping to dispel some of the tension. "But we can definitely work on it tomorrow."

"Sounds good to me," Alex agreed, his grin never faltering. "See you later, then."

As Alex walked away, I could practically feel the air between Ethan and me growing icier by the second. We both knew that my friendship with Alex had stirred up a storm of insecurities and fears, and neither of us was quite sure how to navigate these uncharted waters.

"Are you okay?" I asked hesitantly, feeling the need to address the elephant in the room.

"Fine," Ethan muttered, not meeting my gaze. But I knew him well enough to recognize the hurt simmering beneath his stoic facade.

"Fine?" I echoed, the word hanging in the air between us like a tattered flag on a battlefield. "You don't look fine."

"Maybe because it's frustrating to watch someone flirt with my boyfriend right in front of me," Ethan snapped, finally meeting my eyes.

"Alex and I are just friends," I insisted, trying to keep my voice calm. "He's helping me with my art project, that's all."

"Sure, but does he have to be so touchy-feely about it? And that suggestive tone he uses? It feels like he's trying to piss me off," Ethan argued, his agitation evident in the way he clenched his fists.

"Look, I get that you're feeling insecure, but you have to trust me. Nothing is going on between us," I implored, reaching out to place a hand on his arm. He flinched at my touch, as if burned by the sincerity in my voice.

"Trust you? Like you trusted me when you thought I was spending too much time with Sarah?" Ethan shot back, a bitter edge to his words. I winced at the memory, knowing full well that I had been guilty of the same fears not too long ago.

"That was different," I muttered, kicking myself internally for letting my jealousy get the best of me. "I apologized for that, and I learned from it. Can't you do the same?"

"Maybe if Alex wasn't so damn obvious about wanting more than just friendship with you," he retorted, his anger boiling over. "Can't you see what he's doing? Or are you just enjoying the attention too much to care?"

"Are you seriously accusing me of encouraging him?" I asked incredulously, disbelief flooding through me. "You know how important my art is to me, and working with Alex has given me fresh ideas and inspiration. That's all this is."

"Right, so you're willing to jeopardize our relationship for the sake of some 'fresh ideas'?" Ethan countered, his voice dripping with sarcasm.

"Jeopardize? Ethan, I love you. But I also have dreams and aspirations outside of our relationship," I admitted, my chest tightening with a mix of sadness and frustration. "I'm not going to let my art suffer because you can't handle me having friends who share my interests."

"Wow..." he breathed, hurt flickering across his face. He opened his mouth to respond, but no words came out. Instead, he stared at me, his eyes a swirling storm of emotions that left me feeling more lost than ever before.

The tension between Ethan and I was like a thick fog that had descended upon the cafeteria. It washed over everything, casting a hazy shroud over the once lively atmosphere. The sound of laughter and conversation faded into a dull hum as our classmates picked up on the strained energy radiating from our table.

As I sat there, picking at my food, I could feel the weight of curious eyes on us. I kept my focus locked on my uneaten sandwich, but the knowledge that we were under scrutiny made it impossible to swallow.

"Jordan," Ethan said softly, breaking the silence between us. "I don't want this to come between us. I'm just... I'm scared of losing you."

My heart clenched at the vulnerability in his voice. I knew he was struggling with his own insecurities, just as I was with mine. But I couldn't let fear dictate our relationship.

"Look at me, Ethan," I urged, reaching out to take his hand. He hesitated for a moment before meeting my gaze, his warm brown eyes filled with a mixture of love and uncertainty. "You're not going to lose me. I promise."

"Hey, guys," a familiar, cheerful voice chimed in, causing both Ethan and me to look up. It was our friend Becca, her eyes darting between the two of us with concern. "Everything okay over here?"

"Uh, yeah," I stammered, trying to appear more composed than I felt. "Just... working through some stuff."

"O-kay," she said slowly, clearly not convinced but too polite to pry further. "Well, I just wanted to let you know there's a big party after the football game this Friday, and we're all going to be there. You two should come with us."

"Thanks, Becca," Ethan replied, managing a small smile. "We'll think about it."

"Okay, cool. See you later!" She waved and walked away, leaving us to sit in the wake of her well-intentioned interruption.

As the cafeteria continued to buzz around us, I found myself lost in thought. The world was pulling Ethan and me in different directions, demanding that we each follow our own paths. But as I looked into his eyes, I saw the same fear and longing that echoed within my own heart.

"Jordan, I..."

"Shh," I whispered, silencing him with a gentle finger pressed against his lips. "Let's just get through today, okay? We'll figure everything else out later."

"Okay," he agreed softly, the tension between us slowly dissipating like the morning fog under the warmth of the sun. Our classmates' whispers and curious glances still lingered, but for now, we had each other – and that was enough.

As the lunch bell rang, we gathered our things and made our way out of the cafeteria, our hands clasped together. The hallways were crowded with students rushing to their next classes, but we moved through the throngs like two ships navigating rough waters.

"I love you," Ethan whispered as we stopped outside my classroom. His eyes were intense, filled with the same devotion that had drawn me to him in the first place.

"I love you too," I replied, feeling a small smile play at the corners of my lips. "We'll talk more tonight, okay?"

"Okay," he agreed, leaning in to press a soft kiss to my forehead.

I watched as he walked away. Despite the lingering doubts and fears that had arisen between us, I knew that we would find a way through it. Our love was strong enough to weather any storm – even if it meant navigating uncharted waters.

As I entered my classroom, my mind was already racing with ideas for my art project. I knew that I would have to work hard to prove to Ethan that my friendship with Alex was nothing more than that – a friendship. But I was determined to show him that he had nothing to worry about, that my love for him was unwavering.

The rest of the day passed by in a blur of classes and assignments, but the tension between Ethan and me remained ever-present. We walked to our lockers together, but the silence between us was deafening.

"I'll see you later," he said, his voice barely above a whisper.

"Yeah," I replied, my own voice hoarse with emotion. "Later."

As he walked away, I couldn't help but wonder if this was the beginning of the end. It felt like we were standing at the edge of a cliff, ready to jump into the unknown. But I wasn't sure if we were going to jump together or if we were going to fall apart.

I shook my head to clear my thoughts and made my way to the art room. Alex was already there, hunched over a sketchbook, his fingers moving rapidly across the page.

"Hey," he said, looking up as I walked in. "Ready to get to work?"

I nodded, grateful for the distraction. We spent the rest of the afternoon lost in our own worlds, but it wasn't until the sun began to set that we finally called it a day.

"Thanks for all your help," I said, packing up my supplies. "I couldn't have done it without you."

"Anytime," he replied, flashing me a grin. "You know, you're really talented.

My heart swelled with pride at his words, but I couldn't bring myself to fully accept the compliment. It felt like a betrayal to Ethan, even though I knew it shouldn't.

"Thanks," I said, my voice barely above a whisper. "That means a lot."

AS I WALKED OUT OF the art room, my mind was already racing with thoughts of Ethan. I knew that I had to talk to him, to clear the air between us before it was too late. But I also knew that I needed to be honest with myself about my feelings for Alex.

That night, I sat down with Ethan and we talked for hours. We laid everything out on the table, our fears, our doubts, our hopes, and our dreams. It was a difficult conversation, but it was also cathartic. By the end of it, we had come to a mutual understanding that our love was worth fighting for.

In the days that followed, I worked harder than ever on my art project. I poured my heart and soul into every brushstroke, every color choice, every detail. And when it was finally finished, I presented it to Ethan with pride.

"It's beautiful," he said, his eyes shining with love and admiration. "You're so talented, Jordan."

"Thank you," I replied, feeling a warm sense of contentment settle over me. "I couldn't have done it without you."

As we stood there, looking at the painting together, I knew that we had come out the other side of this storm stronger than ever before. And I also knew that I had found a true friend in Alex – one who shared my passions and understood my creative drive.

In the end, it wasn't about choosing between the two of them. It was about finding a way to balance my passions with my love for Ethan.

Chapter Ten

I stood on the sidelines, watching as Ethan, Mason, and Tyler gathered on the football practice field. Their faces were etched with determination and focus, like soldiers preparing for battle. The sun was setting, casting long shadows across the field and bathing everything in a golden glow. It felt like a dream.

"Alright, let's get to work!" Ethan called out, clapping his hands together. His warm brown eyes sparkled with intensity as he took on the role of team captain. I couldn't help but admire him – not just for his athletic prowess, but for the way he carried the weight of expectation on his broad shoulders and still managed to exude charm and confidence.

"Okay, first up, we're running sprints," he announced, addressing the team. "Mace, Ty, you're up first. Let's see what you got!"

Mason grinned at Tyler, the mischievous twinkle in his green eyes betraying their friendly rivalry. They lined up, side by side, poised to race down the field. At Ethan's signal, they took off like rockets, their powerful legs propelling them forward.

"Go, Mace! Go, Ty!" I cheered, unable to contain my excitement. The thrill of watching them pushed to their limits, striving for excellence, was utterly contagious.

"Next drill," Ethan shouted once everyone had caught their breath, "we're doing tackling exercises. Remember, technique is key. Don't want anyone getting injured!"

As the team began the next round of drills, I marveled at the sheer physicality of it all. The crack of helmets, the grunt of bodies colliding, the pounding of footsteps against the turf – it was like a symphony of strength and determination. And at the center of it all was Ethan, guiding his teammates with unwavering resolve.

"Great job, everyone!" he encouraged, though his voice hinted at exhaustion. "Keep it up! We're not done yet!"

As I watched him push himself to the limit, a pang of longing tugged at my heartstrings. I wished our worlds could merge more seamlessly – his life on the field, my life in the studio. But as much as I wanted to be a part of his world, I couldn't deny the pull of my own passion.

"Alright, team, let's finish strong with some agility drills!" Ethan declared, rallying the troops for one last burst of effort.

I stood there, lost in thought, as the sun dipped lower in the sky. The dreamy haze that had settled over the field seemed to permeate my own thoughts, blurring the lines between love and ambition. And as the day faded into twilight, I couldn't help but wonder if we'd ever find a way to bridge the gap between us.

The sun cast long, golden shadows across the football field as I sat on the bleachers, my sketchbook resting in my lap. The scent of freshly cut grass filled my nostrils, and a gentle breeze ruffled my hair. It was an idyllic afternoon, the kind that felt like it belonged in a painting rather than real life. But there I was, watching Ethan command the practice field with the grace and power of a Greek god.

"Come on, Mace! You're getting slow in your old age!" Tyler teased, his laughter echoing through the air as he raced after Mason during the latest drill.

"Old age? Says the guy who's been complaining about his knees all week!" Mason retorted, effortlessly pulling ahead of Tyler with a burst of speed.

Their banter brought a smile to my face, their easy camaraderie a testament to their lifelong friendship. As they continued their playful competition, I couldn't help but feel an overwhelming sense of admiration for Ethan. He moved so seamlessly between each play, his body a testament to the countless hours spent honing his skills. I wished, not for the first time, that I could capture that raw athleticism on paper, immortalizing his movement in strokes of charcoal and ink.

"Jordan, you daydreaming again?" Mason called out, snapping me back to reality. He grinned at me from the sidelines, sweat streaking his ebony skin as he wiped his forehead with the back of his hand.

"Can't help it," I replied sheepishly, my cheeks warming with embarrassment. "You guys are just fun to watch."

"Fun to watch? Man, you should be out here with us," Tyler chimed in, clapping Mason on the shoulder before jogging over to where Ethan stood. "Ethan, you've got to convince Jordan to join the team!"

Ethan laughed, shaking his head as he glanced up at me. "I think Jordan's better off sticking to his artwork," he said, a fondness in his voice that made my heart swell. "Besides, we wouldn't want him stealing the show out here."

"Speak for yourself, dude," Mason shot back playfully. "I could use some competition!"

As they continued their lighthearted exchange, I felt a familiar ache in my chest – the longing for something just out of reach. The lines between love and ambition blurred, like watercolors bleeding into one another, leaving me torn between two worlds. And as I watched Ethan flash me a smile from across the field, I couldn't help but wonder if there would ever be a way to merge our passions, bridging the gap that seemed to stretch out before us like an endless chasm.

Underneath the scorching sun, I watched as Ethan's sweat-drenched shirt clung to his muscular frame. The football practice had been intense, and during a much-needed water break, I saw my chance to approach him. My heart pounded in my chest like a caged bird, desperate to be free.

"Hey," I said softly as I walked up to him, my voice laced with concern. "Are you okay?"

Ethan frowned, wiping his brow with the back of his hand. "Yeah, why wouldn't I be?"

I hesitated for a moment, searching for the right words. "It's just... I've noticed you've been acting a little distant lately, especially when I talk about my art."

"Really?" he replied, his voice strained. "Because it seems like that's all you ever talk about these days."

The sting of his words cut through me like a knife, leaving me breathless. "Ethan, I didn't realize it bothered you that much."

"Bothered isn't the word, Jordan," he snapped, frustration boiling over. "It feels like your whole world is wrapped up in your art, and there's no room left for us."

I flinched at the raw emotion in his voice - the hurt, the anger, the longing for something more. "Ethan, that's not true," I whispered, my heart aching with the weight of unspoken feelings. "You mean everything to me. I'm just trying to find my own path."

"Your own path?" His eyes blazed with fire as he threw his water bottle down, the liquid spilling across the parched earth like wasted tears. "And what about our path, Jordan? What about the life we're building together?"

"Isn't there room for both?" I asked, my voice trembling. "Can't we support each other's dreams?"

"Of course we can," he replied bitterly, "as long as your art doesn't take precedence over everything else."

As the sun dipped below the horizon, casting long shadows across the field, I felt the chill of doubt creep into my heart. Was it possible to find a balance between our conflicting passions? Or would the rift between us continue to grow, threatening to tear us apart like fragile paper in a storm?

"Let's talk about this later," Ethan said, his voice heavy with resignation. "I've got to get back to practice."

With a sigh, I watched him jog back to the huddle, my heart swelling with love and uncertainty. The taste of unspoken words lingered on my tongue, bitter and sweet, as I contemplated the future that lay stretched out before us like an open road - full of promise, yet shrouded in darkness.

THE GOLDEN RAYS OF the sun brushed against Ethan's face as he glared at me, his eyes narrowing in frustration. I could feel the weight of his gaze like a physical force, pressing down on me as I tried to find the words to explain my devotion to my art.

"Look, Ethan," I began, my voice steady despite the turmoil swirling within me. "My love for art doesn't diminish my love for you. They're separate parts of me, but they can coexist."

"Can they?" he snapped; his hands clenched into tight fists at his sides. "Because it feels like every time you have a choice to make, it's always your art that wins out. What about us?"

"Us? You mean football and me?" I shot back, surprised by the edge in my own voice. The wind picked up, sending a shiver down my spine and rustling the leaves of the nearby trees. I continued, "Ethan, my art is an expression of who I am. It's how I process the world around me, how I understand my feelings. It's not a threat to our relationship. If anything, it strengthens it."

"Strengthens it?" Ethan scoffed, rubbing his forehead with frustration. His sweat-drenched jersey clung to his broad frame, and I couldn't help but admire the strength of his body, even as his words wounded my heart. "How can it strengthen us when all it does is drive a wedge between us? When it takes you away from me and puts you in the arms of people who don't know the first thing about real life?"

"Real life?" I asked, my brow furrowing. "You mean football and this town? Ethan, we're more than just Ada. We're more than just high school sweethearts caught up in the whirlwind romance of adolescence. Our love goes deeper than that. Don't let the expectations of others dictate our relationship."

"Easy for you to say," he muttered, his jaw tense. "You're not the one under the microscope."

"Neither are you," I countered, my voice rising above the distant cheers and grunts from the practice field. "Not when you're with me. When we're together, it's just us – no expectations, no judgment. Remember that."

A heavy silence settled between us, broken only by the sound of our ragged breathing. I could see the hurt in Ethan's eyes, the unspoken fears that lay beneath his anger. And as much as I wanted to reach out and soothe them away, I knew that now was not the time.

"Fine," he said at last, his voice cracking slightly as he turned away from me. "But remember this, Jordan: if you keep pushing me away, eventually I'll stop trying to come back."

A burning sensation filled my chest, as if a match had been struck in the darkness that enveloped the words we'd just exchanged. My eyes couldn't escape Ethan's, locked in place by the hurt and anger swirling within them. The sound of helmets crashing and cleats digging into the turf seemed to fade away, leaving only the sharp edges of our voices cutting through the air.

"Is this what you want, Jordan?" Ethan spat out, his hands clenched into fists at his sides. "To tear us apart with your goddamn insecurities?"

"Of course not!" I shot back, feeling the weight of his accusations like a stone around my neck. "But I won't sacrifice everything I am for the sake of our relationship."

From the corner of my eye, I caught Mason and Tyler exchanging worried glances, their expressions mirroring the storm brewing between Ethan and me. It was as if they could sense the fragile threads holding us together beginning to fray.

"Neither will I," Ethan growled, the words heavy with emotion. "I can't keep trying to balance your world with mine. I have my own dreams and responsibilities, and so do you. Maybe it's time we stopped pretending otherwise."

My heart constricted painfully at his words, but before I could respond, Ethan turned on his heel and stormed off the field, his powerful strides eating up the distance between us. I watched him go, feeling the ragged edges of my breath catch in my throat as the reality of what had just happened settled over me like a shroud.

The sounds of the football practice roared back into focus, filling the air with grunts and cheers that seemed to mock the emptiness left in Ethan's wake. A cold wind whispered across the bleachers, carrying with it the scent of sweat and grass and the bitter taste of loss.

As I stood there, alone amidst the intensity of the training session, I couldn't help but wonder if the love that had once burned so brightly between us was destined to be snuffed out by the shadows of our own ambitions.

A heavy silence settled over me as I watched Ethan's retreating figure, my heart aching with a mix of frustration and longing. The tension between us had been brewing for weeks, but I hadn't expected it to boil over in such a public manner.

The cold wind bit at my skin, numbing my cheeks and sending shivers down my spine. My eyes remained locked on Ethan's back until he disappeared into the locker room, leaving me feeling bereft amidst the organized chaos of the football practice.

"Hey, man." Mason's gentle voice broke through my thoughts, his hand coming to rest on my shoulder. "Don't worry about him, Jordan. He's just stressed."

Tyler appeared by Mason's side, his hazel eyes filled with concern. "Yeah, we all are. Championship season is no joke. But don't take it personally, okay?"

Their words offered a small sliver of comfort, but it was hard not to feel like I was standing on the edge of a precipice, teetering dangerously close to losing everything that mattered most. I knew that Ethan and I both had dreams that reached beyond the confines of our small town, but I couldn't fathom a future where they didn't intersect.

"Thanks, guys," I murmured, trying to offer them a smile that didn't quite reach my eyes. "I know he's under a lot of pressure."

"Listen, Jordan," Mason said softly, his green eyes filled with empathy. "We know how much you two mean to each other. And we also know that things have been tough lately. But you're both strong, and you'll figure it out."

"Exactly," Tyler chimed in, offering me an encouraging pat on the back. "You've both got so much going for you, and there's no way you're letting go of that bond easily."

As their words washed over me, I couldn't help but feel a flicker of hope ignite within. They were right – Ethan and I had faced greater challenges than this before, and we'd always come out stronger on the other side. But at that moment, it felt like we were trapped in a storm with no end in sight, our love being tested by the relentless winds of change.

"Thanks," I whispered again, my throat tight with emotion. "I appreciate your support."

With a final squeeze to my shoulder, Mason and Tyler returned to the field, leaving me standing alone once more. As I watched them rejoin their teammates, their laughter rising above the din of the practice, I realized that they too were tethered by the dreams and expectations that bound us all.

Ethan and I might be standing on the cusp of an uncertain future, but we weren't alone in our struggles. And if we had friends like Mason and Tyler by our sides, perhaps there was still a chance for us to find our way back to each other.

I took a deep breath, feeling the autumn wind brush against my face as it ruffled the leaves on the trees surrounding the football field. The world seemed to stand still for a moment, allowing me to collect my thoughts. My gaze was fixed on the players, their movements fluid like a dance I had witnessed countless times before.

"Alright, let's get back to work!" Ethan's voice carried across the field, snapping me out of my reverie. He returned to the team, his jaw set and eyes betraying his lingering frustration. Despite the turmoil in his heart, he managed to gather his composure, clapping his hands together and calling plays with determination.

"Ready!" he shouted, and the team snapped into position. The sound of helmets cracking against one another punctuated the air, mirroring the tension that weighed heavy in my chest.

"Nice hit, Tyler!" Mason yelled, his voice tinged with laughter despite the seriousness of the situation. It was like watching a movie play out before me, the characters navigating their lives while I stood behind the camera, capturing their stories with each brushstroke on canvas.

"Jordan," I murmured to myself, "what are you going to do?"

As I pondered the future of my relationship with Ethan, my mind wandered to the time we spent together, wrapped in each other's arms, sharing our dreams and fears. We'd always found solace in one another, a safe haven amidst the chaos of our lives. But now, the storm raged within us, threatening to tear us apart.

"Come on, guys! Focus!" Ethan barked at his teammates, his anger and hurt spilling onto the field. His passion for the game was evident, but so too was the emotional turmoil that churned beneath the surface. How could I reconcile my own ambitions with the expectations that burdened him?

"Jordan, you have to trust your heart," I told myself, my fingers clenching the cold metal railing in front of me. "You've faced challenges before, and you'll face them again. But together, you and Ethan are stronger."

The sound of footsteps grew louder as the players charged down the field, their energy mirroring the intensity of my thoughts. In that moment, I knew that whatever lay ahead, I would face it head-on, with love and determination.

"Jordan!" a voice called out, breaking through my contemplation. I turned to see Tyler jogging towards me, concern etched on his face.

"Hey, man," he said, panting slightly from the exertion. "Just wanted to check in. You holding up okay?"

I smiled weakly, my gaze drifting back to Ethan as he led the team through another drill. "Yeah," I replied, my voice barely audible above the sounds of the field. "I'm just... figuring things out."

Tyler nodded, placing a hand on my shoulder. "We're here for you, no matter what happens," he assured me. "And I believe in you and Ethan. You'll find your way through this."

"Thanks, Tyler," I whispered, my throat tight with emotion. As I watched the football soar through the air, caught in the loving embrace of the wind, I couldn't help but feel a flicker of hope ignite within me. Though the path before us was uncertain, there was still a chance for me and Ethan to find our way back to each other.

A bead of sweat trickled down my temple as I continued to watch the practice unfold before me. The sun cast long shadows across the field, painting the scene with a soft, golden hue that belied the tension simmering beneath the surface.

"Nice catch!" Mason shouted as Tyler made a spectacular leap to snag the football out of the air. Their camaraderie brought a brief smile to my face, a stark contrast to the lingering unease that clung to me like a second skin.

"Hey, Jordan? You doing alright?" Mason's voice pulled me back to the present. He stood beside me, his brow furrowed with concern.

I offered a weak nod, my eyes never leaving Ethan as he pushed himself harder than ever before, every muscle in his body taut with determination. "Yeah," I muttered, the word tasting bitter on my tongue. "Just... processing."

"Look, we're all here for you," Mason said, his hand giving my shoulder a reassuring squeeze. "Whatever happens, just know that we've got your back."

"Thanks, Mason," I murmured, feeling a lump form in my throat. My heart ached with longing, but also fear - fear of losing what Ethan and I had built together, and of the consequences our ambitions might bring.

"Alright, everyone, huddle up!" Ethan's commanding voice cut through the cacophony of the field, drawing my attention once more. As the team converged around him, I couldn't help but feel a pang of jealousy at how easily he could command their loyalty, while I struggled to find my own footing in the world of art.

"Jordan, focus," I whispered to myself, forcing my thoughts away from the chasm of doubt that threatened to swallow me whole. Instead, I tried to lose myself in the details of the world around me: the distant hum of cicadas, the scent of freshly cut grass, the way the sunlight glinted off the players' helmets like a thousand tiny stars.

"Let's finish strong!" Ethan shouted, his words resounding across the field like a battle cry. The team erupted in cheers, their voices blending in a harmony that held both hope and defiance.

As I watched them charge back into action, I couldn't shake the feeling that something had shifted between Ethan and me, that this moment marked the beginning of a new chapter in our story – one filled with uncertainty and strife, but also growth and understanding.

"Alright guys, last play," Ethan called out, his voice laced with determination. "Let's make it count."

I took a deep breath, my heart pounding in time with the rhythm of the game, as I braced myself for whatever lay ahead. I knew that our love would be tested by the crossroads before us, but I also knew that we would face it together, hand in hand, guided by the strength of our bond and the unwavering support of our friends.

"Ready... set... go!"

Chapter Eleven

The clamor in Ada High School's hallway was deafening, I stood there, feeling the vibrations of slamming lockers and shuffling backpacks rattle through me. The chaos swirled around me like an ocean current, threatening to sweep me away. But amidst this whirlwind of teenage frenzy, my world halted when Alex approached.

"Hey, Jordan," Alex said, his steps deliberate as he made his way through the bustling crowd. Our eyes met, and it felt like we were locked in a silent conversation, a simmering tension lurking beneath the surface. Unresolved emotions hung between us like unspoken words, heavy and palpable.

"Hi, Alex," I replied, my voice barely audible above the din of the hallway. A strand of curly hair fell across my face, reflecting my own disheveled thoughts.

"Did you, uh, get a chance to work on that sketch for our project?" Alex asked, his fingers nervously playing with the hem of his shirt.

I hesitated, unsure of how to navigate this precarious exchange. "Yeah, I did," I finally answered, my gaze flickering towards the locker-lined walls. The metallic surfaces mirrored my own uncertainty, reflecting fragmented images of passing students. "But I'm not sure if it's any good."

"Can I see it?" There was eagerness in Alex's voice, a genuine interest that both warmed and frightened me. I couldn't help but feel drawn to them, his passion for art resonating with my own.

"Sure," I said, pulling out my sketchbook from my bag. I hesitated for a moment, my heart pounding against my ribcage, before turning to the page where I had sketched our vision. My hands trembled slightly as I handed it over to Alex.

His eyes scanned the drawing, taking in every detail with a mixture of awe and curiosity. "This is beautiful, Jordan," he whispered, reverently. I could see the appreciation in his gaze, an unspoken understanding of the emotions that had poured into each stroke of pencil.

"Thanks," I said quietly, feeling a flush creep up my neck. His praise felt like a soothing balm, calming the storm of doubt that raged within me. But as he handed my sketchbook back, our fingers brushed against each other, and I was reminded of the longing that lay just beneath the surface of our friendship. It was a silent plea, a desperate yearning for something more that we both knew was dangerous to pursue.

"Hey, have you thought more about our collaboration?" Alex whispered, leaning closer to me, his breath warm against my cheek. The hallway was alive with the rhythmic pounding of footsteps and the clamor of a hundred voices, yet in that moment, it seemed as if we were the only ones who existed.

I felt my pulse quicken, the air heavy with unspoken desires. "Yeah," I replied softly, my voice barely audible above the din. "I've been thinking about it a lot, actually."

"Me too." his gaze locked onto mine, green eyes burning with intensity. "I've been wanting to talk to you about it. About...us."

My heart skipped a beat. I knew what was coming. We had danced around this conversation for weeks, ever since we began working on our art project together. Our connection had grown stronger, transcending mere friendship, but I couldn't let myself forget that I was still in love with Ethan.

"Jordan, I need to be honest with you." Alex's words were laced with vulnerability, baring his soul to me. "I can't pretend anymore that this is just about our art. It's become something more for me. And I know it might be wrong, but I can't help the way I feel."

His confession hung in the air between us, a fragile thread threatening to snap. My thoughts raced, weighing the consequences of my decision. I knew that if I chose Alex, it would mean losing Ethan – my first love, my rock in the stormy sea of grief we both navigated after losing a parent.

"Thank you for being honest with me, Alex." The words were sincere, even as my heart ached.

The intensity in Alex's eyes gripped me, pulling me into the whirlwind of emotions that swirled within them. I felt the familiar knot in my stomach tighten as my heart raced with uncertainty. The memory of Ethan's voice, heated and defensive from our argument the previous weekend, echoed through my mind, casting a shadow over the moment.

"Alex, you have to understand," I heard myself saying, my voice tinged with frustration, "Ethan's whole life revolves around football. It's like he doesn't even see my art. And sometimes... sometimes, it feels like he doesn't see me."

I paused, swallowing hard, as if trying to force down the bitterness that threatened to rise and choke me. "It's just... I can't help but feel neglected and unimportant when he talks about winning another state championship or picking the right college."

Alex's gaze held mine, steady and unwavering, as he listened intently to every word. I could see the empathy in his eyes, the understanding that came from knowing what it meant to pour your heart and soul into something only for it to be dismissed or overlooked.

He reached out tentatively, placing a hand on my shoulder. "Jordan," he stated softly, "I know how much your art means to you.

It's a part of who you are, and it deserves to be recognized and appreciated."

His words hit me hard, giving voice to the longing I had struggled to articulate for so long. And yet, I couldn't shake the image of Ethan's warm smile, the way his laughter filled the air like the sun breaking through clouds after a storm. I loved him, but did that love come at the expense of my own dreams?

"Thank you, Alex," I whispered, my chest tight with the weight of unspoken desires and unanswered questions. "You... you get me in a way that no one else ever has."

As the words left my lips, I felt a surge of emotion flood through me – fear and longing, hope and despair, all woven together into an intricate tapestry of feelings that pulled at my heart with every beat. And in that moment, standing there amidst the chaos of the hallway, I knew that whatever path I chose would forever change the course of my life.

"Jordan, you don't have to settle for less than what you deserve," Alex said, his voice calm and steady, like a lighthouse guiding me through the storm of my emotions. "You deserve someone who supports your dreams just as much as you support his."

I looked into his eyes, and it was like gazing into a tranquil sea, endless and full of possibilities. His unwavering belief in me and my art sent shivers down my spine. I found myself drawn closer, our bodies mere inches apart.

"Maybe... maybe we could have something special, you and I," he whispered, his breath warm against my skin. The scent of his shampoo - lavender and vanilla - filled the air around us, a soothing balm to my troubled mind. "We understand each other in ways that others can't. We share the same passions, the same drive to create something meaningful."

My heart raced, torn between the magnetic pull of his words and the memory of Ethan's strong arms wrapped around me, the sound of his laughter echoing through the empty football stands. How could I choose between them? Between the comfort of familiarity and the thrill of uncharted waters?

"Alex..." I began, my voice barely audible above the din of the hallway. Our fingers brushed against one another, a spark of electricity passing between us, igniting a fire deep within my soul. It felt like the entire world had faded away, leaving only the two of us standing together amidst a swirling vortex of desire and uncertainty.

"Jordan, I believe in the possibility of us," Alex continued, his voice firm but gentle. "If you take a chance on me, I promise to always be there for you, to celebrate your victories and lift you up when you fall. We could be something incredible, if you let us."

A warmth spread through my chest, the idea of a future with Alex both exhilarating and terrifying. His presence filled every corner of my being, the intensity of his gaze like a beacon in the night, guiding me toward an unknown destination.

"Alex, I..." My heart pounded in my ears, drowning out the voices and footsteps that surrounded us. The weight of my decision bore down on me, its gravity threatening to crush me beneath its oppressive force. And yet, as I stared into his eyes, I knew that no matter what path I chose, the love that burned within me – for Ethan, for Alex, for my art – would never be extinguished.

My gaze drifted from Alex's intense eyes to the lockers lining the hallway, their cold metal surfaces reflecting the chaos around us. In the back of my mind, I could see Ethan's strong, determined figure on the football field, his blond hair catching the sunlight as he effortlessly threw the ball. The image was a stark contrast to the electric charge that coursed through me in Alex's presence, making it impossible to ignore the weight of the decision I had to make.

"Alex..." I said softly, my heart pounding like a drum in my chest. His eyes met mine again, filled with hope and uncertainty. I took a deep breath, struggling to keep my voice steady. "I need to be honest with you. I... I appreciate everything we've shared, the way you understand my art and the connection we have. And maybe I find the flirting flattering, but... Ethan is my true love."

The words hung in the air between us like a fragile glass sculpture, threatening to shatter at any moment. I watched as Alex's expression shifted, a mix of disappointment and understanding playing across his features. He looked away for a moment, taking in my confession, before meeting my eyes once more.

"Jordan, I... I get it," he whispered, his voice wavering with emotion. "Ethan is important to you. I just thought... maybe there was a chance for us."

"I'm sorry," I murmured, the heaviness of my decision settling over me like a thick fog. "I can't deny that there's something between us, but my heart belongs to Ethan. I can't change that."

For a moment longer, we stood there amidst the whirlwind of students rushing past, our world narrowed down to the space between us. And then, with a small, sad smile, Alex nodded.

"Thank you for being honest with me, Jordan," he said, his voice bittersweet. "I hope you and Ethan find happiness together." He said making a move to turn away from me.

I grabbed his arm, "I want us to stay friends Alex. I don't want to lose what we do have." I pleaded.

Alex's eyes were pools of emotion, mirroring the turmoil I felt inside. His lips parted, and a shaky breath escaped, carrying with it the weight of his heartache. "I... I can't be just friends with you, Jordan," he said, each word laced with the bittersweet tang of longing. "I need more than that. I want more."

My chest tightened, a knot of sympathy and regret forming in my throat. I could feel the pain radiating from Alex, an invisible force that threatened to break us both. And yet, I had to hold firm to my decision. "Alex," I whispered, my voice trembling with emotion. "I understand. I truly do. I can't give you what you're looking for, but I'll always wish the best for you."

His eyes shimmered with unshed tears, but beneath the sorrow, there was a quiet understanding—a recognition of the strength it took for both of us to face this moment. As we stood there, our hearts laid bare, the world began to stir around us once more. The once-muted chatter and hurried footsteps now swelled to a crescendo, signaling the end of our encounter.

"Goodbye, Jordan," Alex murmured, his voice barely audible above the din. "Take care of yourself."

And with that, he turned and walked away, his figure fading into the sea of students as he navigated the aftermath of our conversation. I stood there for a moment longer, the ghost of his touch lingering on my skin like a bittersweet memory.

The class bell rang, its chime echoing through the corridors like a siren call, beckoning us to return to reality. It was time for us to part ways, to navigate the aftermath of our conversation and forge our own paths. As I watched Alex walk away, his shoulders slumped under the burden of unfulfilled desires; I felt a pang of guilt tighten its grip on my chest.

"Jordan, come on, we're going to be late!" someone shouted behind me, pulling me from my reverie. I forced a smile and hurried toward my classroom, the echoes of our words lingering in my mind like the ghostly remnants of a dream.

I couldn't shake the image of Alex's eyes, those beautiful, sorrowful orbs that spoke volumes more than either of our words ever could. His gaze haunted me, a constant reminder of the price we had paid for following our hearts.

"Hey, are you okay?" my friend Sarah asked as we took our seats. Her concern was genuine, but I couldn't bring myself to share the turmoil raging within me.

"Fine, just lost in thought," I lied, offering a weak smile.

"Alright, well if you need anything, you know I'm here," she said, giving my hand a reassuring squeeze before turning her attention to the lesson.

I nodded, grateful for her support but knowing that there were some battles I had to fight alone. The love and longing that burned within me would not be easily extinguished, but I couldn't help but wonder if the flames were destined to consume me.

The remainder of the day passed in a blur, my thoughts consumed by the tension between societal expectations and following my heart. As the sun dipped low in the sky, its golden hues painting the horizon with the promise of another day, I found myself on the football field, Ethan's strong arms wrapped around me in a tender embrace.

"Everything alright?" he asked, his voice soft and filled with concern.

"Fine," I whispered, burying my face in his chest. "Just...thinking."

"About what?" he pressed gently, his warm breath tickling my ear.

"Love," I admitted, my voice barely audible above the gentle rustle of leaves in the distance. "And how sometimes it feels like walking a tightrope between our dreams and the world's expectations."

Ethan pulled back, his eyes searching mine for answers. "You know we'll figure it out, right? Together?"

"Of course," I murmured, my heart swelling with gratitude for the love that bound us together. "Together."

As we stood there, hand in hand, I knew that no matter how messy or complicated life became, our love would be the guiding light that led us through the darkness. For in the end, it was love that mattered most—the love that dared us to dream, to defy convention, and to follow our hearts wherever he might lead. And that, I realized, was worth fighting for.

"I've got to prepare for Friday's game, but do you want to come and watch tape with me?" Ethan asked pulling me from my thoughts.

I smiled, grateful for the distraction. "Sure, I'd love to," I replied, leaning into his embrace once more. Together, we walked off the field, the promise of tomorrow's challenges hovering in the air like a storm cloud. As we made our way towards the locker room, I couldn't help but feel a sense of gratitude wash over me. In a world where love was often met with resistance and doubt, I had found someone who accepted and cherished me for who I was.

As we settled into the dimly lit room, Ethan's fingers expertly navigating the remote, I felt a sense of calm wash over me. The flickering images on the screen were a welcome respite from the chaos of my thoughts, a reminder that sometimes, the simplest moments in life could bring the greatest joy.

As the game played out, Ethan's commentary a steady hum in the background, I found myself drifting off into a peaceful reverie. The love that bound us together was a force to be reckoned with, a beacon of hope in a world that often felt too dark to bear. And as I nestled into Ethan's embrace, I knew that together, we could face anything that came our way.

For in the end, it was love that carried us through the darkest of times, the light that illuminated the path ahead. And as I closed my eyes, the gentle rise and fall of Ethan's chest lulling me into a peaceful sleep, I knew that no matter what the world threw our way, we would always have each other.

Chapter Twelve

The sanctuary of my art studio provided a refuge from the world outside, and as I stepped into the garage, it felt like entering another dimension – one where creativity flourished, and time stood still. The scent of fresh paint mingled with the soft hum of a classical melody, creating an intimate atmosphere that enveloped me like a warm embrace.

Bathed in the warm glow of a desk lamp, I stood before my work, my heart beating in tandem with the rhythm of the music. Canvases in various stages of completion surrounded me, each telling its own story, while shelves filled with meticulously organized jars of paint and an array of well-loved brushes stood as silent witnesses to my artistic journey.

"It's going to be another late-night session Jordan" I murmured to myself, running a hand through my short, curly hair. My thoughts turned to Ethan, my boyfriend – the one person who truly understood what it meant to lose a parent and the solace I found in my art. The love and support we shared were unmatched, yet I couldn't help but feel a tug at my heart when I thought about our future together.

As I dipped my brush into a jar of sapphire blue paint, the bristles gliding across the canvas like delicate wings, I pondered over the choices laid out before me. Would pursuing my passion for art cost me my relationship with Ethan? Was there a way to balance both without losing pieces of myself along the way?

"¿Qué pasa contigo, mi amor?" The sound of my mother's gentle voice pulled me back to reality, her presence exuding warmth and understanding. "Te veo preocupado."

"Hey, Ma," I replied, a smile playing on my lips "Just thinking about some things, that's all."

"¿Qué cosas mi amor?" she asked, her eyes full of concern.

"My art, my relationship with Ethan, my future," I confessed, my voice wavering ever so slightly.

"Ah, entiendo," she nodded. "La vida está llena de decisiones difíciles, pero nunca olvides que tienes el poder de elegir tu propio camino. Pero antes de llegar a esas decisiones, te traje algo para comer," she said, holding out a plate piled high with sincronizadas, the two corn tortillas filled with cheese and slices of ham.

"Gracias, Ma," I murmured, taking a bite of the delicious treat, the cheese melting in my mouth. "Están deliciosas como siempre."

"Me alegra que te gusten," she smiled, her eyes shining with maternal affection. Yet, she could see the turmoil behind my gaze. "¿Y qué pasa, mi hijo? Cuéntame sobre esos pensamientos que se arremolinan en tu cabeza."

I hesitated for a moment, trying to put my swirling thoughts into words. "Estoy luchando con una decisión difícil, Ma," I admitted, the confession feeling like a release of pent-up pressure. "I don't know if I should follow my authentic artistic voice or give in to commercial success."

"La vida es un equilibrio, mi amor," she said gently, her words a soothing balm to my troubled soul. "Tienes que encontrar el camino que te haga feliz sin perder tu esencia."

"And if I can't?" I asked, my voice barely above a whisper.

"Confía en ti mismo, Jordan," she encouraged. "Eres un artista talentoso, y sé que encontrarás la manera de ser fiel a ti mismo mientras persigues tus sueños."

As I mulled over her wise words, my fingers absentmindedly traced the bristles of my paintbrush, the rough texture grounding me in the moment. I knew deep down that my mother was right: finding balance would be essential as I navigated the treacherous waters of success and artistic integrity. But even with her unwavering support, the path ahead seemed daunting.

"Gracias, Ma," I said softly, my heart swelling with gratitude for her guidance. "Siempre sabes qué decir para hacerme sentir mejor."

"Es lo que hacen las madres," she replied with a warm smile, enveloping me in a tender embrace. "¿Recuerdas las primeras veces que pintabas, mi niño?" Mom asked, her voice a gentle melody that hummed through the studio. The scent of homemade sicronizadas filled the air, reminding me of happier, simpler times.

"Of course, Ma," I responded, allowing my eyes to drift over the canvases that lined the walls, each one a testament to my growth as an artist. "I was so young... and so messy."

"Siempre he estado orgullosa de tu talento," she said softly, her hand resting on my shoulder. I felt a warmth spread through me, a comforting reminder of the love that bound us together. "Pero también entiendo que las cosas han cambiado desde entonces."

"Things are just... more complicated now." I sighed, my fingers tapping rhythmically on the edge of my sketchbook. "There's so much more at stake."

"El arte siempre ha sido tu pasión, Jordan," she reminded me, her tone both tender and wise. "No permitas que la presión te haga olvidar eso."

"I know, Ma. But it's hard not to think about all the expectations. From myself, from others..." My voice trailed off, the weight of my words settling heavily upon me.

"Lo sé, hijo," Mom replied, her gaze warm and understanding. "Pero debes recordar que lo más importante es seguir tu corazón y ser fiel a ti mismo."

"Es difícil, Ma" I whispered, feeling the vulnerability in my acknowledgement. "I want so much to be successful, but I don't know if I can have this and everything else that I dream for."

"La vida siempre tiene desafíos, pero tú eres fuerte, mi amor," she reassured me, her words like a soothing balm for my troubled spirit. "Encuentra el camino que te haga feliz sin perder tu esencia."

"¿Y si no puedo encontrar ese equilibrio?" I asked, my voice barely above a whisper.

"Confía en ti mismo, Jordan," she encouraged. "Tu si eres un artista talentoso."

As my mother's comforting words swirled around me, I couldn't help but feel the weight of my decision grow heavier on my chest. She had always been my rock and her unconditional love was a beacon of light in the darkest moments of my life. Her eyes held that same unwavering love as she listened to my fears and doubts.

"Jordan, hijo," Mom said gently, her hands resting on my shoulders, "No importa qué camino elijas, siempre estaré aquí para apoyarte."

"Thank you, Ma," I whispered, feeling the warmth of her support enveloping me like a blanket.

"Lo que importa es que escuches a tu corazón y sigas tus instintos," she continued, emphasizing the importance of staying true to myself.

I turned my gaze towards the shelves filled with supplies, each jar of paint and every brush symbolizing the spectrum of possibilities before me. The room itself seemed to be a canvas, waiting for me to paint my future. As I studied the colorful array of paint and well-loved brushes, I felt both inspired and overwhelmed by the choices that lay ahead.

"Ma, ¿cómo puedo estar seguro de que estoy tomando la decisión correcta?" I asked, my voice choked with emotion.

"Las decisiones nunca son fáciles, Jordan," she replied, her soothing voice carrying the wisdom of years. "Pero debes recordar que lo más importante es seguir tu corazón y ser fiel a ti mismo."

"It's so tough, Ma" I groaned, feeling the vulnerability in my acknowledgement. "I don't want to pick the wrong thing. I feel torn."

My mother's eyes softened, the wrinkles around them deepening in concern. "Tienes que confiar en ti mismo, mi amor. No hay decisiones equivocadas, solo caminos diferentes que te llevarán a diferentes destinos."

Her words were both comforting and daunting, the weight of each one settling heavily on my chest. I knew that whatever path I chose, it would take me on a journey that was uniquely mine. But the fear of making the wrong choice was still there, a nagging voice in the back of my mind.

She continued, ""Me recuerdas a tu padre, Jordan"," she stated quietly, her voice steady and unwavering. "Era un hombre lleno de sueños y miedos."

I nodded, tears springing into my eyes. "I miss him. A lot."

"Estoy aquí para apoyarte, mi amor," she said softly, sensing my inner turmoil. "Siempre estaré aquí para ti, no importa qué camino elijas."

"Thanks, mami," I replied, my voice hoarse with emotion.

"Recuerda que lo más importante es seguir tu corazón y ser fiel a ti mismo," she reminded me, her voice gentle yet firm.

"Mamá, I'm so worried about my relationship with Ethan," I confessed, my voice catching as I tried to put into words the storm brewing inside me. "I'm afraid of losing him, but also of not being able to keep my art because his needs consume me."

"Mi cielo," Mom said softly, her eyes filled with compassion as she placed a comforting hand on my shoulder. "El amor puede resultar aterrador y difícil. Pero puede abrir mil caminos diferentes. Si Ethan siente lo mismo, apoyará tus ambiciones tan ferozmente como apoya las suyas propias."

I took a deep breath, trying to steady my racing thoughts. "But what if I can't have both, madre? What if pursuing success means sacrificing my relationship with him?"

Mom's gaze softened, her hand squeezing my shoulder gently. "Jordan, mi amor, el verdadero amor no existe sin sacrificios. Si Ethan te ama de verdad, apoyará tus ambiciones y te ayudará a alcanzar tus sueños. Y si no lo hace, entonces tal vez no sea el adecuado para ti."

I nodded slowly, feeling the weight of her words settling in my heart. "But how do I know if he really loves me, or if he's just saying it?"

"El amor es una elección, Jordan. Y una elección que se hace todos los días. Si Ethan te elige a ti, a pesar de las dificultades, entonces sabrás que su amor es verdadero."

I closed my eyes, breathing in deeply as I tried to process her words. The fear and uncertainty were still there, but her words gave me a glimmer of hope. "Gracias, madre. Siempre sabes qué decir."

Mom smiled, her eyes crinkling at the corners. "Siempre estaré aquí para ti, mi amor. Siempre."

She continued, "Jordan, tienes un talento increíble," she assured me, her voice a warm embrace. "Pero también eres una persona fuerte y apasionada. No permitas que nada ni nadie cambie eso."

As we spoke, she pulled out an old photo album from one of the shelves, the corners worn and the cover faded. She opened it to reveal pictures of my early art – crayon scribbles and finger paintings that seemed so far removed from the work I was doing now.

"¿Recuerdas cuando hiciste estos dibujos?", she asked, her smile tender as she traced the edges of each picture. "Estos son los primeros pasos de tu viaje artístico, mi amor. Nunca olvides de dónde vienes y lo que te ha llevado hasta aquí."

My eyes lingered on those childhood masterpieces, a flurry of colors splattered across the pages like memories come to life. The nostalgia washed over me like a wave, reminding me of the pure joy and freedom I had felt in those early days, before the world had tried to mold me into something else.

"I hear you, Mom," I answered, my throat tight with feeling. "But when I think of the future, it's overwhelming."

"Entiendo tus miedos, Jordan," she said, her gaze unwavering as she looked into my eyes. "Pero tú tienes la capacidad de elegir tu propio camino. No permitas que las expectativas de otros dicten lo que debería ser tu vida."

"¿Sabes, Jordan?" mom continued, her eyes sparkling with memories. "Cuando era joven, también me enfrenté a decisiones difíciles en mi vida artística." She reached for another photo in the album, revealing a picture of herself standing proudly next to an abstract painting.

"¿En serio, madre? Nunca me hablaste de eso antes," I said with genuine curiosity, captivated by this glimpse into my mother's past.

"Es cierto," she admitted, her smile tinged with a hint of sadness. "Yo también tuve que decidir si seguir el camino del éxito o permanecer fiel a mis ideales artísticos."

"¿Y qué hiciste al final?" I asked, my heart swelling with the knowledge that my mother had once stood where I now found myself.

"Decidí perseguir mi pasión, pero también tener un trabajo estable como enfermera para mantenerme a flote" she explained. "No fue fácil, pero valió la pena. Aprendí que no tienes que sacrificar tu arte por el éxito, y que hay otras formas de encontrar la felicidad."

Her words resonated within me like the notes of a familiar song, stirring a myriad of emotions in my chest. It felt as though I were watching a reflection of my own internal struggle through the lens of her experience.

"Entonces, ¿qué sugieres que haga?" I asked, my voice barely above a whisper as I clung to her every word.

"Recuerda, Jordan, lo que te hizo enamorarte de tu arte en primer lugar," Mom said softly, her eyes glistening with a knowing wisdom. "Es la pureza de tus creaciones lo que te hace único."

Her words wrapped around me like a warm embrace, grounding me in the truth that had been buried underneath my fears and doubts. I closed my eyes for a moment, allowing myself to remember the first time I had picked up a paintbrush, the magic of seeing my thoughts and emotions take shape on a blank canvas.

"Lo sé, mamá," I whispered as my eyes fluttered open. "Pero es difícil mantener esa pureza cuando hay tanto en juego."

"Entonces, quizás deberías recordar por qué empezaste a pintar" she suggested gently, her gaze encouraging me to search deeper within myself.

As we sat there, immersed in our conversation, my hand unconsciously drifted towards a nearby canvas. The rough texture beneath my fingertips seemed to echo the raw vulnerability I felt at that moment, reminding me of the boundless potential that lay dormant within each brushstroke.

"When I paint, I feel as if I can express my feelings and emotions in a way that words cannot" I confessed, tracing the contours of the painted landscape before me. "It's like my soul is speaking through the colors and shapes."

"Y esa es exactamente la razón por la que debes seguir adelante" Mom said with conviction. "No pierdas de vista esa conexión con tu arte, hijo mío. Es lo que te hace especial."

I looked into her eyes, feeling a sense of comfort and reassurance wash over me. In that moment, I realized that although the path before me was unclear and fraught with uncertainty, I had the power to stay true to the essence of my art, even in the face of potential success.

"Gracias, madre" I murmured, my resolve strengthened by her unwavering belief in me. "I promise not to forget what made me fall in love with my art."

"Y yo prometo siempre estar aquí para apoyarte" she replied, her smile a beacon of hope in my darkest moments.

"Madre, ¿qué piensas de la oferta de Marcus Harris?" I asked hesitantly. The name of the gallery owner hung heavy in the air, causing my stomach to churn with a mixture of excitement and dread.

"Creo que es una gran oportunidad" Mom said, her voice cautious yet encouraging. "Pero también entiendo tus preocupaciones."

I closed my eyes, imagining my art displayed within the confines of a pristine gallery. The thought of those sterile white walls looming around my creations made my heart ache. It felt as if they would swallow my work, stripping it of the vibrant soul that flowed through each brushstroke.

"It's just that... I wonder if my art can maintain its essence in a place like that" I confessed, my voice barely above a whisper.

"Tu talento es indiscutible" Mom replied, her eyes filled with conviction. "Y tu arte lleva una parte de tu alma. Esa conexión no se perderá fácilmente."

"But what if recognition comes with too high a price?" I questioned, my fingers absentmindedly tracing the edge of a nearby canvas.

"Entonces tendrás que tomar una decisión" she said gently. "Pero recuerda, hijo mío, que el verdadero éxito viene de ser fiel a ti mismo y a tu arte. El reconocimiento nunca debería costarte esa conexión."

"Es difícil" I admitted, my gaze drifting over to the shelves lined with paint jars and brushes – a tangible reminder of the countless hours spent honing my craft. "No quiero sacrificar lo que amo por algo tan efímero como el éxito."

"Y no tienes que hacerlo" Mom reassured me, placing a comforting hand on my shoulder. "Nunca olvides que tienes el control de tu propio destino. Tu arte es una extensión de ti, y mientras sigas siendo fiel a tu alma, nada ni nadie podrá arrebatarte eso. Nunca me he arrepentido de haber elegido a mi familia en lugar de ser un artista de renombre mundial."

"Gracias, madre" I whispered, feeling the weight of my decision slowly dissipate as her words settled within me.

"Siempre estaré aquí para ti" she said, her smile a beacon in the darkness that had threatened to consume me.

As I sat there, basking in the warmth of her unwavering love and faith in my talent, I knew that no matter what path I chose, I would never allow the lure of recognition to sever the connection between my soul and my art.

The room fell into comfortable silence, with only the radio playing, as I pondered the gravity of the decision before me. With each note, my emotions swirled and danced like leaves caught in a tempest, threatening to engulf me in their chaotic embrace.

"Jordan, mi amor," Mom whispered softly, her voice barely audible above the delicate melodies that filled the air. "Siempre estarás en mi corazón, no importa qué decidas."

"Gracias, madre," I replied, my heart aching with the weight of my choice. My fingers traced the rough edges of the canvas before me, its vibrant colors a testament to the passion and love I'd poured into every stroke.

"Recuerda, siempre tendrás el apoyo de tu familia y tus amigos." Her words hung in the air like a balm, soothing the raw edges of my uncertainty. "El mundo está esperando verte brillar."

"Lo sé," I murmured, my gaze drifting to the shelves lined with jars of paint and well-loved brushes. Each object seemed to call out to me, urging me to embrace the artist within and let my soul soar free.

"¿Y Ethan?" Mom asked gently, probing at the tender wound that lay at the heart of my struggle. "Él te ama, Jordan. No permitas que esta decisión te aleje de él."

"I love him too much to let him go," I admitted, my voice laced with longing. "But I can't help but wonder if I'm choosing between my art and my relationship with him."

"Las elecciones nunca son fáciles, hijo mío. Pero debes confiar en tu corazón y saber que siempre encontrarás la manera de equilibrar lo que más importa en tu vida."

I closed my eyes, allowing the soothing rhythm of her words to wash over me like a gentle rain. In that moment, I knew that no matter which path I chose, the love and support of those closest to me would see me through.

"Thank you, mom," I whispered, my heart swelling with gratitude. "Your love and guidance will always be my beacon in the darkness."

"Y tú eres el mío" she replied, her voice filled with warmth and pride.

As the last strains of the music faded into silence, the room contracted around me, its walls closing in like a vice. The choices before me loomed larger than ever, casting long shadows that threatened to swallow me whole. And as the weight of my decision pressed down upon me, I knew that only time would reveal the true consequences of the path I would choose.

"Te amo, madre" I said, my voice barely audible above the quiet murmur of the world outside.

"Te amo, hijo" she responded, her voice a lifeline that anchored me amidst the stormy seas of doubt and fear.

Chapter Thirteen

Moonlight crept through the gaps in the curtains, casting an eerie glow on the walls of Ethan's room. The air was heavy with anticipation, as if the room itself held its breath, waiting for something to happen. I couldn't help but feel that it echoed the turmoil unfurling within me.

Ethan sat perched on the edge of his bed, his fingers drumming impatiently against the mattress. His eyes were fixed on the door, every muscle in his body tensed like a coiled spring. It seemed as though each second that passed brought us closer to an emotional collision we could no longer avoid.

"Hey," he whispered, his voice barely audible as I stepped inside. Our eyes met for a moment, and I saw a reflection of my own emotions mirrored in his warm brown gaze - love, fear, and the ever-present battle between our dreams and the world's expectations.

"Hey," I replied softly, my heart racing as I crossed the threshold into his sanctuary. The room felt charged with an energy that crackled like static electricity. We both knew what was coming, but neither of us was ready to face it head-on.

"Have you been waiting long?" I asked, trying to keep my tone light despite the tension prickling my skin. I desperately wanted to reach out and touch him, to assure myself that he was still there, still with me, even as the storm grew darker around us.

"Feels like forever," he murmured, his fingers still tapping out a nervous rhythm. "But I know it hasn't been that long."

"Time has a funny way of playing tricks on us," I said, trying to smile. But the words felt hollow, like they were suspended in the air between us, a fragile bridge we were too afraid to cross.

Ethan's thoughts seemed to be racing, his inner conflict evident in the furrow of his brow and the tight clench of his jaw. I could sense his fear, a shadow that threatened to engulf us both, but what choice did we have? We were on a collision course with our own desires, and no amount of denial would save us from the inevitable crash.

"Jordan, I... I need to tell you something," he started, his voice shaking. "I love you. I do, more than anything. But I'm scared."

"Scared of what?" I asked, even though I knew the answer.

"Of everything," he admitted, his eyes glassy with unshed tears. "Of what it means for my future in football, for us, for our dreams."

Moonlight cast ethereal shapes upon the walls, the room pulsating with an energy that mirrored my own trepidation. Ethan's gaze was heavy on me, his shoulders tense as he sat perched on his bed. I swallowed hard, trying to steady myself before delving into the heart of our conversation.

"Listen, Ethan," I began, my voice shaking slightly. "We have to talk about where this is all going. Our future."

"Jordan, I... I don't know what to say," he confessed, those warm brown eyes now clouded with uncertainty.

"Neither do I, but we can't avoid it any longer." I took a deep breath, feeling the knot in my stomach tighten. "I'm scared of losing myself, my art, if I continue down this path with you."

His eyes widened in surprise, and for a moment, he seemed lost for words. But then, his lips parted, and he uttered a confession that struck me to my core. "I'm terrified too. Terrified of not getting into a good college because of... well, us."

The air crackled with tension, our fears finally laid bare before each other. My heart ached as I watched Ethan grapple with his vulnerability, a side of him hidden from everyone else but me.

"Jordan, I love you so much," he whispered, his voice barely audible over the thrumming of my heartbeat. "But I can't help but feel like everything is slipping away."

"Then... do you really love me?" I dared to ask, my chest tight with apprehension. "Or are you just afraid of being alone?"

"Of course I love you!" Ethan's outburst filled the room, his expression a mix of hurt and disbelief. "How could you even doubt that?"

"Because sometimes," I said, struggling to keep my composure, "it feels like you're holding back, like there's a part of you that can't fully commit to us."

"Jordan..." He hesitated for a moment before continuing. "You're wrong. I'm distracted yes, but it doesn't mean I love you any less. We both have so much at stake here, and I'm terrified of the unknown."

Our eyes locked, an unspoken understanding passing between us. Our love was as undeniable as the storm brewing within us – a tempest of doubt, fear, and longing. And yet, in that instant, we had no choice but to confront the chasm that threatened to swallow us whole.

"Whatever happens," I told him, my voice unwavering despite the tremor in my heart, "we'll face it together. We'll find a way to make this work. I need to tell you something," I said, my voice wavering as the truth hung heavy on my tongue.

"What?" Ethan asked, his brows furrowed with concern.

"Marcus Harris approached me. He wants me to commit to his gallery and start working for him. I would work as an 'artist-in-residence' from Thursdays to Sundays." The words felt like a betrayal, spilling from my lips.

"Are you serious?" Ethan's voice was sharp, the hurt in his eyes unmistakable. "And what did you say?"

"I haven't given him an answer yet. But... it's tempting, Ethan. It's a chance for me to pursue my art and make a name for myself."

"Is that all it is?" he challenged. "Or are you using this as an excuse to escape the pressure of us?"

"Of course not," I replied, my heart aching at the thought. "But I can't deny the fact that working for Marcus would mean freedom from everything that's holding me back."

"Jordan, how could you even consider leaving me when I need you the most? We were supposed to face these challenges together!" Anger flared beneath the surface of Ethan's words, but I saw the vulnerability in his eyes.

"What are you talking about? I would be at school every day. I just won't be at every game. You know how important this is to me."

"I do. But at the cost of losing each other?" he whispered, the pain in his voice cutting through me like a knife.

"I don't have the answers," I admitted. "All I know is that I love you, and I'm scared."

"Then let me be your anchor, Jordan. Let's weather this storm together, no matter how difficult it may be."

Ethan stood up from the bed and approached me by the door. As he drew closer wrapping me in his arms, our embrace was a mix of longing and desperation, a brief respite from the tempest of emotions swirling around us. I could feel the beat of his heart against my chest, a constant reminder of the love that tethered us together.

"Promise me," I whispered into his ear, "that no matter what path we choose, our love will never waver."

"I promise," he murmured, his breath warm against my skin. "No matter how many obstacles stand in our way, our love will remain strong."

For a moment, we found solace in each other's arms, the storm within momentarily quelled by the strength of our bond. But as we parted, the weight of our choices loomed heavy over us, the shadows of uncertainty creeping in from all sides.

"Whatever happens," I said, my voice barely audible, "just remember that I'll always love you, Ethan Parker."

"Always," he echoed with a sad smile, his eyes glistening with unshed tears.

The room seemed to close in on us as the silence settled like fog, amplifying our inner conflict. I couldn't help but feel like we were standing on a battleground, our love pitted against the harsh realities that threatened to tear us apart. The moonlight streaming through the window cast long shadows across the floor, a stark reminder of the world outside and the expectations that loomed over us.

"Jordan," Ethan said stepping back, his voice barely above a whisper. "Do you... do you ever feel like we're trapped between two worlds?"

I looked into his eyes, seeing my own turmoil mirrored in their depths. "Sometimes," I admitted, my heart heavy with the weight of unspoken fears. "Like we're caught in the eye of the storm, just waiting for it to swallow us whole."

His fingers grazed mine, tentative yet needing the connection. "And what if the storm never passes, Jordy? What if we're forced to choose between our hearts and the lives we've built?"

The questions hung in the air, charged and unyielding like bolts of lightning. I searched for the words to ease the tension, but they remained elusive, locked away behind the wall of uncertainty that had risen between us.

"Maybe..." I trailed off, feeling the pressure of our dreams and fears crashing together like thunderheads in the night. "Maybe we need to trust that our love is strong enough to weather the storm, no matter how fierce it becomes."

Ethan's gaze held mine, desperate for reassurance. "But can it, Jordan? Can our love truly withstand the pressures of football and art, your commitment to Marcus Harris, and everything else that's thrown our way?"

"Of course it can!" I insisted, my passion surging like a tidal wave. "Our love has been forged by fire, and nothing – not football, not art, not even Marcus – can extinguish the flame that burns within us."

"Then why does it feel like we're drifting further apart every day?" His words cut through me, exposing the raw wound that had been festering beneath the surface.

"Maybe... maybe it's because we're both trying so hard to hold onto what we have that we're suffocating each other in the process." The truth of my words reverberated throughout the room, a stark reminder of the delicate balance we were struggling to maintain.

"Then how do we find our way back to each other?" Ethan asked, his voice laced with desperation. "How do we bridge the gap that's grown between us?"

I reached for his hand, our fingers intertwining as I sought solace in his touch. "We fight, Ethan. We fight for our love with everything we have, even when the world tries to tear us apart."

The silence that followed our words hung in the air like a tenuous truce, the weight of our unresolved conflict pressing down upon us. The room seemed to hold its breath, waiting for one of us to break the uneasy peace.

Ethan's eyes searched mine, his brow furrowed as if trying to read the thoughts swirling within my mind. I couldn't bear to look away, my heart pounding as the tension between us stretched thin, threatening to snap at any moment.

"Jordan..." Ethan whispered, his voice cracking under the strain of his emotions. "I... I don't want to lose you."

"Neither do I," I replied, the knot in my chest tightening as I fought to keep my voice steady.

"I know you think we should fight" he said, desperation creeping into his tone. "But I don't know if I have the energy."

The statement hung in the air, our answers as elusive as the shadows cast by the moonlight streaming through the window.

"I don't know, Ethan," I admitted, my fingers absently tracing the pattern on the bedspread beneath me. "But I think... I think we need to be honest with ourselves about what we really want. And what we're willing to sacrifice to make this work."

Ethan's eyes flickered with something that I couldn't quite place. Was it fear? Anger? Resignation? I couldn't tell, but his grip on my hand tightened as he searched my face for answers.

"What are you saying, Jordan?" His voice was low, a rumble in his chest that left me breathless.

"I'm saying that we need to be honest with ourselves," I repeated, my voice barely above a whisper. "We need to figure out what we want, and what we're willing to give up to make it happen."

"And what if what we want is incompatible?" Ethan's words were slow, measured, as if each one weighed heavy on his tongue.

"Then... then we'll have to find a way to let go," I said, the words catching in my throat. "For both our sakes."

Ethan's eyes held mine for a long moment, the silence between us thick with unspoken emotion. I could feel the weight of his gaze, the pain and longing and love that he couldn't put into words. And I knew, with a sinking feeling, that we were at a crossroads.

"Jordan..." Ethan's voice was hesitant, as if he was afraid of what he was about to say. "There's something I need to tell you."

My heart skipped a beat, a sense of foreboding creeping up my spine. "What is it?"

"I... I've been offered a scholarship," Ethan said, his voice trembling. "To play football for Penn State."

The words hit me like a sucker punch, knocking the breath out of me. Penn State. One of the top football programs in the country. The offer was a dream come true for Ethan, but it also meant that he would have to leave me behind.

"Oh, Ethan," I whispered, my eyes filling with tears. "I'm so happy for you, but... what about us?"

"I don't know," he admitted, his eyes searching mine for understanding. "I don't know what this means for us. But I know what it means for me."

The weight of his words settled on my chest like a leaden blanket. We had always talked about a future together, but now it seemed like that future was slipping away. The silence stretched between us, heavy with the weight of unspoken fears and doubts.

"I love you, Jordan," Ethan said, his voice breaking with emotion. "But I don't know if I can give up football. I could be the first openly gay quarterback in a major program. This would be everything that I've worked my whole life for."

"I understand," I said, the words tasting bitter in my mouth. "I can't ask you to give up your dreams for me."

The reality of our situation hit me like a ton of bricks. We were facing an impossible choice, between love and ambition, between passion and practicality. The weight of it all threatened to crush us, to tear us apart at the seams.

We sat in silence for what felt like hours, lost in our own thoughts and emotions. The moon had shifted in the sky, casting long shadows across the room. The night seemed endless, stretching out before us like an infinite expanse of uncertainty.

His hand found mine, the warmth of his touch seeping into my skin as he held on tight. "I've never wanted anything more than I want you," he murmured, his voice barely audible. "But I'm scared, Jordan. I'm scared of losing everything I've worked so hard for."

"Me too," I whispered, my heart aching at the vulnerability in his eyes. "But I can't help but wonder if we'll lose even more if we don't take the risk."

"Are you saying...?" His question trailed off, the unspoken words hanging between us like a ghost.

"Maybe," I said, the word tasting bittersweet on my tongue. "But only if we're both willing to fight for it."

The moment stretched on, taut with anticipation, before Ethan surged forward and captured my lips in a searing kiss. It was passionate, desperate, our love and longing entwined with the bitterness of our unresolved conflict.

The intensity of our kiss seemed to swell with every passing moment, each caress carrying more emotion than the last. My heart raced and my mind spun as I realized the enormity of what we were feeling. This was our love, a force so strong it could move mountains.

We moved together as if in a dream, the world around us disappearing until it was just the two of us in the stillness of this moment. Our lips spoke volumes without words, whispering promises of eternity and assurance that no matter what happened tomorrow, tonight we were one.

Eventually, our kiss slowed and we slowly pulled apart. Ethan's eyes remained closed as he rested his forehead against mine, his breath coming in shallow gasps as he struggled to regain control. I felt tears stinging my eyes as I studied his face, my heart swollen with love for this man who had come into my life and forever changed it for the better.

"I don't want to lose you," he murmured eventually, his voice raw with emotion. "But I'm scared, Jordan."

"Me too," I said softly. "But maybe if we take this chance together, we won't have to lose anything at all."

He took a deep breath and opened his eyes. His gaze seemed to pierce right through me; it was like he was looking straight into my soul. The weight of our kiss still lingered on my lips as I pulled away, the air in Ethan's room growing heavy with unspoken fears. My eyes searched his face for reassurance, but all I found was a reflection of my own doubts and struggles.

Ethan whispered, his voice strained. "I want to fight for us, but sometimes it feels like the world outside is trying to tear us apart."

A gust of wind rattled the window, as if to emphasize his point. My fingers twisted the hem of my shirt nervously, my thoughts racing. We were standing at the edge of a vast gulf, the distance between our dreams and the harsh realities outside threatening to swallow us whole.

"Everything we want... it feels so... impossibly far away," I admitted, my voice trembling. "But I can't imagine my life without you, Ethan."

"Neither can I," he replied, his hand reaching out to touch mine. As our fingers intertwined, sparks of electricity crackled in the air around us. It was as if the conflict within us had taken on a tangible form, a storm brewing just beyond our reach.

"Then what do we do?" I asked, my heart aching with the weight of our dilemma. "How do we choose between our love and our dreams?"

Ethan sighed, his grip on my hand tightening. "I don't know, Jordan. But I do know that I don't want to be the reason you give up your art."

"Your football career means so much to you too, Ethan," I reminded him, my chest constricting as I struggled to keep the tears at bay. "It's not fair for either of us to sacrifice everything."

"Maybe there's a way we can have it all," Ethan suggested, a note of hopefulness in his voice. "Or at least find a balance between what we want and what the world expects of us."

"Is that even possible?" I asked, my voice barely a whisper.

"Maybe," Ethan replied, his eyes locking onto mine with fierce determination. "I don't have any answers. But I know that I want to try. I want to fight for us, for our love, for our dreams. And if that means breaking down barriers and defying expectations, then so be it."

I nodded, feeling a sense of relief wash over me. It wasn't a solution, but it was a start. We could face this together, as a team. And maybe, just maybe, we could find a way to have it all.

As his words washed over me, I felt a glimmer of hope take root in my heart. Our connection was undeniable, but so was the conflict threatening to tear us apart. And though the road ahead was uncertain, I knew that I couldn't walk away from the love that had come to define my very existence.

As we laid there, hands intertwined, our thoughts drifted off into the future. The possibility of what could be if we were both able to pursue our own passions and still be together. A world where love and ambition could coexist.

But for now, in this moment, we were content to simply be together. To hold on tight and let the world outside melt away. Because in the end, that was all that truly mattered.

"Alright," I agreed, my voice wavering with emotion. "Let's fight for this, Ethan. For our love, for our dreams... for everything we hold dear."

Ethan's arms wrapped around me, shielding me from the coldness of the world outside. Our embrace felt like a sanctuary, a haven where we could hide from the expectations and pressure that weighed heavily upon us. But our haven was also a prison, one we had unwittingly fashioned ourselves.

"Jordan," Ethan whispered into my ear, his voice trembling with emotion. "I can't do this without you. I need your love, your support... but I also need to be true to myself."

I closed my eyes, my heart aching as I considered the gravity of the situation. The uncertainty of our future together hung in the air, a specter that haunted every corner of my thoughts. "I know," I murmured, feeling the tears well up in my eyes. "But sometimes, love alone isn't enough, Ethan."

His grip on me tightened, as if he were trying to hold onto something slipping through his fingers. "Isn't it worth fighting for?" he asked, desperation lacing his words.

"Of course it is," I replied, my voice cracking under the weight of my emotions. "But the question is, how do we fight for our love while still staying true to ourselves and our dreams?"

Ethan buried his face in my hair, his breath warm against my neck. "I don't know," he admitted, his voice barely audible. "But I do know that I can't imagine my life without you by my side."

"Neither can I," I agreed, even as my mind raced with the countless challenges we faced. Football had always been such an integral part of Ethan's life, whereas art was my passion, my very soul. How could we reconcile these seemingly incompatible worlds?

"Promise me," Ethan said suddenly, his brown eyes searching mine with intensity. "Promise me that whatever happens, we'll never give up on each other."

I hesitated, the enormity of the promise weighing heavily upon my heart. Could I really make such a vow, knowing the storm that was brewing on the horizon? But as I looked into Ethan's eyes, seeing the love and vulnerability that lay within, I knew that I had no choice.

"I promise," I choked out, my voice thick with emotion. "No matter what comes our way, we'll face it together."

"Thank you," he whispered, his lips brushing against mine in a bittersweet kiss. As our mouths met, I felt the rawness of our love, a love that was both beautiful and painful in its intensity.

We held onto each other, our bodies clinging together in an attempt to combine into something new. The feeling was both a safe haven from the outside world and a prison of our own making, fraught with both solace and agony.

Moonlight washed over us like a wave, bathing the room in an ethereal glow. We remained entwined on the bed, our breaths coming in shuddering gasps as we clung to each other, neither one of us willing to let go just yet.

"Jordan," Ethan murmured, his voice barely audible above the distant rumble of thunder. "I don't know what's going to happen, and it scares me."

"Me too," I confessed, my heart feeling as though it was caught in a vice. The storm outside mirrored the tempest within - a maelstrom of love, fear, and uncertainty that threatened to consume us both.

"Can you promise me something?" He asked, his warm brown eyes searching mine for reassurance.

"Anything," I said, trying to steady my shaky voice.

"Promise me that we'll always be honest with each other, no matter how difficult or painful the truth might be."

I hesitated, the enormity of the promise weighing heavily upon my heart. Could I really make such a vow, knowing the storm that was brewing on the horizon? But as I looked into Ethan's eyes, seeing the love and vulnerability that lay within, I knew that I had no choice.

"I promise," I choked out, my voice thick with emotion. "No matter what comes our way, we'll face it together."

"Thank you," he whispered, his lips brushing against mine in a bittersweet kiss. As our mouths met, I felt the rawness of our love, a love that was both beautiful and painful in its intensity.

We clung to each other, our bodies pressed together as if trying to meld into one being. In that moment, our love was both a refuge from the external world and a cage of our own making, a paradoxical blend of comfort and pain.

The heat of our tangled bodies contrasted with the cool air that seeped through the cracks in the window. Our breaths mingled, hearts pounding like a thousand drums in unison.

"I can't believe you got an offer from Penn," I admitted, my throat tight with emotion. "Signing day is soon so I wouldn't be surprised if you get more offers."

Ethan's eyes softened as he looked at me, his fingers tracing lazy circles on my bare skin. "I know, but Penn is like a dream school. I can't pass up this opportunity," he said, his voice tinged with regret.

I nodded, understanding his dilemma all too well. Pursuing one's dreams often meant making difficult choices and sacrifices, and we were both facing that reality head-on.

"I'm proud of you," I said, my voice filled with genuine admiration. "You've worked so hard to get here, and you deserve all the success in the world."

He smiled, the warmth of his expression melting away the tension that had been building between us. "I couldn't have done it without you, Jordan. You're my rock, my inspiration."

I felt my heart swell with love, a fierce protectiveness taking hold of me. I would do anything to support Ethan's dreams, even if it meant sacrificing my own aspirations.

"But what about your art?" he asked, his brow furrowing in concern. "I don't want you to give that up for me."

I took a deep breath, the weight of the conversation bearing down on me. "I won't give up my art, Ethan. It's a part of who I am, just like football is a part of you."

He nodded, the understanding between us palpable. "I know," he said quietly. "But what does that mean for us? How can we make this work?"

I took his hand, our fingers interlacing as if we were trying to anchor each other to the present moment. "I don't know." I reached around and pulled him closer to me.

As we held each other, the storm within us grew fiercer, love and conflict grappling for dominance. Our connection was undeniable, but so were the challenges we faced: the weight of societal expectations, the future of Ethan's football career, and my own fear of giving up my art.

But in that moment, none of those external factors mattered. All that mattered was the love that we shared, a love that was both fragile and resilient.

"We'll figure it out," I said, my voice resolute. "Together."

Ethan's eyes softened, his fingers tracing the contour of my cheek. "I believe you," he whispered, his breath warm against my skin.

The storm outside raged on, but within the confines of our embrace, we found a sense of calm. A sense of belonging.

As the night wore on, we drifted off into a restless sleep, our bodies still entwined. In the morning, the sun would rise, and with it, the challenges we faced. But for now, we were content to hold onto each other, to revel in the love that had brought us together.

For better or for worse, we were in this together.

Chapter Fourteen

I stood there on the sidelines, my camera hanging heavy around my neck. The Ada High School football field sprawled beneath the vast, tumultuous sky, a battleground where dreams and tensions collided. Towering bleachers loomed like ancient coliseums, filled with passionate spectators who seemed to feed off the anticipation in the air. The energy was electric, setting the stage for the inner conflicts that I knew were brewing within me.

I felt a pang of guilt as my thoughts turned to Ethan. I knew that he was doing everything within his power to make his dream come true, and I couldn't help but admire him for it. But at the same time, I felt anxious about what this meant for us. Would the distance between us grow too large? Would our relationship be able to survive the strain of college?

As I peered through the viewfinder, I couldn't help but feel overwhelmed by the sheer grandeur of it all. The giant floodlights cast long, dramatic shadows across the field, their glow making everything appear larger than life. With every snap of my camera, I captured not just the players on the field, but also the relentless, pulsating spirit of our school.

"Come on, Cougars! Let's go!" The roaring crowd became a symphony of passion, each cheer and chant an embodiment of our collective spirit, echoing through the stadium like a tidal wave. It was deafening and exhilarating all at once.

"Jordan, you got this shot?" asked Coach Thompson as he clapped me on the back, jolting me out of my reverie.

"Y-Yeah, Coach. I got it," I assured him, though my heart raced as fast as the athletes sprinting before me.

"Good. We need some great shots for the newspaper and yearbook, son. Keep it up."

"Thanks, Coach." I swallowed hard, trying to focus on my task amid the chaos.

The atmosphere was charged with both excitement and tension. Fans waved banners, shouted their allegiance, and painted their faces with team colors. Everything felt like it was teetering on the edge of something monumental, and yet, my thoughts couldn't help but drift to Alex.

I couldn't help but wonder where he might be at that moment. Was he watching the game from the bleachers, cheering for the opposing team? Or was he somewhere else entirely, doing god-knows-what with god-knows-who?

I shook my head, trying to banish the thoughts from my mind. I had to focus on the game, on capturing every moment, every emotion, every detail. I shifted my weight, adjusting my camera's focus as the players on the field collided with a deafening thud.

The Cougars were ahead, but only by a few points. The tension was palpable, and every play felt like a life-or-death situation. I watched as Ethan sprinted across the field, his body a blur of motion. He was so fast, so agile, so determined. I couldn't help but feel a surge of pride and admiration for him.

But then my eyes caught something else. A figure in the bleachers, watching intently. It was Alex.

My heart skipped a beat as I realized that he was looking directly at me. Our eyes met, and for a moment, time seemed to stand still. I felt a mix of emotions wash over me: fear, anger, sadness, longing. But mostly, I felt a deep, aching desire.

I tore my gaze away from him, trying to focus on the game once more. But the image of him lingered in my mind, like a haunting memory that refused to be forgotten.

During a timeout in the second quarter, I caught Ethan's eye from where I stood amidst this sea of fervor. Our gazes locked, and for a brief moment, everything else faded away. I saw the determination etched in the lines of his face, but beneath it, a vulnerability that mirrored my own - a mix of love, fear, and longing.

"Great pass, Ethan!" I shouted, trying to offer some encouragement as he jogged back onto the field.

"Thanks, Jordan," he called out, flashing me a smile that made my heart skip a beat.

As I returned my attention to the camera, I couldn't help but feel like a spectator in my own life. Everything around me buzzed with excitement, yet I was standing on the sidelines, watching it all pass me by. I wanted to be out there with Ethan, sharing every triumph and defeat as we navigated this tumultuous journey together.

But instead, here I stood, my finger trembling over the shutter button as I tried to capture these fleeting moments of happiness before they slipped through our fingers. And as the game raged on, and the crowd's symphony reached its crescendo, I knew that soon, we would have to confront the storm that had been brewing between us - a storm that threatened to tear us apart.

The scent of freshly cut grass wafted through the air, a bittersweet reminder of summer's end. I inhaled deeply, savoring the earthy aroma as it mingled with the adrenaline and sweat of the players around me. It was a sensory overload, grounding and exhilarating all at once. With every deep breath, I felt a surge of energy, ready to capture the challenges on the field.

"Jordan!" Ethan called out, his voice barely audible over the roar of the crowd. "Are you okay?"

"Of course," I replied, forcing a smile. "Just taking it all in."

"Good," he said, clapping me on the shoulder. "We've got this, right?"

"Absolutely," I agreed, trying to mask the tempest of emotions roiling beneath the surface.

As halftime began, Ethan and I stood side by side on the field, our shoulders almost touching. To the world, we were a team, a fairy-tale love story playing out beneath the stadium lights. But beneath that veneer lay a simmering storm of emotions, our shared history a weighty mantle that threatened to pull us under.

"Remember summer camp?" Ethan asked, his voice tinged with nostalgia.

"Like it was yesterday," I murmured, my heart aching at the memory. "You were so amazing, and I captured it all on film."

Ethan laughed, a sound that once brought warmth to my soul but now seemed to echo like a distant memory. "And look at us now," he said, gesturing to the packed stadium. "On the brink of another championship."

"Wouldn't miss it for the world," I replied, hoping my words rang true.

"Jordan, there's something I need to tell you," Ethan said, his voice suddenly serious.

I looked into his warm brown eyes, shadows cast by the stadium lights only deepening their intensity. "What is it?"

"Whatever happens tonight, whatever comes next... I want you to know that I'll always be here for you," he said, his voice barely a whisper.

I swallowed hard, feeling my throat constrict with emotion. "And I'll always be here for you, Ethan."

As halftime came to an end and the players returned to the field, Ethan and I shared one last look, our eyes reflecting both love and longing. Our hands brushed against each other briefly, a fleeting moment of connection amidst the chaos of the game. And as we stepped back into our respective roles, I couldn't help but wonder if this would be the last time we stood together, side by side, as the sun set on our fairytale.

The final quarter of the game was a blur, our school's team fighting tooth and nail for every yard. I could see the determination etched on Ethan's face as he led the Cougars with unwavering focus, the weight of his father's legacy pushing him forward. The crowd roared like the ocean during a storm, their cheers and jeers blending into a symphony that both invigorated and unnerved me.

"Come on, Ethan!" I shouted, my voice joining the cacophony, even as my heart pounded with conflicting emotions. My camera clicked in rapid succession, capturing the moments of triumph and despair as they played out on the field.

With seconds left on the clock, Ethan threw a Hail Mary pass, the ball arcing through the air like a comet. The stadium held its collective breath, time seeming to slow as we all watched, our hearts in our throats. And then, miraculously, the ball found its way into Mason's hands, who crossed into the end zone just as the buzzer sounded. Victory was ours.

The crowd erupted into chaos, a tidal wave of euphoria sweeping over us all. I stood there amidst the celebration, my heart swelling with pride for Ethan but also heavy with the secret I had been harboring. It was now or never.

I pushed my way through the throng of cheering students, my eyes locked on Ethan as he basked in the glory of his win. As I approached, he turned to me, his face flushed with excitement, his brown eyes alight with joy.

"Jordan! We did it!" he exclaimed, pulling me into a tight embrace.

My heart raced, pounding against my chest like a trapped bird. I knew what I had to do, what I owed both of us. "Ethan," I stammered, my voice cracking. "I need to tell you something."

His smile faltered, the celebratory din around us fading into a distant murmur. "What's wrong?" he asked, concern flickering across his face.

"Alex," I whispered, the name feeling foreign on my lips. "I... I think I have feelings for him."

The words tumbled out of me like stones, and I braced myself for the impact, the hurt that would inevitably register in Ethan's eyes. But to my surprise, his expression remained unreadable, as if he were trying to process what I had just said.

"Jordan..." he began, his voice barely audible over the roar of the crowd. "Are you sure?"

I hesitated, contemplating the enormity of my confession. But deep down, I knew the truth. "Yes," I replied, my voice wavering. "I'm sorry, Ethan. I never meant for this to happen."

For a moment, we stood there, our world crumbling around us as the stadium lights cast long shadows across the field. The cheers of victory rang hollow in my ears, the joyous cacophony a stark contrast to the storm raging in my heart. And as I looked into Ethan's eyes, searching for some trace of understanding, I knew that nothing would ever be the same again.

As Ethan's eyes darkened, the stadium lights cast ominous shadows on his face. His jaw clenched, and I could see the emotions churning within him, building like a storm as he tried to comprehend my confession.

"Are you really doing this now, Jordan?" he spat, his voice low and furious. The conflict between us intensified amidst the deafening roar of the crowd, our world shrinking down to this battleground of hurt and betrayal.

"Look, I didn't plan for this," I replied, desperation seeping into my voice. "I thought I owed it to both of us to be honest."

"Right," Ethan scoffed, "and you couldn't have waited until after the game? Until after we sealed our place in the championships?"

He shook his head, his anger mounting. "I can't believe this is happening."

"Neither can I," I admitted, my heart aching with regret. "But we can't ignore this, Ethan. We need to figure out what it means for us."

"Us?" he snarled. "What about me, Jordan? What am I supposed to do with this information?"

For a moment, uncertainty flickered across his face, and I could see the weight of his decision pressing down on him. It was a heart-wrenching choice - give me the space I needed or cling desperately to a relationship that seemed to be crumbling. The consequences loomed large in his mind, like a storm on the horizon.

"Maybe..." I hesitated, searching for the right words. "Maybe we need to take a step back and evaluate our relationship."

Ethan stared at me, his eyes blazing with a mix of betrayal and confusion. "So that's it, then? You drop this bombshell on me, and now we're supposed to just walk away from each other?"

"Think of it as giving us some room to breathe," I suggested, though my voice trembled with fear. "We both need time to process this."

"Jordan, you're asking me to let go of what we've built together," he said, the hurt in his voice cutting through me like a knife. "I don't know if I can do that."

"Neither do I," I whispered, my heart heavy with the weight of our shared pain. "But we owe it to ourselves to figure out who we are and what we truly want."

As we stood there, our relationship hanging in the balance, the relentless cheers of the crowd continued, oblivious to our inner turmoil. The world around us seemed so distant, as if the dreamy haze of victory had obscured the harsh realities of life beyond the football field. And yet, in that moment, I knew that nothing would ever be the same again.

"Fine," Ethan said finally, his voice barely audible over the din. "I'll give you your space. Just don't expect me to wait around forever."

"Thank you," I choked out, my heart breaking at the strain in his voice. "I promise I won't take too long."

As the cheers of victory washed over us like ocean waves, I couldn't help but feel as if Ethan and I were standing on the edge of a precipice, the ground crumbling beneath our feet. The crowd's ecstatic cries punctuated our conversation, a stark reminder that we were caught in a vortex of emotions, spinning wildly amidst the chaos of the world.

"Is this really what you want?" Ethan asked, his voice trembling with barely-contained anger. "You're willing to throw away everything we've built together... for what? Just so you can figure out who you are? Or you feelings for some guy?"

"Maybe," I admitted, my heart heavy with guilt and confusion. "But it's not just about me, Ethan. It's about us. We've been through so much together, and I think we owe it to ourselves to make sure we're making the right choices."

"Right choices?" he scoffed, his eyes narrowing as he stared at me. "What's right about tearing us apart, Jordan? What's right about leaving me when I need you the most?"

"Sometimes, what's right isn't always what's easy," I whispered, feeling a mixture of sadness and determination washing over me. "I don't want to see us grow apart, Ethan, but I also don't want to live a lie. I have to find out who I really am, outside of our relationship. And maybe... maybe you need to do the same."

The crowd swirled around us, jubilant and intense. It was as if the universe itself were trying to drown out our pain, the cacophony of voices amplifying the turmoil within our hearts.

"Jordan..." Ethan hesitated, his eyes searching mine for the love that had once sustained us, the love that now seemed as fragile as glass. "I don't know if I can do this. I don't know if I can let you go."

"Neither do I," I admitted, tears welling in my eyes as I looked at him – the boy who had been my rock, my anchor in a sea of uncertainty. "But maybe... just maybe... this is what we need to do, in order to find our way back to each other."

The stadium was a frenzy of students and parents. The game was over and perhaps, our era. The world around us seemed to shimmer and fade, as if we were caught in a dream, suspended between the past and the future.

"Fuck," Ethan said finally, his voice barely audible above the din. "I can't believe you're doing this."

"I'm not doing this to hurt you, Ethan," I said, my voice barely above a whisper. "I'm doing this because I need to figure out who I am, and what I want."

"And what about me?" Ethan demanded, his voice rising with anger. "What about what I want? What about who we are?"

I could feel the tears streaming down my face as I looked at him, the boy I had loved for so long. "I don't know, Ethan," I said, my voice breaking. "I don't know what the future holds for us. But I can't keep pretending everything is okay when it's not."

Ethan's face softened for a moment as he looked at me, his anger giving way to sadness. "I just don't want to lose you," he said, his voice barely above a whisper.

"I don't want to lose you either," I replied, my voice trembling with emotion. "But maybe... maybe we need to take a step back for a while. Just to figure things out."

Ethan nodded slowly, his eyes still filled with pain. "Okay," he said finally. "I'll give you your space. But I hope you know that I still love you, Jordan. And I always will."

"I love you too, Ethan," I said, my heart heavy with emotion. "And I always will."

As we stood there, both of us on the verge of tears, the world around us seemed to blur into nothingness. The only thing that mattered was the love we shared, the bond that had sustained us through so many trials and tribulations. And yet, despite all of that, we were standing on the brink of a new chapter in our lives, one that we could not ignore or deny.

"I think we should end things now," I said, my voice barely above a whisper. "Before it gets any harder."

Ethan nodded slowly, his eyes glistening with tears. "I understand," he said, his voice choked with emotion. "But it's going to be hard to let go."

"I know," I replied, my own voice trembling with sorrow. "But we can't keep pretending that everything is okay. We have to be honest with ourselves and with each other."

For a moment, we just stood there, holding each other tightly, neither of us wanting to let go. The crowd around us had dissipated, leaving us alone in our grief and our pain. It was a moment of raw vulnerability, a moment that would stay with us for the rest of our lives.

And then, slowly but surely, we began to pull away from each other, our embrace fading into nothingness. It was a painful moment, a moment of letting go, but it was also a moment of acceptance. We had both come to the realization that our relationship was no longer sustainable, that we needed to move on and find our own paths in life.

"I guess this is it," Ethan said finally, his voice barely audible above the din of the other students.

"I should go." I nodded towards the exit. "And you need to be with your team."

Ethan nodded slowly, his eyes filled with sadness and regret. "Yeah," he said, his voice barely above a whisper. "I'll see you around, Jordan."

As I walked away from him, my heart heavy with sorrow and longing, I knew that this was not the end of our story. It was merely the beginning of a new chapter, one that would be filled with uncertainty and change.

As I reached the stadium parking lot, I stood there, alone in the darkness, my heart heavy with regret and uncertainty. I had just broken up with Ethan, my best friend and the love of my life. It felt like I had made a huge mistake - one that would have far-reaching consequences. And yet, deep down, I knew that this was the right thing to do. I needed space to figure out who I was and what I wanted, and Ethan deserved the same.

But as much as it hurt to let go of him and our relationship, I also felt a strange sense of peace. This decision had taken tremendous courage, and although it hurt in the short term, it was going to help us both in the long run.

As I walked away from the stadium, something inside me changed. A small spark of hope ignited within me and suddenly I knew that everything was going to be alright. The future may be uncertain but at least now we were both free to pursue our own paths without having to worry about each other's expectations or feelings getting in the way.

As tears streamed down my face, all I could do was take comfort in this thought and trust that everything would eventually work out for the better.

Chapter Fifteen

Sitting in the stands as the former boyfriend of the star quarterback, I remember how the world seemed to hold its breath that Friday night, the football field at Ada High School ablaze with dazzling lights. The roar of the crowd filled the air like a tidal wave, drowning out any other sound. My heart pounded in tandem with the drumline, anticipation coursing through my veins. Beside me, Alex fidgeted nervously, his artistic fingers tapping against his thigh.

"Are you alright?" I asked, leaning closer.

"Of course," Alex replied, his eyes flickering from me to the field. "Just excited for the game."

"Me too," I admitted, though my excitement was more rooted in the figure we both watched.

Ethan led the team onto the field, his confident stride and unwavering gaze the embodiment of determination. The sight sent a shiver down my spine. I knew what this game meant to him. The weight of expectations rested heavily on his broad shoulders, and yet there he was, shining brighter than the stadium lights above us.

"Go, Ethan!" I shouted, joining the chorus of voices that echoed around us.

"Did you bring your camera, Jordan?" Alex asked, nudging me in the ribs.

"Always," I replied, patting the bag that hung by my side. "Wouldn't miss a moment of this."

"Good," Alex grinned. "You're going to want to capture every second."

As the first quarter progressed, I found myself torn. Every play had my attention glued to Ethan, but a tension hung in the air between Alex and me. I couldn't shake the feeling that something remained unresolved, a conversation left unfinished. But it would have to wait. For now, all that mattered was the game, the glory, and the boy who held my heart.

"Come on, Ethan!" I yelled, clutching the railing in front of me. "You've got this!"

"Man, he's incredible," Alex murmured, admiration clear in his voice. "The way he moves on that field... it's like poetry."

"Isn't it?" I agreed, my chest swelling with pride. "He was born to do this."

"Seems like you were born to capture it all," Alex replied, nodding at the camera around my neck. "Your photos of him are amazing."

"Thanks," I said, feeling a flush rise to my cheeks. "I just want to show the world what I see in him."

"Jordan," Alex whispered as the crowd erupted around us. "We should talk."

"Later," I replied, my eyes glued to Ethan. "Right now, I need to be there for him."

"Alright," he agreed, his mouth a tight line. "But we can't put it off any longer."

"Promise," I assured him, crossing my heart.

The moment the second quarter started, a deafening roar filled the stadium. It was as if a tidal wave had crashed against the stands, lifting everyone to their feet. I shivered, feeling the energy of the crowd course through my body like electricity. This was it—the championship game. The culmination of countless hours of sweat, determination, and sacrifice for Ethan.

"Can you believe this?!" Alex shouted over the noise, his eyes wide with excitement.

"Absolutely incredible," I replied, my voice raw with emotion.

On the field, the sound of cleats pounding the grass echoed like thunder. Each brutal collision between players sent tremors through my chest, a display of force that was both breathtaking and terrifying. It was a dance of strength and agility, each powerful tackle a testament to the sheer physicality of the game.

"Did you see that hit?" I yelled to Alex, gripping his arm as Ethan sprang back up after being tackled.

"Fuck!" Alex responded, mirroring my awe. "How do they survive that?"

"Pure adrenaline...and probably a little bit of insanity," I laughed, watching as Ethan dusted himself off and prepared for the next play.

As the quarter wore on, I found myself lost in thought, my mind wandering to the intimate moments shared between Ethan and me. Our quiet conversations in the art room, when the rest of the world seemed to fade away. The way his eyes lit up when he spoke about football, a passion that burned within him like an unquenchable flame.

"Hey, Earth to Jordan!" Alex snapped me out of my thoughts, leaning in close so I could hear him over the din of the crowd. "You've been zoning out a lot lately. What's going on?"

"Nothing," I lied, forcing a smile onto my face. "I'm just so proud of Ethan."

"Of course you are," Alex said, his voice softening. "But something's been bothering you. I can tell."

"Maybe we can talk about it later?" I suggested, not wanting to delve into my internal conflicts while the championship hung in the balance.

"Sure," Alex agreed, though I could see the concern etched on his face.

As the final minutes of the quarter ticked away, the tension in the stadium was palpable. Each yard gained or lost felt monumental, as if the entire fate of our town rested on the outcome of the game. The cheers and groans of the crowd became a symphony of emotion, rising and falling with each play.

"Come on, Ethan!" I whispered under my breath, my fists clenched in anticipation. "You can do this."

Suddenly, time seemed to slow as Ethan released a perfect spiral pass, arcing through the air and landing in the outstretched arms of Mason right at the goal line. Touchdown! The stands erupted into pandemonium, the collective euphoria washing over me like a warm wave.

"YES!" I screamed, embracing Alex in a tight hug. "We did it!"

"Amazing, isn't it?" Alex shouted back, his face flushed with excitement. "I've never seen anything like this before."

"Neither have I," I agreed, my heart swelling with pride for Ethan and the team. In that moment, I knew that memories of this night would stay with me forever—wistful remembrances of love, longing, and the indomitable spirit of the human soul.

The crowd roared with excitement as the second half kicked off, but I remained silent. Lost in my thoughts, I could hardly take in the tense energy of the stadium. All my attention was focused on Ethan, and my mind was awash with memories of our time together.

Suddenly, Alex broke into my thoughts, clapping his hands together. "I'm going to get us some snacks," he announced cheerfully, pushing himself up from his seat.

"Sounds good," I replied absentmindedly, still lost in thought.

Alex returned a few minutes later with two hotdogs and two cups of soda. We sat in silence as we ate—not an uncomfortable one, but one filled with the weight of all that had passed between us before. When we finished our meal, Alex cleared his throat and spoke softly: "You know I'm here for you if you want to talk."

I nodded. "Thank you," I said quietly. There was so much to say—so many emotions stirring inside me—but how could I put them into words? Nevertheless, knowing that Alex was here for me was enough; it made me feel less alone in what felt like an impossible battle with myself.

With renewed determination, I focused my attention back on the game and cheered along with the rest of our school as Ethan drove us towards another victory. The tension was palpable as the clock ticked down, and I couldn't help but notice Alex's reactions to every play—his eyes widening, his hands gripping the edges of his seat. It was impossible to ignore the unresolved tension that hung between us.

"Did you see that pass?" he exclaimed, leaning toward me. "Ethan's really giving it his all out there."

"Yeah," I agreed, watching as Ethan expertly maneuvered around a defender. "He's put everything into this game."

On the field, Ethan's journey played out before our eyes, each movement etching a story of determination and dreams. The weight of the championship game rested heavily on his shoulders, and yet he carried it with grace and resilience.

"Get out of there Ethan!" Alex shouted, and I could hear the strain in his voice. It was clear that he was just as invested in this game as I was, though our reasons differed.

"Almost there," I muttered, my heart pounding in my chest. At times like these, I wished I could be more than just a bystander, cheering from the bleachers.

"Can you believe this?" Alex asked, turning to me with a mixture of excitement and concern. "It's so... intense."

"Welcome to Ada High School football," I said with a wry grin. "This is what we live for around here."

As the fourth quarter progressed, I found myself lost in the rhythm of the plays, the sound of cleats digging into the grass, the roar of the crowd as they cheered for their hometown heroes.

"Jordan," Alex said hesitantly, breaking through my reverie. "I, um, I wanted to talk to you about... us."

"Later," I replied, not ready to face the unresolved feelings that lingered between us. "Right now, let's just focus on the game."

"Alright," he agreed, but I could see the concern etched on his face.

The stadium filled with an overwhelming anxiety as the clock wound down. Every inch gained or lost felt like a milestone, and the tension rose with each play. The crowd sung together in unison with cheers and gasps of despair, amplifying the emotions until our entire fate lay in the balance of the game.

"Come on, Ethan!" I whispered under my breath, my fists clenched in anticipation. "You can do this."

The cold air filled my nostrils as the crowd roared around me. I clenched my fists, feeling the cold metal of the bleachers beneath my fingers.

"Can you believe this?" Alex shouted over the din, his eyes locked on the field. "It's like watching a movie!"

I nodded, my heart pounding in my chest. The game had been a rollercoaster of emotions, the momentum swinging back and forth like a pendulum. I could feel the tension in every fiber of my being, the weight of each play bearing down on us all.

Ethan stood at the line of scrimmage, sweat glistening on his brow as he surveyed the field. He barked out a series of commands, his voice strong and resolute amidst the chaos.

"Come on, Ethan!" I whispered under my breath, willing him to succeed. As he caught the snap and dropped back to pass, time seemed to slow down. The ball arced through the air, a beacon of hope against the darkening sky.

"Intercepted!" a voice screamed next to me, and my heart sank. A player from the opposing team had jumped the route and snatched the ball from the air, dashing our hopes for victory.

"Damn it," Alex muttered, running a hand through his hair. "We needed that."

I chewed my lip, anxiety knotting in my stomach. The clock ticked down mercilessly, each second bringing us closer to the end of the game. Ethan's dreams of a championship hung in the balance, and I couldn't help but think of how much was riding on these final moments.

"Jordan, are you okay?" Alex asked, his concern genuine.

"I'm just... worried about Ethan," I admitted, my voice tight with emotion. "He's worked so hard for this, and I don't want to see him lose."

"Hey," Alex said, placing a reassuring hand on my shoulder. "He's got this. Trust me."

As the game continued, I watched as both teams fought with everything they had, their resilience and determination etching a story of triumph and heartbreak onto the field. Each tackle, each play, a testament to the human spirit.

"Fourth down!" Tyler shouted from the sideline, his eyes burning with intensity. The huddle broke once more, and Ethan took his place behind the center.

"Let's go, boys!" he roared, his voice echoing across the field. As the ball snapped into his hands, I held my breath, praying for a miracle.

"Go, Ethan, go!" I screamed, unable to contain my emotions any longer. He scrambled to his right, looking downfield for an open receiver.

"Pass it!" Mason yelled, his arms outstretched and ready.

The football spiraled through the air, its trajectory uncertain. As it fell towards Mason's waiting hands, I squeezed my eyes shut, unable to watch.

"Did he catch it?" I whispered to Alex, fear tightening my chest.

"Touchdown!" Alex exclaimed, his voice filled with disbelief and joy.

My eyes flew open, and I saw the players on the field erupt into celebration. Ethan held his arms aloft in victory, his face lit up with pure happiness.

"See?" Alex grinned, clapping me on the back. "I told you he'd pull through."

"Thank you," I murmured, tears pricking at my eyes. "For believing in him."

"Always," Alex replied, his gaze softening. "Now let's go celebrate with our champion."

In that moment, a surge of love and pride for Ethan swept through us all, binding us together in a shared celebration of his triumph. His leadership had brought us to this point, a testament to his dedication and talent. He was the embodiment of everything we cherished about the game, a symbol of hope and strength in a world that often felt cold and unforgiving.

I couldn't help but beam as I watched Ethan bask in the adoration of the crowd, his eyes glistening with unshed tears. It was a moment I would never forget, a glimpse of the man he was destined to become – strong, resilient, and true to himself.

The final whistle pierced the air, and the scoreboard declared us victorious. A roar of elation erupted from the stands as my classmates leaped to their feet, a tidal wave of euphoria washing over us all. We had done it - back-to-back championship seasons, a feat that seemed impossible mere months ago.

"Can you believe it?" Alex shouted, his words barely audible amidst the cacophony of cheers and applause. His eyes sparkled with excitement, mirroring the fervor that coursed through my veins.

"I knew he could do it," I replied, beaming as I watched Ethan embrace his teammates on the field below, their faces alight with pure joy. It was a sight to behold, like a painting come to life, each brushstroke imbued with love and triumph.

"Jordan!" someone called, and I turned to see a group of friends beckoning me over, their arms laden with confetti and streamers. I glanced at Alex, sensing the unspoken invitation in his gaze.

"Go on," he said softly, a wistful smile tugging at the corners of his mouth. "Celebrate."

"Alright," I agreed, my heart swelling with gratitude for his understanding. But just before I turned to join the others, our eyes locked once more, a flicker of unresolved tension passing between us. The world fell silent around us, the roar of our classmates fading into the background as the weight of the moment settled upon us.

"We should talk," I murmured, my voice tinged with hesitation. The words hung in the air, heavy with the knowledge of what they signified - an acknowledgment of the unspoken feelings that had blossomed between us, despite the bonds we shared with others.

"Yeah," Alex agreed, his gaze never leaving mine. "We should."

"Later," I promised, breaking away from his intense stare and taking a deep breath to steady myself. The noise of the stadium rushed back in, filling my ears with the sounds of laughter and exultation as I joined my friends in their jubilant revelry.

As we tossed confetti into the air, our voices raised in triumphant song, I couldn't help but steal glances at Alex, his presence a magnet that drew my gaze like a moth to a flame. During our joy, I knew that our conversation loomed on the horizon, a storm cloud threatening to dampen our victory. But for now, I allowed myself to bask in the glow of success, my heart swelling with pride for Ethan and the journey we had all undertaken together.

"Here's to us," I whispered, raising an imaginary glass in toast to the future, whatever it may hold.

With my camera in hand, I made my way to the locker room, eager to capture the victorious smiles and euphoria etched across the faces of Ethan and his teammates. The air was thick with the scent of sweat and adrenaline, the staccato rhythm of laughter and excited chatter bouncing off the walls.

"Hey, Jordan!" called one of the players, striking a pose as I snapped a shot of him grinning triumphantly. "Make sure you get my good side!"

"Of course," I replied with a smile, my heart swelling with happiness for their hard-won victory.

As I turned to snap another pic, Alex caught my arm, pulling me into a secluded corner. The world around us seemed to fade away as our eyes locked, heat radiating between us. Before I could say anything, he wrapped his arms around me, drawing me in for a passionate kiss that sent shivers down my spine. His teeth grazed my lower lip, biting softly and leaving a tingling mark that would remain long after our lips parted.

"Alex..." I whispered, breathless and stunned by the intensity of our connection. He simply nodded, a silent acknowledgement of the conversation we still needed to have before slipping back into the celebratory fray.

I took a moment to steady myself, my pulse racing as I reluctantly left behind the warmth of Alex's embrace to rejoin the jubilant celebration unfolding within the locker room. As if drawn by an invisible force, I found myself face-to-face with Ethan, his smile bright but his eyes clouded.

"This changes everything," he murmured, running a hand through his damp hair. I knew he wasn't referring to the victory, but to the unknown future that stretched out before us.

"Tell me what you're thinking," I urged gently, searching his eyes for answers.

Ethan leaned against the lockers, his shoulders sagging under the weight of his dreams. "I've been considering multiple football scholarships to really good schools, but it's... complicated," he confessed, his voice barely audible above the noise of the celebration.

"Complicated how?" I inquired, my heart aching for him as I sensed the burden of his ambitions.

"Choosing the right school, the pressure to perform... and everything, Jordan," he admitted, reaching out to take my hand. "I don't know if I want to stay closer to home or go far away."

"Hey," I said softly, squeezing his hand reassuringly. "You'll figure it out. You've worked so hard for this."

Ethan looked at me, gratitude shining in his eyes. "Thank you, Jordan. That means everything to me."

The locker room was overflowing with laughter and cheers, the scent of sweat and victory hanging in the air. I stood there, camera in hand, trying to capture the essence of the moment, but my thoughts were elsewhere. The taste of Alex's kiss lingered on my lips, a sweet poison that threatened to unravel everything I held dear.

"Hey, Jordan!" Mason shouted from the other side of the room with a wide smile plastered on his face.

"What's going on? Can you believe it?" I asked, unable to contain the excitement in my voice.

"No way!" he exclaimed, "Come on, let me get a cool picture of me with the winning ball." He beamed.

"Yeah, no problem," I said, raising the camera to look through its lens.

As I focused on Mason and the football in his hands, my mind couldn't help but wander back to Alex. The kiss we shared had been electric, a promise of what could be if we allowed ourselves to explore our feelings. But the weight of our unspoken attraction hung between us like a veil, threatening to shatter the bonds we had built with others.

"Jordan, are you okay?" Mason asked, his voice bringing me back to the present.

"Yeah, sorry. Just lost in thought," I replied, shaking my head to clear away the fog of my conflicted emotions.

"Hey, I wanted to ask you something," Mason said, his voice dropping to a whisper. "Why did you and Ethan break up?"

The question caught me off guard, and I felt a flush of heat rise to my cheeks as I considered my answer. "I... I don't know if I want to talk about it," I stammered, feeling suddenly exposed.

"Come on, Jordan," Mason urged, his eyes shining with mischief. "Is it Alex? The way he looks at you, the connection you guys have... It's obvious."

"I didn't break up with Ethan because of Alex," I protested weakly, my heart aching.

"It had to be something. Ethan is gutted." Mason countered, his words planting a seed of doubt in my mind. "And I saw that kiss, Jordan."

With those words ringing in my ears, I made my way back out to the field, my mind whirling with the possibilities of what could be. The euphoria of my kiss with Alex still pulsed through my veins, and I wanted to find him to have that chat.

I made my way towards him, the roar of the locker room fading into the background as we stood face to face once more.

"We need to talk," I said softly, my voice barely audible above the noise.

"I know," he replied, his eyes never leaving mine. "But not here."

I nodded, understanding the need for privacy. We slipped out of the stadium, the cool night air a balm against my fevered skin.

Alex led me to an empty corner of the athletic fields, the only sounds the distant echoes of the celebration. He turned to face me, his eyes intense and searching.

"I can't stop thinking about you," he said, his words a confession of the desire that had been simmering between us for so long.

"I know," I replied, reaching out to touch his cheek. "I broke up with Ethan."

"I know." Alex leaned in, his lips seeking mine in a kiss that set my body ablaze. We clung to each other, the only thing that mattered in the world the heat of our passion.

As we parted, breathless and dizzy with ecstasy, I knew that everything had changed. The future loomed before us, an unknown path that could lead to either joy or heartache. But in that moment, all I wanted to do was embrace the possibilities and see where the journey could take us.

Chapter Sixteen

The Marcus Harris Art Gallery was a kaleidoscope of colors and emotions, each piece on display a testament to the unique visions of its creators. Paintings captured moments frozen in time, while sculptures reached out into the room as if to touch the hearts of those who stood before them. The air hummed with a quiet reverence, punctuated only by the soft footsteps of patrons who wandered the exhibits with hushed awe.

"Jordan Torres," I whispered to myself, seeing my name printed on the small label beneath my painting. My heart swelled with pride and anxiety as I looked at my art, hanging there for all to see. This was the moment I had been working toward for so long, yet now that it was here, I couldn't shake the feeling that it was all just a dream.

"Quite remarkable, isn't it?" A velvety voice broke through my thoughts, and I turned to find Marcus Harris standing beside me. His dark eyes were locked onto my painting, his face a mask of intrigue. He was older than me, in his early forties, but he carried himself with a grace and sophistication that made him seem ageless. Like his gallery, he was a work of art in his own right.

"Thank you," I said, my throat tight. "I'm really honored to have my work displayed in your gallery."

"Your talent speaks for itself," Marcus replied, turning to look at me. "You have a rare gift, Jordan. Your ability to capture emotion and convey it through your art is truly extraordinary. I particularly like the way you've incorporated the football motif. It's not often we see such a blend of sports and fine arts."

"Football has always been a part of my life," I confessed. "But art has allowed me to explore another side of myself, one that's less bound by society's expectations."

"Indeed, that's what makes your work so compelling," Marcus said, gesturing to the crowd that had begun to gather around my painting. "Your art is a window into your soul, and it's clear you have a story to tell."

I glanced at the people who had stopped to admire my work, their eyes filled with appreciation and curiosity. It felt like a weight balanced precariously on my shoulders, as if my future hinged on their approval. I wanted to be true to myself, but I also couldn't help but wonder how far my art could take me.

"Jordan, I want you to know that I believe in you and your art," Marcus said, placing a hand on my shoulder. "And I would be honored to help guide you along this journey. Together, we can take your career to new heights."

His words were like a lifeline, offering hope and validation in equal measure. But as much as I longed for his guidance, I knew that my heart belonged to someone else. I thought of Ethan, his unwavering support, and our shared love that transcended the boundaries of our respective worlds. The choice before me was one of career and love, and the path forward seemed as uncertain as ever.

"Thank you, Marcus," I told him, my voice barely audible above the pounding of my heart. "I'll think about it."

The hushed murmurs of admiration and anticipation in the gallery were like the first whispers of a symphony, gradually building to a crescendo. The air was infused with the scent of fresh paint and the soft rustling of expensive clothing as visitors moved from piece to piece, their eyes alight with curiosity and wonder.

"Jordan, this is incredible!" a woman exclaimed, her voice barely containing her excitement. "Your use of color and texture is simply breathtaking."

"Thank you," I replied, my cheeks flushed with pride. The feeling of having my work admired by others was intoxicating, leaving me giddy and elated.

"Ah, there you are, Jordan." A familiar voice broke through the thrum of conversation, and I turned to see Malcolm Foster, an accomplished artist and my mentor, weaving his way through the crowd toward me. His silver hair gleamed under the gallery lights, and his eyes sparkled with warmth and wisdom.

"Professor! What do you think?" I asked, eager to hear his opinion.

"I've just arrived, but I'm impressed," he said, clasping my shoulder. "I can't wait to see your art and I'm proud that you are exhibiting tonight."

"Thanks to your guidance, sir," I answered, genuinely grateful for his mentorship. He had been instrumental in helping me navigate the complexities of the artistic world while staying true to myself.

"But now, it's up to you to decide where you want to take your art next," he continued, his gaze locked onto mine. "You have a gift, Jordan. Don't be afraid to use it."

"Thank you, Professor," I whispered, his words settling deep within me like a mantra. As the evening wore on, I felt simultaneously different emotions – one giddy of the promise of a glittering career in the world of art, and two distraught over my relationship with Ethan.

As I walked around lost in thoughts, the air in the gallery was thick with anticipation, as if it were a tangible force pressing in on me. I took a tentative step closer to my art on display, feeling a sense of reassurance settle over me at the sight of Alex.

"Your work is stunning, Jordan," Alex whispered, his eyes wide with admiration as they followed the curves and lines of my paintings. "You've poured your heart into these pieces, and it shows."

"Thank you, Alex," I murmured, but my voice was barely audible over the thrum of hushed conversations swirling around us. My thoughts felt heavy, laden, as if dipped in molasses, and my chest tightened with each breath. This was a pivotal moment for me – a crossroads between my dreams of artistic success and the love that tethered me to Ethan.

"Are you nervous about tonight?" Alex asked gently, his gaze softening with concern. He knew this wasn't just another exhibition for me; it was the culmination of years of hard work and self-discovery.

"Terrified, actually," I admitted, my fingers twisting together involuntarily. "But also... excited. It feels like anything could happen from here on out."

"Embrace that feeling, Jordan," Alex urged, his hand resting lightly on my arm, grounding me as my pulse raced beneath my skin. "This is your moment to shine. Don't let fear hold you back."

"Easy for you to say," I said with a wry smile, recalling how effortlessly Alex seemed to navigate the world of art and academia. But then again, he hadn't experienced the same tumultuous journey I had – the loss of a parent, a relationship built on shared pain, and the relentless struggle to find my own voice amidst a mountain of expectations.

"Jordan, listen to me," Alex insisted, his tone firm yet gentle. "You have an incredible gift. You're not just an artist; you're a storyteller. And the world needs to hear your stories."

I swallowed hard, his words resonating within me like a struck chord. He was right – I had something unique to offer, and it was time for me to embrace my own potential.

"Thank you, Alex," I whispered, feeling a newfound determination flare within me. "I promise I won't let fear hold me back. No matter what happens tonight, I'll keep moving forward."

"Good," he said, his eyes sparkling with pride. "Now, let's go show the world what Jordan Torres is capable of."

As we continued around the gallery together, I felt the weight of this night settle on my shoulders, a burden both heavy and exhilarating. My heart raced, and yet, for the first time, I knew I could face whatever the future held.

Marcus Harris approached me, his eyes radiating an air of sophistication and a deep appreciation for art. He wore a charcoal suit that accentuated his lean frame, and as he drew closer, I could sense the power and influence he wielded in the art world.

"Jordan, your works are truly intriguing," he said, one hand resting casually in his pocket. "I must say, you have a unique way of expressing yourself through your art."

"Thank you, Mr. Harris," I replied, my voice wavering slightly under the weight of his compliment. "I try to tell stories through my paintings, to share my thoughts and emotions with the world."

"Art is, after all, a reflection of the artist's soul," Marcus mused, his gaze drifting over the vibrant colors and intricate brushstrokes of my work. "And I can see a great depth within yours."

As we spoke, I noticed Professor Malcolm Foster weaving through the crowd, a proud smile plastered on his face. His eyes met mine, and he beckoned me over.

"Excuse me, Mr. Harris," I said politely, stepping away from him to join my mentor.

"Jordan, my boy," Malcolm began, placing a firm hand on my shoulder. "Your work tonight has truly outdone itself. The raw emotion, the honesty – it's something I haven't seen in years."

"Thank you, Professor," I responded, warmth spreading through me like a sunbeam breaking through storm clouds. "Your guidance has helped me find my own voice."

Malcolm's eyes twinkled as he studied my artwork more closely. "This piece, in particular," he said, pointing to a painting depicting a football game fading into a soft, romantic embrace. "It speaks volumes about your journey – not just as an artist but as a human being."

"Football was always a refuge for me," I admitted, my voice tinged with nostalgia. "But then I discovered that love could also be a sanctuary – even amidst the chaos of this world."

"Your art is a testament to that," Malcolm said, nodding in agreement. "Never forget where you came from, Jordan. And never be afraid to embrace your heart's true desires."

With Malcolm's words resonating within me, I felt a renewed sense of purpose blossoming in my chest. I understood then that my art had the power to touch others – to evoke memories and emotions that lay dormant beneath the surface of their consciousness.

"Thank you, Professor," I murmured, feeling an immense gratitude for his mentorship. "I promise to keep pushing myself, to explore new depths and share my stories with the world."

"Good," he replied, clapping me on the back. "The art world is lucky to have you, Jordan."

My heart swelled with gratitude as Malcolm's words echoed in my mind. As I glanced around the gallery, my gaze fell upon his familiar face again – Alex Reynolds, his eyes holding a hint of mischief as he studied one of my paintings. He was an enigma, someone who had managed to worm his way into my life and offer me a different perspective on my art and myself.

"Hey, Jordan," Alex said casually, a warm smile playing on his lips. "Your work is really something else."

"Thanks, Alex," I replied, feeling a strange mix of excitement and apprehension whenever we spoke. It was difficult to put my finger on it, but there was an underlying tension between us that seemed to grow with each encounter.

"Seriously, though," he continued, gesturing towards a piece depicting a football soaring through a stormy sky. "This one's my favorite. It's like you've captured the essence of freedom – that moment when you break free from the chains that bind you."

I couldn't help but smile at his interpretation; he always seemed to see things in my art that others couldn't – or wouldn't. "That's exactly what I was going for," I admitted. "It's about finding the courage to defy expectations and choose your own path."

"Sounds like a story worth telling," he mused, his eyes never leaving the painting. "You're a gifted artist, Jordan. You have a rare talent for making people feel something."

"High praise coming from you," I said, recalling the intricate sketches adorning Alex's sketchbook. He was an artist in his own right, albeit a more private one. "I appreciate the support."

"Of course," he replied, finally tearing his gaze away from the canvas to look at me. "We may be different, but I think we understand each other on some level."

As our conversation continued, I found myself lost in a sea of indecision – torn between the life I had built with Ethan and the allure of an untethered existence, free from the constraints of society. It was a decision that weighed heavily on my heart, even as the gallery buzzed with excitement around me.

"Jordan," Alex said gently, his voice pulling me back into the present. "Whatever you decide to do with your art – just remember that it's yours. Don't let anyone else dictate what you create or how you express yourself."

His words calmed me, adding fuel to the fire that burned within my soul. As I gazed at the vibrant colors and bold brushstrokes that adorned the walls, I knew that my future as an artist hung in the balance. The choice was mine to make – and the consequences were mine alone to bear.

"Thanks, Alex," I whispered, my voice tinged with determination. "I promise I won't forget that."

"Good," he replied, his eyes softening as he offered me a reassuring smile. "You're stronger than you think, Jordan. Just trust yourself – and your art."

The murmurs around us continued, but the world seemed to slow down as I locked eyes with Alex. His gaze was steady, unwavering, and full of understanding. The tension between us was palpable, like the charged air before a storm.

"Jordan," Alex said softly, his voice barely audible over the hum of conversation. "I know how much this means to you. Your art is beautiful, honest, and it speaks to people."

"Thanks," I replied, my throat tightening with emotion. We stood side by side in the gallery, our shoulders brushing against each other, our proximity intensifying the connection that had been growing between us ever since we met.

"Your work has touched so many, and it will continue to do so no matter what path you choose," he continued, his words echoing through my mind like a haunting melody.

"Alex," I breathed out, not knowing what else to say. Our eyes met again, and for a moment, it felt as if time had stopped. My heart pounded in my chest, feeling both heavy and light all at once.

"Sometimes," he whispered, leaning in closer, "the most important decisions are the ones that scare us the most. Because they're the ones that have the power to change everything."

As his lips brushed against mine, the world around us seemed to fade away. The vibrant colors of the artwork, the hushed conversations – all of it disappeared, leaving only the raw intensity of this moment. The kiss was gentle, yet passionate; a collision of emotions that sent shivers down my spine.

"Jordan," Alex murmured against my lips, pulling back slightly. "No matter what happens, remember that you're not alone. You have people who care about you, who believe in you." His hand found mine, our fingers intertwining as if they were always meant to fit together.

"Thank you, Alex," I whispered, my heart swelling with gratitude. Our connection had deepened, the roots of our friendship growing stronger with each passing day. And in that moment, amidst the art that had been my life's work, I felt both terrified and invigorated by the unknown future that lay before me.

As we stepped back from our embrace, the gallery came into focus once more, the vibrant artwork and hushed conversations a vivid reminder of the decision that still loomed. The anticipation hung heavy in the air, a knot of unresolved tension that bound us all together as we awaited the outcome.

"Whatever you decide, Jordan," Alex said quietly, his eyes shining with unwavering support, "I know it'll be the right choice."

I nodded, feeling the weight of the decision that still needed to be made – a choice that would forever alter the course of my artistic journey and the relationships I held dear.

Chapter Seventeen

The starlit sky above mirrored the turmoil within me as Ethan and I stood in my yard, the distant sounds of Ada fading into insignificance. In that moment, our emotions drowned out everything else. It was the following Sunday night after the championship game, and Ethan had learned about Alex's kiss at the stadium and that I had been sitting with him during the game.

"Jordan," Ethan's voice erupted like a storm – his anger, long simmering beneath the surface, finally bursting forth. "Did you cheat on me with him? How long have you been sneaking around with Alex?"

His words were a torrent of resentment and hurt, echoing through the night and piercing my heart. My chest tightened as I tried to find the words to explain my interactions with Alex; to tell Ethan that it wasn't what he thought. But I struggled, my throat closing and choking back my own pain.

"Tell me, Jordan," he demanded, brown eyes blazing with intensity. "How long has this been going on?"

I swallowed hard, feeling the weight of his stare bearing down on me. The cool grass beneath my feet suddenly felt like a bed of nails, every blade digging into my skin, a reminder of the pain I'd caused. This wasn't how I wanted things to go, but I couldn't hide the truth any longer.

"Since the beginning of the school year," I admitted, the words barely audible. "But it wasn't like that, Ethan. We were just friends, and then... that kiss happened. I didn't plan for it. It just... happened."

Ethan clenched his fists, knuckles turning white as he grappled with the enormity of my revelation. I had never seen him look so betrayed, and I would have given anything to take away the hurt in his eyes.

"Friends?" he scoffed bitterly. "Is that what you call it? Sitting together during the most important game of my life, letting him kiss you?"

I wanted to reach out and touch his arm, to reassure him that our love was still real and worth fighting for. But the invisible barrier between us seemed impenetrable, a chasm that had grown wider with every lie I'd told.

I hesitated for a moment, my heart pounding like a drum in my chest. I knew that laying out the truth was the only way to salvage what was left of our relationship. Swallowing hard, I began, "Alex and I met in art class at the beginning of the school year. We were just friends—really good friends."

Ethan's eyes darkened, but he didn't interrupt, and I continued, "He understood my art in ways that no one else seemed to, and it was... refreshing. Our friendship turned to subtle flirting, as you know. But when he asked me to take it further, I denied him."

"Then how did you end up kissing him?" Ethan demanded, his voice choked with hurt.

"You and I had broken up and Alex invited me to sit with him during your championship game," I explained, my voice trembling. "He said he wanted to see the game with me. I didn't know that he still had feelings for me. When I went to leave, he... he kissed me. It caught me off guard."

As I confessed, I could see Ethan's face contorting in pain, a portrait of raw betrayal. The weight of my words hung in the air between us like a dark cloud, suffocating our intimacy. And as much as it pained me to admit it, I knew that we were both grappling with the enormity of what had happened.

"Jordan," Ethan whispered hoarsely, his fists clenched involuntarily, knuckles turning white. "How could you let this happen? I trusted you."

"Please, Ethan," I begged, my tears blurring my vision. "I told you I needed space to figure this out. You said you would give it to me."

But my pleas seemed to fall on deaf ears, drowned out by the storm of emotions raging inside him. I reached out to touch his arm, desperate to bridge the chasm that had opened between us, but he pulled away, the coldness in his eyes cutting deeper than any blade ever could.

"Trust is everything, Jordan," he said, his voice hollow and devoid of warmth. "And you've shattered mine."

As I stood there under the starlit sky, my heart aching with regret, I couldn't help but wonder if our love could ever be repaired.

Tears streamed down my cheeks, each drop a testament to the internal struggle that tore at my heart. Ethan's anger was palpable, drowning out my pleas for understanding like the roaring waves of a tempestuous ocean.

"Can't you see how unfair you're being?" I choked out, my voice trembling with emotion. "If you hadn't been so caught up in chasing your father's ghost, trying to win another state championship, maybe I wouldn't have even noticed Alex."

The night sky held its breath as I spoke, the stars shimmering like the last vestiges of hope in our crumbling relationship.

"Is that what you think, Jordan?" Ethan's voice reached a crescendo, the sharpness of his words cutting through the air like shards of shattered glass. "You think I'm the one who pushed you into the arms of someone else?"

He took a step forward, his eyes blazing with fury. "You're the one who shattered our trust, Jordan. You threw away everything we had – everything we built together – with a reckless disregard."

My heart thudded painfully in my chest as he continued, his voice low and filled with disdain. "And don't even try to use your art as an excuse. Your feelings for Alex have nothing to do with your talent. He could never be half the man that I am."

His cruel words sliced through me like a knife, leaving fresh wounds in their wake. I knew he only said them to hurt me, but they stung all the same. How could he not understand the turmoil I felt in my soul? The torment of wanting to follow my dreams while knowing it would take me away from him?

"Maybe you're right," I whispered, my tears falling unabated as I stared into the depths of his brown eyes. "Maybe I was wrong to think that love could survive the storms life throws at us."

"Jordan," he breathed, the anger in his voice giving way to something far more painful – resignation. "I just... I can't do this anymore."

The weight of his words settled heavily on my shoulders, crushing me with their finality. As I stood there, my heart splintered into a thousand pieces, and I couldn't help but wonder if our love could ever be repaired.

"Stop, Ethan," I cried, my voice strained and desperate, tears blurring my vision as I stared into his eyes. "I didn't cheat on you, I swear."

"It's not just about Alex!" I continued, my hands shaking with emotion. "You're the one who destroyed us! You became so obsessed with winning another state championship that you pushed me away! You stopped caring about anything else!"

"Jordan," he whispered, his voice filled with disbelief and hurt. But I couldn't hold back any longer; the pain inside me had been festering for too long.

"Look at what you've done to me!" I shouted, pulling up the sleeve of my shirt to reveal the scars that marred my arm. The evidence of my depression and self-harm that I had tried so desperately to hide from him.

Ethan's eyes widened in shock, and I could see a flicker of guilt flash across his face before it hardened once more. He reached out and grabbed my arm, his fingers digging into my skin as he inspected the scars.

"Is this what you want? To blame me for your own pain?" he spat venomously, his face inches from mine.

"Let go!" I screamed, using my free hand to slap him across the face. The echo of the impact rang through the night air, leaving us both stunned by the intensity of my action.

For a moment, we stood there, locked in a tableau of pain and betrayal. Then, Ethan took a step back, releasing his grip on my arm. A wall of ice seemed to form around his resolve as he looked at me with a mixture of disappointment and anguish.

"Fine, Jordan," he said, his voice cold and distant. "If that's how you feel, then our love is dead."

His words pierced my heart like a dagger, their finality ringing in the night air. And in that moment, I knew that nothing I could say or do would be enough to bring him back.

The cold earth beneath me seemed to absorb the shock of Ethan's words, and my body crumpled to the yard, like a discarded piece of paper. The pain in my chest mirrored the agony in my soul as the last remnants of hope shattered into a thousand pieces. I couldn't breathe, couldn't think; all I could do was feel the weight of this moment pressing down on me.

"Jordan," Ethan's voice wavered, but he didn't look back. Instead, he took another step away from me, his footsteps echoing through the night as a testament to the bond we had lost.

"Please," I managed to choke out, my heart aching with each breath, "don't go."

He hesitated for the briefest of moments, as if considering whether to turn around and face our broken love head-on. But then, with a sigh that carried the weight of regret and disappointment, he continued walking away. It was then that I realized I was grappling with an impossible choice – reach out and beg Ethan to stay or let him go.

My voice trembling, I whispered, "Ethan, was it all a lie? All those evenings when we talked under the stars about our hopes and doubts? Was it all just an illusion?"

I felt a small flicker of hope that asking these questions would restore our relationship. But at that moment, I needed to understand how we had managed to come to this point—where the love we'd shared had turned into dust.

"It wasn't a lie, Jordan," Ethan said without turning towards me. "But sometimes, even love isn't enough."

His words cut through the silence like a knife, leaving me feeling more alone than ever before. How could love not be enough for us? We had defied expectations, fought against the constraints of our small town, and bared our souls to one another. And yet, here we were, standing on opposite sides of an insurmountable chasm.

I begged, my voice quavering, "Please, don't go. Let us talk this out. Our relationship is too valuable to just throw away."

But Ethan didn't stop. He continued walking away, his footsteps growing fainter and fainter as he disappeared into the darkness. I was left with nothing but the memories of our love and the haunting question of whether we could ever find our way back to each other.

"Goodbye, Ethan," I breathed, my heart heavy with longing and regret.

My trembling hand hovered in the air, caught between the impossible choice of reaching out for Ethan or letting him go. My heart ached with the need to have him stay, to work through the pain and find our way back to each other. But words failed me, and my hand became a silent plea, a desperate hope that he would turn around and give our love another chance.

"Wait," I whispered into the night, but the wind carried away my voice before it could reach him.

Ethan's retreating figure faded into the shadows, until all that remained was the deafening silence his absence left behind. The once comforting darkness of my yard now felt like an endless abyss, swallowing the remnants of our love. Even the stars above seemed to dim, as if mourning the loss of what we once had.

I clenched my fists, fighting back the urge to scream, to break the quiet that had settled over me like a shroud. Instead, I turned my gaze toward the sky, searching for answers among the constellations that had been our silent witnesses on countless nights spent together. But they offered no solace, their distant glimmers only serving to remind me of the emptiness that had replaced the warmth of Ethan's embrace.

The memories of our shared laughter and whispered confessions played like a film reel in my mind, each scene a testament to the love that had bloomed between us. Every touch, every stolen kiss, was embedded in my soul, indelible marks that connected me to Ethan even as he walked away.

"Was it all for nothing?" I asked myself, my chest tightening with the weight of unspoken regrets.

But there was no answer, only the cold realization that our love, like the fleeting beauty of a sunset, had come to an end. It was a truth I couldn't escape, no matter how much I wished to turn back time and rewrite our story.

My knees buckled, unable to support the weight of a love that had been shattered. I crumpled to the ground, my anguished cries tearing through the stillness of the night. My tears blurred the edges of the world around me, transforming the stars above into streaks of light that seemed to blend with my own grief.

"Please," I whispered, my voice shaking as it dissolved into the darkness. "Why?"

The stars stared down at me, their brilliance only serving to highlight the devastation that lay below. They were cold and distant, a cruel reminder of the beauty that once existed in our love. A love that had been nurtured by tender touches and shared dreams, a love that had blossomed against all odds.

"Is this really the end?" I asked myself, my chest tightening with the weight of unspoken regrets.

But there was no answer, only the cold realization that our love, like the fleeting beauty of a sunset, had come to an end. It was a truth I couldn't escape, no matter how much I wished to turn back time and rewrite our story.

"Goodbye, Ethan," I murmured, my voice barely audible over the sound of my own heart breaking. "I love you."

And with those final words, I let go of the hope that had kept me tethered to him, watching as it vanished into the night like a dying star.

As I knelt there on the damp grass, the anguish of my loss threatened to consume me. But amid the pain, I clung to the memories of our love, seeking solace in the echoes of laughter and the warmth of stolen kisses. Each memory was like a brushstroke on the canvas of my heart, a testament to the passion and tenderness that had once defined us.

"Will I ever feel that way again?" I wondered, my thoughts drifting like leaves on a breeze. "Or am I destined to live in the shadow of what we once had?"

The night offered no answers, its silence only amplifying the emptiness that now enveloped me. And as I gazed up at the starlit sky, I couldn't help but think of Ethan, his absence a void that seemed to stretch across the universe.

"Is he looking at the same stars?" I thought, my heart aching with longing. "Does he feel this same crushing loneliness?"

But even as I pondered these questions, I knew that the answers didn't matter. Our love, like the stars above, was now out of reach, a distant light that could never again warm my soul.

I pulled myself up from the damp grass, my legs trembling with the effort. My heart felt as if it would shatter into a million pieces, each one carrying the weight of our love's demise. I stumbled towards the front porch, feeling as lost and broken as the relationship that had once been my guiding light.

The stars above offered no solace, their cold indifference cutting deeper than any blade. I sank onto the wooden steps of the porch, my hands running over the grain, seeking comfort in its familiar roughness.

"Jordan," I heard Ethan's voice echo in my memory, recalling the way he used to say my name, his touch as tender as a brushstroke on canvas. "You're the most beautiful thing I've ever seen."

"Was I really?" I asked the silent night, my tears falling like raindrops onto the weathered wood beneath me. "Or was that just another lie?"

I clenched my fists, the pain grounding me in the agonizing present. For a moment, I wished I could trade my artistic talent for the power to turn back time, to rewrite our story and erase the mistakes that had led us here.

"Remember when we used to watch the stars together, Ethan?" I murmured, my gaze fixed on the glittering sky above. "We'd lay side by side on the field after practice, our dreams as boundless as the universe."

"Touchdown!" I could almost hear him shout, his laughter contagious as he celebrated another victory. Football had always been more than just a game for him; it was a connection to his father, a link to the man he longed to make proud.

"Is that what drove us apart?" I wondered, my heart heavy with regret. "Did I fail to understand the depths of your devotion, blinded by my own insecurities?"

"Jordan, you're amazing just as you are," his voice whispered in my mind, a ghostly memory that brought both comfort and pain. "You don't need to change for anyone."

"Was that true once?" I asked the darkness, my soul crying out for an answer. "Or was our love always doomed, a beautiful illusion destined to fade like the colors of a sunset?"

The night remained silent, leaving me to grapple with the haunting questions and the uncertainty that gnawed at my heart. And as I sat there on the front porch, my eyes fixed on the stars, I knew that I would never stop searching for the answers – even if it meant wandering forever in the shadow of our love.

"Will we ever find our way back to each other?" I whispered into the void, my voice a desperate plea for hope. "Or is this truly the end?"

The stars twinkled coldly above me, offering no solace or guidance as I faced the daunting unknown.

Chapter Eighteen

The sun-drenched school courtyard seemed to shimmer like an enchanted oasis, the golden light filtering through the leaves and casting intricate patterns on the ground. It felt as though the world had slowed down just for us, allowing time to breathe and embrace the beauty around us.

"Hey, let's sit over there," Alex suggested, pointing to a bench hidden in the shade of a large tree. Weaving our way through the bustling students, we found our moment of solitude amidst the chaos.

"Whew, I needed a break from all that," I confessed as we settled onto the bench. "School can be so overwhelming sometimes."

"Tell me about it," Alex agreed, his eyes meeting mine, offering a sense of understanding I hadn't realized I longed for. "What do you do when everything seems to be too much?"

"Well," I hesitated, shrugging. "I paint. It helps me escape from reality and pour out everything I'm feeling onto the canvas."

"Yeah me too," Alex said, his face lighting up with genuine interest. "I've always felt that my best work comes from when I'm feeling more emotional than normal."

"Exactly," I replied, blushing slightly at his enthusiasm. Every time Alex spoke I felt butterflies. "What else do you do to deal with the weight of the world?"

"Stargazing," Alex admitted with a wistful smile. "There's something about the vastness of space that makes our problems seem so insignificant. It's comforting to know that we're not alone in the universe."

"That makes sense, I've noticed stars in your artwork" I agreed, intrigued by this new side of Alex. "So, what do you want to do with your life? I mean, after high school and everything."

"Good question," Alex pondered, his eyes fixed on a distant point as if seeing into the future. "I think I want to study astronomy and maybe work at a planetarium or something. I want to paint too. I don't know, so many options," he laughed. "What about you?"

"An artist, of course," I laughed, but the weight of my dreams felt heavy in my chest. "At least, that's what I hope for. Sometimes it feels like I'm reaching for something just out of my grasp."

"Hey," Alex said softly, his hand brushing against mine, sending a jolt of electricity through my body. "Don't be modest. You're incredibly talented, Jordan. Don't let self-doubt hold you back."

"Thank you," I whispered, feeling my heart swell with gratitude for this newfound connection. We sat there, side by side, basking in the warmth of the sun and the magic of our shared dreams. For the first time in a long while, I felt truly understood. And as we continued to talk and laugh, the world seemed to fade away, leaving only the two of us and the boundless possibilities laid out before us.

The atmosphere in the courtyard had shifted ever so slightly, with a warm tranquility wrapping around us like a gentle embrace. A breeze meandered through the leaves above, scattering dappled sunlight across our faces and carrying the sweet scent of blooming flowers. The distant laughter of students seemed to blend into the soothing backdrop, their voices softened by the golden haze of the afternoon sun.

"Sometimes, I wonder if we're just the sum of our dreams," Alex mused, his eyes reflecting the light as he looked up at the swaying branches. "You know, the hopes and fears that keep us moving forward." He wore a simple T-shirt and jeans, his muscles straining underneath the fabric.

I contemplated his statement for a moment before responding. "I think you're right. Our dreams shape who we are and what we become."

"Exactly!" Alex exclaimed, his enthusiasm infectious. "What's your biggest dream, Jordan?"

"Besides being a successful artist?" I chuckled, feeling a little vulnerable as I shared my deepest aspirations. "I've always wanted to travel the world, experience different cultures, and maybe find some inspiration along the way."

"Wow, that sounds amazing," Alex said, his eyes shining with genuine interest. "I'd love to do something like that too. Do you have any specific places in mind?"

"Everywhere," I admitted, my thoughts drifting to far-off lands and exotic adventures. "But I guess the top of my list would be Paris, Rome, and Tokyo. How about you?"

"Those are great choices," Alex agreed. "For me, it's more about seeking out the hidden gems, the places most people overlook. There's something magical about discovering the lesser-known corners of the world."

"Definitely," I nodded, feeling a sense of hope as our dreams intertwined. We continued to share our aspirations, fears, and hopes for the future. It was as if our conversation peeled away the layers that separated us, allowing us to connect on a deeper level.

"Jordan, I have to confess something," Alex said hesitantly, his gaze shifting away from mine. "I've always been drawn to the stars, like they're calling out to me in some way."

"Really?" I asked, intrigued by this new insight into Alex's inner world.

"Yeah, it's hard to explain," he continued, his voice softening. "Sometimes I look up at the night sky and feel this overwhelming sense of wonder. Like there's so much more out there, just waiting to be discovered."

"Maybe you're meant to explore the universe," I suggested, smiling at the thought of Alex charting a course through the stars.

"Maybe," Alex said with a small laugh. "It would be an adventure, that's for sure."

As we sat there, basking in the warmth of the sun and the magic of our shared dreams, I felt a connection unlike any I'd experienced before. We were two souls reaching for the stars, bound by the hope and longing that fueled our journey. And as the shadows lengthened and the sunlight faded, I knew that together, we could conquer the world.

"Hey, do you remember the first time we met?" I asked, breaking the comfortable silence between us.

Alex leaned back on the bench and looked at the sky. "Of course, it was in the art room."

As he spoke, I couldn't help but notice how Alex's eyes lit up when talking about our shared passion for art. "You know," I began hesitantly, "I've been thinking a lot about that day, and how much has changed since then."

Alex turned to me, his gaze curious yet gentle. "What do you mean?"

I took a deep breath, trying to untangle the whirlwind of emotions inside me. "Well, I guess what I'm trying to say is that... I feel like my feelings for you have changed. Like, it's gone beyond art, and I can't deny that there's this connection between us."

Alex's eyes widened slightly, and he paused before responding. "Jordan, I think I've loved you from the moment I first saw you." He reached out, his fingers lightly grazing mine.

Our hands brushed against each other, sending an electric current through my body. My heart raced, and I knew that I couldn't ignore the growing intimacy between us any longer.

"Is it... Is it wrong to feel this way?" I asked, my voice barely more than a whisper.

Alex shook his head slowly, his eyes never leaving mine. "No, Jordan." He shook his head.

"It feels so fast," I started.

Alex interrupted me, "There's nothing wrong with feeling a connection with someone. There's no timeline on these things either. It doesn't take away from your relationship with Ethan. It just means that you're growing as a person, and that's okay."

I felt a wave of relief wash over me, followed by an undeniable warmth that radiated from Alex's presence. We sat there, our shoulders brushing against one another, sharing meaningful glances as the world around us seemed to fade away. I turned towards him and looked into his eyes.

"Jordan," Alex whispered, breaking our shared gaze. "I know this is new for you and that you only recently broke up with Ethan, but you can embrace this. Don't be afraid or caught up in feelings of guilt. There is nothing bad about this."

"Thank you, Alex," I murmured, my voice barely audible amidst the distant laughter of students and the rustling leaves above us. "That means more to me than you know."

The sun dipped lower in the sky, casting a warm golden glow over the courtyard as if it were spun from dreams. Shadows stretched and danced upon the ground, weaving intricate patterns that told stories of his own. Alex and I lingered on the bench beneath the old oak tree, our conversation ebbing and flowing like the gentle breeze that rustled the leaves above us.

"When did you start having feelings for me?" Alex asked suddenly.

I hesitated, my fingers tracing the worn grooves of the wooden bench. "I don't know," I admitted, my voice soft and wistful. "I think it's been building for a while now. Every time we talk or spend time together, I feel this pull towards you. It's like you're the missing piece of my puzzle."

Alex smiled at me, his eyes crinkling at the corners. "I know the feeling. I tried to ignore it for a long time, but I can't deny it anymore."

We sat in silence for a while, lost in our own thoughts. The air around us was heavy with the weight of our unspoken desires, and I felt a sense of anticipation building inside me.

"Jordan," Alex said suddenly, breaking the silence. "Can I kiss you?"

I turned to him, my heart racing with a mixture of excitement and fear. "Yes," I whispered, leaning in towards him.

Our lips met in a soft, gentle kiss, and I felt a rush of heat flood through my body. It was like nothing I'd ever experienced before, a heady mix of desire, passion, and connection. Alex's arms wrapped around me, pulling me closer to him as if he never wanted to let me go.

As we broke apart, I looked into his eyes, feeling a sense of wonder at what had just happened. "Wow," I breathed, feeling a smile spread across my face.

Alex grinned back at me, his eyes alight with happiness. "Yeah, wow."

Our shoulders lightly touched as we leaned in closer together, our voices a soft hush amidst the sound of rustling leaves and faraway students' laughter. I felt my heart beat faster due to our proximity.

I couldn't help but giggle as Alex recounted a story from one of his ill-fated night sky-viewing expeditions. "And there I was, perched on the rooftop with my telescope, when my foot slipped and I almost flew off!"

"Wait!" I exclaimed, laughing. "You were on the roof? That's dedication!"

"Hey, you do what you gotta do for the perfect view," Alex grinned, his eyes twinkling like the stars he adored.

As we laughed together, our shoulders brushed against each other, and I felt a warmth that had nothing to do with the sun shining above us. Our connection seemed to deepen with every word we exchanged, and it was difficult to ignore the growing affection within me. I wondered if Alex felt it too.

"Jordan," said Alex, his voice softening. "Do you ever think about combining your art with astronomy? Like, creating something that captures the beauty of the universe?"

"I haven't thought about it before," I admitted, intrigued by the idea. "But it sounds amazing. I'd love to try it out sometime."

"Really?" Alex asked, his face lighting up. "That would be incredible! I could show you some constellations and galaxies to use as inspiration."

"Deal," I agreed, smiling. As we continued to chat, Alex's hand found its way to my back, offering a gentle touch that sent shivers down my spine.

The sun's warm rays bathed the courtyard in golden light, casting intricate patterns on the ground. The scent of blooming flowers filled the air, while the distant laughter of students provided a soothing backdrop to our conversation. In that moment, I couldn't imagine being anywhere else.

My thoughts swirled around me – the comfort of Alex's presence, the excitement of exploring new artistic horizons, and the curious feeling that had blossomed between us. What was this strange connection? This safety I felt? I couldn't be sure, but I knew one thing: I didn't want this moment to end.

"Jordan?" Alex's queried. "You seemed lost in thought for a moment there."

"Sorry," I said, shaking my head slightly. "I was just thinking about how much I've enjoyed getting to know you and how... special our connection feels."

Alex's smile grew wider, his eyes meeting mine. "I feel the same way, Jordan. There's something about you that makes me feel like I can truly be myself."

"Likewise," I murmured, my heart swelling with warmth and affection.

"Have you ever thought about what might happen between us in the future?" Alex said softly, his eyes never leaving mine.

I hesitated for a moment, my heart skipping a beat as I considered his question. "I... I haven't really allowed myself to think too far ahead," I admitted, my voice cracking slightly. "But I know that I want to be around you, to see where this connection between us leads."

Alex nodded, his fingers brushing against mine as we sat side by side. "I feel the same way. It's hard to put into words, but... there's something about us that feels so right, so inevitable."

As we spoke, I couldn't help but be aware of the growing stillness around us – the quieting of voices, the gentle rustle of leaves as the breeze picked up. It was as if the world had paused, holding its breath in anticipation of our next move.

"I don't know, though," Alex continued, his gaze steady and sincere, "I just want more. Time. Kisses. Everything, really."

"Me too," I whispered, feeling a shiver run down my spine at the thought of what lay ahead for us.

In that moment, the air seemed to sparkle with possibility, alive with the promise of unspoken dreams and untapped potential. My heart was beating faster. Out on the far horizon, birds were circling in slow spirals against a clear blue sky. Half-hidden behind a cloud, sunlight caught the red tip of an airplane's wing.

"This maybe got deeper than I thought it would," Alex said, laughing at how serious the conversation had turned. "So, tell me about your latest art project."

I hesitated for a moment, feeling the weight of my dreams in every brushstroke. "Well," I began slowly, "it's an exploration of identity, I guess. The layers we build up over time and the masks we wear to protect our true selves."

"Sounds fascinating," Alex replied, his eyes bright with genuine curiosity. "Do you ever feel like you're still discovering who you really are?"

"Sometimes," I admitted, surprised by the vulnerability in my own words. "But isn't that what life is all about? Constantly evolving and growing?"

"Exactly," Alex said, nodding in agreement. "And that's the beauty of art, too – it helps us understand ourselves and the world around us."

The sun was just beginning to set, casting a warm golden glow across the courtyard as Alex and I sat there. A sea of students ebbed and flowed around us, his laughter dancing through the air like a carefree melody. But in our little oasis, time seemed to slow down, allowing us to savor this rare moment of solitude.

"Hey, remember the first time we really talked?" Alex asked, his eyes sparkling with mischief. "You were so focused on your sketchbook that you didn't even notice me until I sat right next to you."

I laughed, my cheeks flushing at the memory. "I was so embarrassed! But you just smiled and started talking about art, and it felt like we'd known each other for years."

"You were so flustered," Alex said, leaning closer to me, his gaze intense and curious. "And so cute."

"Stop," I said, running a hand through my curly hair. "I don't even want to think about the awkwardness of that moment."

He chuckled and tapped the tip of my nose with his finger. "Okay, I'll stop – but only if you kiss me."

My heart skipped a beat at his words, but I couldn't help but smile. "Is that a bribe?"

"Maybe," he said, his eyes full of mischief. "But it's a good one, right?"

I bit my lip, trying to hide my growing excitement. "I don't know..."

"Come on," Alex said, his voice dropping to a whisper. "I'm dying here."

Without a word, I leaned in and pressed my lips against his, feeling a jolt of electricity run through my body as our mouths met. For a moment, everything else fell away, leaving only the sensation of his lips on mine and the warmth of his body against mine. It was as if we were the only two people in the world, lost in our own private universe.

When we finally pulled away, gasping for breath, Alex smiled at me. "Wow," he said softly. "That was... incredible."

I nodded, unable to find words to describe the rush of feelings that was still coursing through me. All I knew was that I wanted more of this – more of him, more of us.

As the world around us slowly came back into focus, I couldn't help but feel like everything had shifted in that one moment. A new energy pulsed through my veins, a desire to explore this connection with Alex in every way possible.

As the sun dipped further below the horizon, casting intricate patterns of light and shadow onto the ground, I realized how deeply my feelings for Alex had grown. We'd bonded over our love for art and shared dreams, but it was more than that – he understood me in a way nobody else ever had.

"Alex," I said hesitantly, my heart pounding in my chest, "I have to tell you something."

"Go ahead," he murmured, his eyes never leaving mine.

"I think... I think I'm falling for you."

There was a moment of silence as my words hung in the air between us, fragile and delicate as a spider's web. And then, to my surprise, Alex smiled – a warm, genuine smile that lit up his face like the first rays of sun after a storm.

He spoke in a gentle voice, his fingers entwining with mine, "Jordan, I've been in love with you for an eternity," he murmured.

As we sat there, hand in hand, bathed in the glow of the setting sun, I knew that our journey had only just begun. We would face challenges, of course, but together we could overcome anything. For the first time in my life, I felt truly alive – not just existing, but living, thriving, and growing.

And as the last remnants of daylight faded into twilight, I couldn't help but think that perhaps, just perhaps, the best was yet to come.

Chapter Nineteen

The early evening sun filled the art studio with a gentle glow, bathing it in an orange-ish hue. I worked carefully to get it ready for Alex's visit, setting out easels and laying out paintbrushes and paints on the table. I went about my tasks with precision, eagerness surging through my veins as I tidied up.

Yesterday we had talked about our dreams and worries; that conversation felt like a turning point. I was sure that I was falling for Alex and his arrival this day held so much potential.

When Alex knocked on the door, I inhaled deeply and welcomed him into my garage that had been transformed into a makeshift studio. We hugged and then started discussing art.

"Have you ever tried using oil pastels?" I asked, holding up a stick of vibrant blue. "I've been experimenting with them lately."

"Ah, I prefer acrylics," Alex replied, his voice full of passion. "There's something about their versatility that really speaks to me."

Our conversation flowed effortlessly as we discussed various art techniques and shared thoughts on our favorite artists. Alex's eyes sparkled with enthusiasm as he spoke, and I found myself becoming more and more captivated by his artistic perspective.

"Art has such an emotional impact," I mused, running my fingers along the edge of a canvas. "It can evoke feelings that are otherwise impossible to express."

"Absolutely," Alex agreed, nodding intently. "A piece of art can communicate so much without ever saying a word."

Feeling the trust and understanding that had blossomed between us, I took a deep breath and opened up about my own creative struggles and fears. "Sometimes, though... I worry that I'm not doing enough. That I'm not pushing myself artistically."

Alex listened attentively, his eyes full of empathy. "I think we all feel that way at times. But remember, it's important to be patient with yourself. Growth takes time."

As Alex and I continued to discuss our shared passion for art, we found ourselves immersed in deep conversation. Our experiences and feelings about art aligned beautifully, and the emotional connection between us only seemed to deepen as we conversed. We explored ideas of artistic expression and the impact it had on our lives and identities.

"Isn't that what makes art so powerful?" Alex asked, his eyes shining with intensity. "The ability to transcend boundaries and bring people together?"

"Exactly," I agreed, feeling a warmth spread through my chest. "It's what I've always loved about it."

Our conversation eventually slowed, and a comfortable silence fell upon us, filled with unspoken words and tension. As we exchanged meaningful glances, I could feel the raw emotions simmering beneath the surface, threatening to overflow.

"Jordan," Alex whispered softly, his voice barely audible.

"Alex," I replied, my heart pounding in my ears.

In that moment, all pretense vanished, and we gave in to the desire that had been building between us. Our lips met tentatively at first, but soon the kiss deepened, fueled by a mixture of longing and curiosity. My hands traced the contours of Alex's body, noting the firmness of his muscles and the smoothness of his skin.

As our kiss intensified, our bodies moved together in perfect harmony. We clung to each other as though we would be torn apart if we let go. Our hearts raced in time with one another, and I felt an overwhelming swell of emotion rising within me.

"Your body is like a work of art," I murmured, my fingers lingering on the curve of his shoulder. "Each line and curve tells a story."

"Show me your heart, Jordan," he whispered, his breath hot against my ear. "Let's create something beautiful together."

As our bodies intertwined, I marveled at the intimate dance we shared, each touch and movement exploring new depths of our connection. The room seemed to fade away, leaving only the rhythm of our hearts and the quiet sound of our breaths mingling in the air.

"Alex..." I breathed, lost in the sensation of our bodies becoming one, the world around us fading to nothing but our passionate embrace. The emotions we shared in that moment were raw and palpable, a testament to the bond we had formed through our love for art and each other.

"Jordan," he whispered back, his eyes locked on mine as if searching for something deeper within me.

As his lips continued to explore my body, I felt the soft brush of Alex's fingertips across my skin. The sensation sent shivers down my spine, and I welcomed it with a contented sigh.

"Jordan," he whispered against my neck, his voice husky with need. "I want to make you feel good."

"Please," I gasped, my body aching for him.

We moved to the antique chaise lounge near the window, the plush pillows providing a cushion beneath us as we continued our exploration of each other's bodies. The dim light filtering through the sheer curtains cast a warm glow over the room, illuminating the artwork surrounding us. Each piece seemed to come alive with emotion, as if they too were sharing in the intimacy of this moment.

Alex drew a deep breath as he stood and admired me, his gaze lingering on my body. His fingers were gentle but firm as they brushed my hair away from my face, the gesture sending shivers down my spine. He then leaned in to capture my lips in a passionate kiss before carefully undoing the buttons of my shirt.

With each button that came undone, I felt more exposed and vulnerable. But Alex's touches were gentle and reassuring, and I knew that he would never hurt me. As he pulled away, I glanced down at his own shirt, now unbuttoned revealing a smooth expanse of skin beneath.

He noticed my gaze and smiled, slowly pulling his shirt off before guiding me back onto the chaise lounge. He stood there for a moment, just admiring me as the light of the setting sun streamed through the window. I felt myself blush as every inch of me became visible in the golden light.

I was suddenly aware of how close we were and how much trust we had placed in one another to take this step together. With shaky hands I began to take off the rest of my clothes before Alex followed suit and unfolded himself next to me on the chaise lounge.

We lay there side by side, skin against skin with our limbs tangled together as if they belonged there all along. Our hearts beat in perfect harmony as we explored each other's bodies under the warm embrace of twilight's glow. My eyes closed as waves of pleasure rolled over me with each touch from Alex's fingertips and lips until finally I could resist no longer - surrendering myself wholly to him for what would be our greatest work yet...

His hand slid down my back, pulling me impossibly closer to him. As he entered me, a wave of pleasure washed over me, and my mind went blank for a moment. My heart raced, my breath coming in shallow gasps as we moved together, our bodies perfectly in sync. Time seemed to stand still, as if the universe itself was holding its breath, waiting for the climax of our passionate encounter.

"Ah, Ethan..." I sighed, my thoughts momentarily lost in the overwhelming sensations that flooded my senses.

Alex pulled away from me, his eyes filled with surprise and pain. Confused, I looked up at him. "What's wrong? Why did you stop?" I asked, attempting to draw him back to me.

"I'm not him," Alex replied quietly.

"Who are you talking about?" I questioned.

"I'm not Ethan," he said again.

My heart dropped as I realized my mistake, and the weight of what I had done came crashing down on me. The name that had slipped from my lips was not Alex's, but Ethan's. The man I loved – the man I couldn't have. Panic filled my chest, and I struggled to find words that would somehow mend the hurt that I had caused.

"Alex, I'm so sorry," I stammered, my voice barely a whisper. "I didn't mean... It just happened."

The air in the studio grew heavy, a suffocating silence descending upon us. Alex's breath hitched, his movements stilling as he pulled further away from me. I blinked, my mind racing to understand why our passionate embrace had come to such an abrupt halt.

"Alex?" I whispered, confusion lacing my voice.

"Jordan, I..." He swallowed hard, unable to meet my gaze. "You just called me Ethan."

Shame and regret washed over me like a tidal wave, threatening to pull me under. The name had slipped past my lips without warning, betraying the depth of my feelings for Ethan. My heart ached with the realization that I had wounded Alex so deeply. I sat up on the chaise leaning forward.

"Alex, I'm so sorry," I murmured, reaching out to touch his arm. "I don't know why I said that. It was a mistake."

He flinched at my touch, retreating further from me. His eyes, once filled with warmth and understanding, now held only hurt and disappointment. "I'm not Ethan, Jordan," he whispered, his voice cracking. "I can't be him, no matter how much you want me to be."

"Please, let me explain," I pleaded, desperate to salvage what was left of our connection. But the more I tried to reach out, the more he withdrew, his defenses rising like a fortress around him.

"You need to figure things out, Jordan. And I... I can't be the one to help you do that," Alex suggested quietly, his voice barely audible as he began to gather his clothes.

As he dressed and moved towards the door, I could feel our friendship – our brief romance – slipping away like sand through my fingers. The wistful, nostalgic tone of our earlier conversation seemed like a distant memory, replaced by the cold sting of reality.

"Alex, talk to me," I pleaded.

"Fine, Jordan?" His voice cracked, and he looked away, unable to hold my gaze. "You call out another man's name while we're... together, and you want to talk about it?"

I closed my eyes, wincing at the hurt that laced every syllable. "I didn't mean to say Ethan's name, Alex. It just... it slipped out. You have to believe me."

"Of course it slipped out," he said, his voice heavy with sarcasm. "Because deep down, that's who you really want, isn't it? Ethan, your golden boy."

"Alex, it's not like that," I protested, my heart racing. "Yes, I love Ethan, but I also care about you. So much. More than I can put into words."

"Then why did you say his name?" Alex demanded, his eyes brimming with unshed tears.

"Because I'm scared, okay?" I admitted, my own voice trembling. "I'm scared of losing him, of not being good enough for him. And when I felt your touch, it was like a lifeline, a reminder of what I might lose if I don't fight for him."

"Jordan," he whispered, shaking his head as though he couldn't comprehend what I was saying, "you can't just use me as a stand-in for Ethan. That's not fair to either of us."

"I know, and I'm sorry. I never meant for it to be this way." The weight of my confession hung heavy in the air between us, filling the room with a palpable tension.

"Look, I get it" - Alex took a deep breath - "I understand that you're in love with Ethan. But I can't be the one you turn to when things get tough with him. I have my own heart to protect."

"Alex, I never meant to hurt you," I said softly.

"You need to figure things out." Alex stated again, his voice barely audible as he touched the doorknob.

I couldn't help but feel a knot of guilt tightening in my chest as I studied Alex's face, searching for some semblance of forgiveness. He managed a weak smile, and despite the hurt that lingered in his eyes, there was an undeniable grace to his demeanor.

"Jordan, it's alright," he said gently, the corners of his mouth trembling ever so slightly. "We all make mistakes, and we can't help who we love."

"Thank you, Alex. I just wish... I wish I hadn't messed things up between us." Goosebumps prickled on my skin as I wrapped my arms around myself, seeking comfort in my own embrace.

"Sometimes things don't work out the way we want them to," Alex murmured, his gaze shifting to the floor. "But that doesn't mean we can't still be friends, right?"

"Of course," I replied, my heart swelling with gratitude for his understanding. "I'd like that."

"Good," he said, offering me another small smile "Take care of yourself, Jordan. And remember - you deserve to be happy."

"Thank you, Alex," I whispered, struggling to hold back the tears threatening to spill down my cheeks. "You do too."

With a final, lingering glance at me, Alex stepped through the doorway and disappeared from sight. As I listened to door closing, I couldn't help but feel a deep sense of loss - not only for the friendship that had been irreparably altered, but for the simple clarity of knowing where my heart truly belonged.

As the sun dipped below the horizon, casting the room in shadow, I found myself alone with nothing but the memory of Ethan's touch to keep me company. And as much as it scared me to admit it, I knew then that I was utterly, irrevocably wrecked for him.

Chapter Twenty

Almost two months had passed since I broke up with Alex, and February's icy grip held the town of Ada in its frosty grasp. The high school gym was a haven from the cold, buzzing with anticipation as everyone gathered for Ethan's college decision announcement. Warmth radiated from the bodies packed into the stands, the smell of sweat and old sneakers permeating the air.

I sat among my classmates, their energy contagious and infectious, as they whispered excitedly about the possibilities laid out before our star quarterback, Ethan Parker. He stood tall and proud on the basketball court, his blond hair catching the light, his warm brown eyes scanning the crowd. The staff and faculty, beaming with pride, surrounded him, and the entire student body was present to bear witness to this momentous occasion.

"Can you believe this is happening?" a girl behind me gushed. "Ethan's going to make it big, just you wait and see!"

"Of course," her friend replied. "He's got talent and determination. And he's such a great guy too."

Their words struck a chord within me. Even though we were not together at that moment, my heart still beat for Ethan. I longed to be close to him again, to share his triumphs and support him through his struggles. But we were separated by the divide created when I chose to end things with him and explore my connection with Alex, and now we were both left standing on opposite sides, trying to find our way back to each other.

"Hey, Jordan!" someone called out, snapping me out of my thoughts. I turned to see a few familiar faces – friends and fellow students who had come together to celebrate Ethan's achievements.

"Hey," I replied, forcing a smile. Despite the excitement in the air, I couldn't shake the feeling of loneliness that enveloped me like a thick fog.

"Isn't this incredible?" one of them asked, unable to contain their enthusiasm. "I wonder where he's going to choose?"

"Only a few more minutes until we find out," another chimed in, eyes glued to the clock ticking down on the wall.

All around me, the gym erupted with speculation and predictions, the energy in the room reaching a fever pitch as the moment of truth drew near. And through it all, I couldn't help but feel a sense of longing – for the past, for the future, and for the boy who had captured my heart with his strength, determination, and unwavering love.

The news crews had descended upon our gym, their cameras and microphones poised to capture every moment of Ethan's college decision. He was ranked in the top of the nation's high school quarterbacks. In some rankings he was first. This might be the biggest choice Ethan would make this early in his career. The weight of anticipation hung heavy in the air, like a thick fog that refused to dissipate. Reporters from local stations mingled with national sports journalists, all eager for the exclusive scoop on where the Ethan would be taking his talents next.

At the center of it all was a table adorned with an array of college caps, each one representing a potential future for Ethan. He stood beside it, flanked by his mother, coaches, and teammates – a united front showcasing the support he'd garnered throughout his high school career. A hush fell over the crowd as he took his seat, his fingers brushing against the microphones before him.

"Are you ready?" his coach asked, clapping him on the shoulder with a reassuring smile.

"Ready as I'll ever be," Ethan replied, his voice steady but tinged with nerves.

As I sat in the stands, my heart raced in time with Ethan's every breath. This moment felt like a culmination of everything we'd been through together – the love, the loss, and the bittersweet memories that made up the tapestry of our shared experiences. And now, as he prepared to make a choice that would shape the course of his life, I couldn't help but feel a profound sense of loneliness.

"Good luck, man! You got this!" one of his teammates shouted, breaking the silence that had settled over the gym.

"Thanks," Ethan responded, flashing a nervous grin that seemed to light up the room.

"Hey, Jordan," someone whispered from behind me,. "How are you holding up?"

"Fine," I lied, forcing a smile. "I'm just... here to support him, you know?"

"Of course," they replied, placing a consoling hand on my shoulder. "We all are."

But deep down, I knew that my presence in the stands held a greater significance than simple camaraderie. For Ethan and me, our love had always been about more than just football or art – it was a testament to the power of connection, of finding solace in one another amidst the chaos of life.

So as he sat at that table, his future laid out before him like a roadmap, I couldn't help but hope for a sign – some indication that our paths would converge once more, bringing us back together against all odds. And although the distance I had created between us felt insurmountable, I clung to the belief that love could bridge even the widest chasms, guiding us home to each other's arms once again.

The crowd's energy vibrated through the gym, anticipation hanging heavy in the air. Murmurs and whispers of speculation swirled around me.

"Is he going to OU?" someone asked nearby.

"Definitely not," another person chimed in. "I heard he's considering LSU."

"Really? I thought for sure he'd choose Alabama... or maybe even Florida State," someone else added to the flurry of guesses.

As the thrum of voices continued, I could feel the suspense building within me, my heart pounding against my chest with every beat. It was torturous – the waiting, the wondering, the uncertainty of it all.

Ethan sat at the table, surrounded by caps from various colleges. He looked down at them, scanning each one carefully as if trying to read some hidden message within their embroidered logos. His fingers brushed lightly over the brims, hesitating for a moment before moving on to the next one.

"Hey, Ethan!" a voice called out from the crowd. "You got this, man! We believe in you!"

"Thanks!" he replied, looking up and flashing a smile that sent a jolt of warmth through my chest. Somehow, despite the pressure of the moment, he seemed almost serene – like he was completely at peace with whatever decision he was about to make.

"Man, I can't believe we're really here," a friend beside me sighed, shaking his head in disbelief. "Feels like just yesterday we were all little freshmen running around, trying to figure out where our classes were."

"Time flies, huh?" I agreed, my gaze never leaving Ethan as he took a deep breath and finally began to speak.

"First off, I just want to say thank you," he started, his voice strong and steady. "To everyone for being here. You've all supported me through everything – the wins, the losses, the highs and lows. And I wouldn't be here today without you."

As Ethan continued, his eyes locked with mine for a split second, and I felt a shiver race down my spine. It was as if he were speaking directly to me, reminding me of all the times we'd spent together – the laughter, the tears, the moments that felt like they would last forever.

"Choosing where to go for college is never easy," he said, turning back to the caps in front of him. "But I know that the choice I've made isn't just about football. It's about being true to myself."

"First and foremost, I want to thank my teammates. You guys are my brothers on and off the field, and I couldn't have achieved anything without each and every one of you," Ethan began, his voice filled with warmth and gratitude. I could see the genuine appreciation in his eyes as he scanned the sea of faces before him.

"Next, I'd like to thank my coaches who have pushed me to be the best player I can be, both physically and mentally. Your guidance has been invaluable," he continued, offering a respectful nod to the men standing behind him.

"Of course, none of this would be possible without the unwavering support of my mom. You've been my rock through everything, and I love you more than words can express," Ethan said, turning to his mother, who stood next to him with tears glistening in her eyes.

"Finally, I want to say thank you to my friends. You've been there for me through thick and thin, always ready to lend an ear or offer a kind word when I needed it most. You all mean the world to me."

Ethan's gaze traveled over the crowd, and I felt my heart skip a beat as our eyes locked again for a brief moment. There was something unspoken in that glance, a message meant for me alone.

"Deciding on which university to attend has been difficult, because it's not just about football—it's about following my heart as well. And so, the university I am choosing is a signal to the most important person in my life, that I am willing to do anything, to sacrifice everything for them."

As he spoke those words, I knew deep down that he meant me. The room seemed to fade around us, leaving only Ethan and me, connected by a bond that distance and time could never break.

Ethan picked up the UCLA cap from the table and placed it firmly on his head, smiling with a rare vulnerability. The cameras went off in a frenzy, capturing the pivotal moment that would define the next chapter of our lives.

"UCLA," I whispered to myself, my heart swelling with love and longing for the boy who had chosen to follow his heart, even when it led him far away from home.

The sudden explosion of camera flashes momentarily blinded me, as I tried to process the shock that rippled through the gym. Disbelief and confusion spread across the faces of staff, faculty, and students. Conversations erupted, a collision of questions and speculation filling the air.

"UCLA? Seriously?" someone behind me muttered. "Why wouldn't he go to Oklahoma or Alabama? This doesn't make any sense."

"Maybe he just wants to be in California," another voice chimed in doubtfully.

As the murmurs and whispers swirled around me, I clung to the knowledge that Ethan had chosen UCLA for a reason that transcended football.

"Hey, Jordan!" a familiar voice called out. My best friend, Lucy, pushed her way through the crowd to stand beside me. "Did you hear? Ethan's going to UCLA!"

"Yeah, I heard," I replied softly, my heart aching with a mixture of joy and sorrow. "He's trying to be closer to CalArts, I think."

"Wow," she breathed out, her eyes wide with surprise. "That's... really sweet, actually."

I nodded silently, biting back the tears that threatened to spill over. I knew this was Ethan's way of showing how much he cared, how he was willing to give up the prestige of playing for a powerhouse football team just to be near me. But it also underscored the painful reality of our situation—of two people bound by love but separated by their dreams.

"Jordan, are you okay?" Lucy asked, her eyebrows knitting together with concern.

I forced a smile, swallowing the lump in my throat. "Yeah, I'm fine. Just... surprised, like everyone else."

"Look," she said gently, placing a hand on my shoulder. "I know things have been tough between you and Ethan lately. But maybe this is a sign that you're meant to be together, y'know? A chance for a fresh start."

I wanted to believe her, to cling to the hope that we could still find our way back to each other. But my heart remained heavy with uncertainty.

"Maybe," I murmured, my gaze drifting back to Ethan as he was swarmed by reporters and well-wishers. "I just don't know if it's enough."

"Hey," Lucy said firmly, gripping my shoulder. "Don't give up on him, Jordan. Not when he's willing to do this for you."

"Okay," I whispered, nodding my determination. "I won't."

As the gym filled with excited chatter and speculation, I clung to the lingering warmth of Ethan's unspoken message, a beacon of hope in the uncertain waters of our future. And though I knew there would be challenges ahead, I vowed to fight for the love we shared, no matter the cost.

The gym suddenly erupted into questions shouted and camera flashes, reporters racing to get the first exclusive interview with

Ethan. He was swarmed by a sea of microphones, all pointed at him like weapons, waiting for his next words.

"Mr. Parker, how did you come to this decision?" one reporter asked, her voice barely audible over the frantic buzz of the room.

"Can you tell us more about your relationship with Jordan? How does it feel to be the first out D1 quarterback?" another inquired, catching me off guard. My heart skipped a beat as I realized that they were piecing together Ethan's message, too. There wasn't any way to keep our story hidden now.

"UCLA is an unexpected choice for someone with your talent," a third reporter chimed in. "Why not choose a school more known for its football program?"

Ethan, still wearing the UCLA cap, raised his hands to silence the barrage of questions. His eyes scanned the crowd, finally landing on me. Our gazes locked for a moment, and it felt like time stood still. I could see the determination burning in his brown eyes, and I knew he meant every word of his earlier declaration.

"Listen, everyone," Ethan called out, his voice firm yet gentle. "I made this decision because it's what's best for me, and for the people I care about most. I couldn't be happier with my choice."

As the media continued their frenzy, faculty members began ushering students back to class, while others exchanged hushed whispers about the implications of Ethan's announcement. Throughout the commotion, I couldn't help but focus on the single question that lingered in my mind: What would become of us?

"Jordan," Lucy said, leaning in close so only I could hear her. "You know you have to talk to him, right? After everything that just happened, there's no turning back."

I nodded, my heart pounding in my chest. "I know. But how can I just walk up to him with all these reporters around?"

"Leave that to me," she replied with a mischievous grin.

"Lucy, wait!" I said quickly grabbing her arm before she enacted her plan. "Let Ethan have this moment. I'll talk to him later tonight." I said quietly.

"Really?" She asked incredulously.

"Really." I smiled.

Lucy nodded, understanding the gravity of the situation. "Okay. Just don't wait too long, okay? You don't want to lose him again."

"I won't," I promised, watching as Ethan made his way towards the exit, his entourage of reporters trailing behind him like a pack of hungry wolves. "I'll talk to him tonight."

With a heavy heart, I turned away from the chaos of the gym and made my way back to my class room, my mind whirling with unanswered questions and unspoken fears. I knew that Ethan's decision to attend UCLA was a gesture of his love for me, but I also knew that it was just the beginning of a long road ahead—one filled with obstacles, challenges, and heartache.

But as I settled into my desk, staring up at the chalkboard, I felt a flicker of hope ignite within me. For the first time in a long time, I felt a renewed sense of purpose and determination—the kind that came from knowing that, no matter what, I was not alone. Ethan was with me, every step of the way.

Chapter Twenty-One

My stomach was tied in knots as the sun set and I made my way down the road to Ethan's house. The twinkling stars above me seemed to be mocking me, their gentle light making me feel more alone than ever. I knew this conversation had to take place; Ethan had chosen a future at UCLA, and he had chosen us. But the closer I got to his door, the more doubts started to creep in. What if he had changed his mind? What if he regretted his decision? With trembling fingers, I knocked on the door, my heart pounding so loudly that it felt like it would burst from my chest.

The moment the door swung open, I couldn't help but drink in the sight before me. There stood Ethan, shirtless, his sculpted muscles glistening beneath the soft moonlight. His warm brown eyes met mine, and I could see a mix of surprise and apprehension swirling within their depths.

"Jordan," he said, "What are you doing here?"

I could feel my cheeks flush as I quickly looked away from Ethan's captivating gaze. "Um, I wanted to talk," I said, my voice barely audible. "If that's okay?"

"Of course," he said, stepping back to let me inside. He glanced around the room nervously before gesturing for me to have a seat. We both sat down on the couch, a few feet apart, neither of us speaking a word.

"Uh, I..." I stammered, momentarily losing myself in the contours of his body. "I needed to talk to you. About...you know, your choice."

"UCLA?" he asked, his tone cautious. I hesitated for a moment, allowing myself to take a deep breath and collect my thoughts.

"Yeah," I replied, "Why did you choose UCLA? It came out of nowhere."

Ethan paused, choosing his words carefully. "I thought...I thought it was what you wanted," he confessed, his voice tinged with uncertainty. "But now, I don't know. I'm not sure about anything anymore."

"Why aren't you sure anymore?" I asked, unable to hide the hurt in my voice.

"I mean it was a big decision, and I wanted to show you that you mattered more than football." he said, his eyes conveying a sincerity that I couldn't deny. "But I don't know if that's good enough."

"Why?" I pressed, my emotions bubbling just beneath the surface. "Why choose UCLA then? If you aren't sure that it was good enough?"

"Because sometimes, following your heart means making difficult choices," he whispered, his gaze locked on mine. "And now I'm thinking that I haven't kept my word about giving you space to figure out your feelings for Alex. I don't know if this complicates things for your relationship with him."

"Alex?" The name tasted raw on my tongue, and I could feel the sting of tears threatening to spill over. "Ethan, I don't want Alex. I want you."

"Really?" He blinked, his surprise evident in the way his eyebrows shot upwards.

"Really," I confirmed, my voice barely audible. "I love you, Ethan. Alex will always be special and we have an undeniable connection. But it's you."

Ethan sat back on the couch. I could feel my heart hammering in my chest as I waited for Ethan's response. He rubbed a hand across his forehead, and I felt a hint of panic rising within me. Maybe he couldn't process that I wasn't with Alex, or maybe he didn't feel the same way about me...could this all be for nothing?

Suddenly, Ethan shifted and looked at me. His eyes were serious, yet filled with a warmth that reassured me. He reached out and took both of my hands in his, our fingers entwining together in a comforting embrace.

"Jordan," he said softly, "I love you too."

A wave of relief washed over me and I smiled back at him, not daring to break our gaze. We stayed like that for what seemed like an eternity before finally pulling away from each other.

After a moment Ethan stood up and mumbled, "I need something to drink." And walked to the kitchen.

I followed him and took a set at his dining table. Taking a deep breath, I mustered the courage to address our issues head-on. "Ethan, we need to talk."

"Jordan, what happened with you and Alex?" Ethan turned and asked softly, his eyes searching mine for answers. "You two seemed perfect for each other."

"Alex is great," I replied, running my fingers along the edge of the wooden table. "He understands me on so many levels, but... he's not you, Ethan." My voice trembled as I spoke, raw emotions swirling within me like storm clouds.

"Then why did you push me away?" Ethan questioned, his brow furrowing with confusion and hurt.

"Because I was scared," I admitted, my heart feeling heavy in my chest. "I didn't want to lose you, but I didn't know how to balance my passion for art with our relationship. I didn't feel like there was space for both of our dreams."

Ethan nodded slowly, his brown eyes filled with empathy. "I've been there too, Jordan. The pressure to follow my father's footsteps in football, to live up to everyone's expectations... it's suffocating. But that doesn't mean I don't care about you or our future together."

"Sometimes it feels like football is all that matters to you," I confessed, my words spilling out like floodwaters breaching a dam. "Like everything else, including me, comes second."

"Jordan, that's not true," Ethan insisted, coming to the table and taking a seat. "But I understand why you might feel that way. I guess we've both been so focused on our own dreams that we haven't made enough time for each other." He said pushing a glass of water over to me.

"Maybe," I agreed, my fingers still tracing the table's edge. "But Ethan, if we're going to make this work, we need to find a way to support each other's passions without losing sight of what really matters—our love for one another."

Ethan reached across the table, his hand covering mine, the warmth of his touch sending a shiver down my spine. "You're right, Jordan. We can't let fear hold us back any longer. It's time for us to face our challenges together and show the world that we're stronger as a couple than we ever were apart."

The air in the room grew heavy, a tension building between us as I hesitated to share my heart. My voice wavered, unsure of how to put into words the emotions that swirled within me like a turbulent storm. "Ethan," I began, swallowing hard, "there was this moment in my studio with Alex... we were... together. And I called out your name instead of his."

A flicker of sadness flashed across Ethan's face, but he remained silent, willing me to continue.

"God, it wrecked Alex, you know? He knew then that he was just a stand-in because I couldn't have you. And it hurt him so much, because he really cared for me." My chest tightened, guilt and regret mingling with the longing that still burned for Ethan.

As I looked into Ethan's eyes, I saw a mirror of my own emotions: the vulnerability, the love, the fear. His eyes seemed to darken, filled with an intensity that sent shivers down my spine. Slowly, he leaned toward me, his lips parting slightly as if ready to claim mine. He put his hand around my neck to pull me forward.

But something held me back, a nagging feeling that there was more we needed to say, more we needed to understand before we could move forward. So I gently placed a hand on his chest, stopping him mid-motion.

"Wait, Ethan," I whispered, my voice barely audible over the pounding of my heart. "We need to talk about this. We need to figure out what all of this means, for both of us."

"You said my name?" He whispered lustily, his eyes never leaving mine.

"Yes. That's not the point. Please, Ethan," I begged, my voice wavering as I tried to hold back the tears that threatened to spill. "I need you to listen to me. I can't go on like this anymore."

He hesitated for a moment, his eyes searching mine as if trying to decipher the meaning behind my words. And then he nodded, sitting back and folding his arms across his bare chest. His eyes still blazed with a heat that made me shiver.

"Alright," he said, his tone guarded but curious. "Go ahead."

"Even though I was with Alex, all I could think about was you," I admitted, my heart pounding in my chest as I spoke. "I'm so wrecked for you, Ethan. But it's not fair how consumed you've been with football, and how little time you've made for me. I've felt abandoned because of your obsession."

His brow furrowed as he listened, the muscles in his jaw tightening as he struggled to keep his emotions in check.

"Jordan, you know how important football is to me," he replied, his voice strained. "It's not just about the game. It's about honoring my dad and everything he wanted for me. I thought you understood that."

"Of course I understand," I shot back, frustration flaring within me. "But it doesn't change the fact that I feel like I come second to your sport. When you went to summer camp and you started focusing on the upcoming season, I felt like you didn't care about me."

My voice cracked as I laid bare the deepest corners of my soul, revealing the insecurities and darkness that had haunted me for so long.

"I started cutting again. I showed you the scars. I'm not blaming you, but the stress of our relationship and the loneliness that I felt left me empty." I said my voice cracking. "Ethan, there were times when I felt so worthless and alone that I... I thought about ending it all."

His eyes widened in shock, and for a moment, I saw the raw pain that my confession caused him. But instead of pulling away, he reached out and grasped my hand, his fingers warm against my skin.

"Jordan, I'm so sorry," he whispered, his voice thick with emotion. "I never meant to make you feel that way. I love you more than anything, and I promise that I'll do better. But you have to believe me when I say that I never stopped caring about you, even during the most intense moments of football season."

"Then show me, Ethan," I implored, my eyes locked on his as I fought to convey the depth of my need. "Show me that you're willing to put us first, to prioritize our relationship over everything else."

He nodded, his grip on my hand tightening as if to anchor us both to this moment, to the promises we were making under the starlit sky.

"I will, Jordan," he vowed, his voice firm with conviction. "I will do whatever it takes to make sure you never feel abandoned or unloved again."

And as we sat there in the stillness of the night, our words echoing around us like a symphony of hope, I knew that we had taken the first step toward healing the wounds that had threatened to tear us apart.

Ethan's eyes filled with unshed tears, and I could see the cracks forming in his strong facade. His voice trembled as he began to speak, finally laying bare his own fears and doubts.

"Jordan, you have to know that I love only you," he pleaded, desperation lacing his words. "It kills me that you would believe anything different. These last few months, when you asked for space to explore your feelings for Alex... it was like a piece of me was missing."

He looked down at the table, his fingers fidgeting with the edge of the tablecloth. "I felt lost without you by my side. I tried to throw myself into football, but it just wasn't the same anymore. It felt empty, hollow. And at night, when I was alone with my thoughts, I couldn't help but wonder if I had pushed you away for good."

His gaze met mine again, his eyes pleading for understanding. "Sometimes I would be filled with rage, with this bottomless jealousy. I pictured you laying beside him. Or him inside of you. Or, I don't...just ugly things. But even during those darkest moments, I never stopped loving you, Jordan. Not for a second."

My heart ached as I listened to his confession, my own emotions swirling as I struggled to process everything he was saying. I reached across the table, tentatively placing my hand on top of his. His fingers twitched beneath my touch before curling around my hand, holding onto me like a lifeline.

"Thank you for telling me that, Ethan," I whispered, my voice softening as I tried to convey the depth of my gratitude. "I'm sorry I ever doubted your love for me. I know we both have our insecurities to work through."

He nodded, a small smile ghosting over his lips. "Yeah, maybe we do. But we can work through them together, right?"

"Right," I agreed, my heart swelling with love and hope as we reached this turning point in our relationship.

And as we sat there, our hands clasped together, I knew that we had taken an important step toward healing and understanding. We were learning to navigate the complexities of love together, our bond growing stronger with each passing moment.

As the silence between us grew, I found the courage to voice my gratitude for Ethan's choice of college. "Ethan, I just wanted to say... thank you for choosing UCLA," I began hesitantly, my fingers playing with the edge of the tablecloth as I spoke. "It means a lot to me that you picked a school close to where I'll be studying."

His brown eyes widened in surprise, his lips parting slightly as he processed my words. "You got into CalArts?" he asked, his voice tinged with awe and excitement.

I nodded, my chest swelling with pride as I confirmed the news. "Yeah, I did. So we'll both be heading to California."

"Wow, Jordan, that's amazing!" Ethan exclaimed, putting his head down on the table and pumping his fist. "I'm so proud of you. You deserve it more than anyone."

"Thanks," I murmured, feeling a warmth spreading through my chest at his praise. "And I'm grateful that we'll still be close to each other."

"Me too," he agreed, his gaze softening as he looked at me. "I know football has always been a big part of my life, but you've become an even bigger part, Jordan. And I don't want to lose that."

I swallowed hard, touched by the sincerity in his voice. "Neither do I," I admitted quietly, my heart constricting with emotion.

Slowly, tentatively, Ethan reached out across the table, his hand hovering just above mine. I glanced down at our hands, my breath catching in my throat as I saw the vulnerable uncertainty in his gesture. Then, with a burst of determination, I lifted my own hand and intertwined our fingers, feeling the familiar roughness of his skin against mine.

As our hands connected, I felt a surge of warmth and belonging coursing through me, the sensation grounding me in the moment. This was real, I realized. This was us, finally beginning to heal and move forward together.

"Jordan, I promise you," Ethan whispered, his voice filled with conviction as he squeezed my hand gently, "we'll make it work. We'll face our challenges and insecurities together, and we'll come out stronger for it."

"Promise?" I asked softly, seeking the reassurance I needed to put my faith in our love once more.

"Promise," he confirmed, his eyes locked on mine, and in that moment, I knew that we were truly ready to take this next step in our journey together, hand in hand.

I felt Ethan's breath on my lips, and we both hesitated for a second, our eyes searching each other's. It was as if time stopped, waiting for us to make our move.

"Jordan," Ethan whispered, his voice barely audible, but filled with longing.

"Ethan," I replied, my own voice tinged with emotion. We leaned in, closing the gap between us, our lips meeting in a tender kiss that sealed our renewed commitment to each other. The world around us seemed to fade away, leaving only the two of us and the comforting embrace of the Parker dining room.

We pulled away slowly, our eyes locked on one another, a shared understanding passing between us. In that moment, it felt like the weight of the world had been lifted from our shoulders. Our love had been tested, but it had endured, and now we could face whatever challenges lay ahead, together.

"Thank you," I said softly, my heart brimming with gratitude for everything Ethan had done to prove his love for me. "For choosing a school close to mine, for never giving up on us, and for always being there when I needed you the most."

Ethan smiled gently, his warm brown eyes filled with love. "You're worth it, Jordan. You always have been, and you always will be. I swear I'll do better."

I reached out to touch his face, tracing the familiar lines and contours that I'd come to know so well. My fingers lingered on the curve of his cheek, marveling at the warmth of his skin.

"I'm sorry," I whispered, feeling tears prick at the corners of my eyes. "I'm so sorry for doubting you, for not trusting in what we had."

"Hey," Ethan said softly, taking my hand in his. "It's okay. We both made mistakes, but we'll learn from them. That's what matters."

I nodded, swallowing the lump in my throat. "You're right," I agreed, drawing strength from his unwavering support. "We'll face whatever comes our way, as long as we have each other."

"Always," Ethan promised, his voice filled with conviction. "Do you want to stay?" He asked quietly nodding towards his room.

I smiled shyly and nodded. The night around us seemed to hum with the promise of a brighter future, one where we could chase our dreams and still hold onto the love that had brought us together. As the stars above continued their silent vigil, I knew that no matter what life threw our way, Ethan and I would always find our way back to each other.

The bed creaked softly as Ethan and I sat side by side, the night air cool against our skin. Through Ethan's window, the stars twinkled like diamonds strewn across a velvet sky, their light casting a serene glow that seemed to envelop us in a cocoon of tranquility.

"Feels like forever since we just sat together like this," I murmured, leaning my head against Ethan's shoulder. His strong arm wrapped around me, pulling me closer.

"Too long," he agreed, his voice rumbling in his chest. "I missed this."

"Me too." I closed my eyes, savoring the closeness between us. For a moment, all the pain and heartache of the past few months seemed to fade away, replaced by the comforting familiarity of Ethan's presence.

We sat in silence for a while, the only sounds the gentle rustling of leaves in the breeze and the distant hum of traffic. It was a rare moment of stillness in our otherwise hectic lives, a chance to reconnect and find solace in each other's company.

"Do you want one of my shirts?" Ethan asked, breaking the silence with a smile in his voice.

I laughed softly, "Yeah, that would be nice."

He got up and walked over to his dresser. grabbing a shirt for me. I began to remove my shoes and take off my clothes.

Ethan walked back over to me, holding out a plain grey v-neck shirt in his hands. "Here," he said softly, a small smile playing on his lips.

I smiled back and took the shirt from him, slipping it over my head. It was soft against my skin and smelled like Ethan: a combination of cologne and laundry detergent. I closed my eyes, relishing the comfort that enveloped me as I inhaled deeply.

"Feels nice," I murmured contentedly, snuggling closer into Ethan's embrace. He hummed in agreement, pressing his lips to my forehead in a sweet kiss. We settled down onto the bed together, still wrapped up in each other's arms.

"We should get some sleep," Ethan suggested after a few moments of peaceful silence had passed between us.

"Mm-hmm," I agreed, already beginning to drift off into dreamland. "Promise me something, Ethan," I said, my voice thick with emotion. "Promise me that no matter what happens, we'll never lose sight of this moment. That we'll always find our way back to each other."

"Jordan," he began, his voice low and earnest. "I promise. No matter what life throws at us, you are the one I want by my side through it all. And I'll do whatever it takes to make sure we never lose sight of that."

"Thank you," I whispered, my heart swelling with love for this incredible man beside me. We laid there, wrapped in each other's arms, and drifted off to sleep.

Chapter Twenty-Two

The moment we stepped onto the field, I felt a tidal wave of emotion wash over me. Nostalgia mixed with excitement as Ethan and I donned our caps and gowns, the deep red fabric draped over our shoulders and billowing in the gentle breeze.

"Can you believe it's finally here?" I asked, my voice tinged with both awe and disbelief.

Ethan's warm brown eyes sparkled as he grinned at me. "Honestly? No," he admitted, running a hand through his slightly longer blond hair. "But man, what a ride it's been."

We joined our classmates in the designated area, the buzz of anticipation palpable in the air. The sound of applause swelled around us as families and friends gathered in the stands to celebrate our achievements.

"Hey, Jordan! Ethan!" one of our friends called out, waving enthusiastically. We waved back, exchanging smiles and laughter with those we'd grown up with, forged friendships with, and survived the gauntlet of high school alongside.

"Remember when we were just freshmen?" Ethan mused, his gaze drifting across the sea of red gowns. "Feels like a lifetime ago."

I nodded, the memories playing like a movie in my mind. "We've come a long way since then, haven't we?"

"Damn right, we have," he agreed, squeezing my hand gently.

As we stood there, side by side, the weight of all we'd experienced together settled on my heart. From the unspoken understanding of losing a parent to the shared passion for sports and art that had brought us closer, we'd weathered countless storms.

"Hey, Jordy?" Ethan said softly, using the affectionate nickname only he was allowed to call me. "No matter where life takes us, promise me we'll always find our way back to each other."

My throat tightened, but I managed a smile, my hand reaching out to touch the pendant that hung around my neck – a reminder of the love we'd built and the future we were chasing together.

"Promise," I whispered, the word feeling like both an anchor and a lifeline. And as the applause continued to ring in our ears, I knew one thing for certain – whatever challenges or triumphs awaited us beyond this field, we would face them hand in hand, hearts filled with love and determination.

"Hey, you two!" I heard Bella's voice call out, and I turned to see her waving excitedly at us. "Can't believe this is finally happening!"

"Neither can we," Ethan replied, grinning as he high-fived Mason.

"Remember freshman year?" asked Mason, joining us in line. "Feels like it was just yesterday."

"More like a lifetime ago," I said with a nostalgic sigh.

"True, but look how far we've come since then," he added, pulling me into a quick hug. "Wishing you both all the best."

"Thanks, Mason," I said, my heart swelling with appreciation for the friendships that had been forged over these four years.

"Jordan! Ethan!" Roger called out, jogging over from across the field. "You guys made it!"

"Of course we did," Ethan chuckled. "Wouldn't miss this for the world."

Roger, our class clown, struck a comical pose as he stood beside us. "Well, don't forget us little people when you're off being famous artists and football stars."

"Never," I promised, laughing along with him.

As more classmates approached, exchanging hugs and words of encouragement, I couldn't help but feel a sense of unity and camaraderie amongst us all. We'd grown together, learned together, and now we were stepping into the unknown together.

"Attention, everyone!" The principal's voice boomed through a microphone, signaling the start of the ceremony. "Please find your seats!"

"Guess it's time," Ethan whispered, his hand giving mine a gentle squeeze.

"Time to face the future," I agreed, feeling both excited and wistful as we took our seats among our classmates.

I scanned the rows of familiar faces, each one holding a piece of my high school journey. As the first notes of "Pomp and Circumstance" began to play, I closed my eyes, allowing the swell of emotions to wash over me – pride, gratitude, love, and just a touch of sadness for the chapter we were about to close.

"Hey," Ethan nudged me gently, his eyes shining with unspoken understanding. "No matter what comes next, we've got this."

I smiled at him, feeling a surge of warmth fill my chest. "Yeah, we do."

Together, we faced the stage, our hearts full to bursting as we prepared to take that first step into the rest of our lives.

The sun filtered through the trees, casting dappled shadows on the rows of chairs as Principal Miller took to the stage. A hush fell over the crowd, and I felt Ethan's hand brush against mine, anchoring me in this moment.

"Good evening, ladies and gentlemen," Principal Miller began, her voice wavering with emotion. "It is with great pride that I stand before you today, celebrating the accomplishments of this extraordinary group of young adults."

My gaze lingered on Ethan as he listened attentively, the sunlight catching the golden strands of his hair. He looked back at me, his warm brown eyes conveying a depth of understanding that I knew only we shared.

"Throughout their time here at Ada High School," Principal Miller continued, "these students have faced numerous challenges – both on and off the field – and emerged stronger for it. Their resilience and determination are truly inspiring."

I thought back to the countless hours spent in the art studio, striving to express my innermost thoughts and feelings through color and form. I recalled the nights when Ethan would come home bruised and battered from football practice, yet never once did he let his spirit waver.

"Each and every one of you has a unique story to tell," said Principal Miller, her eyes scanning the sea of graduates. "You've formed bonds that will last a lifetime, discovered passions that will shape your futures, and found love in the most unexpected places."

Ethan's hand found mine again, and he squeezed it gently. In his touch, I felt the memory of our first tentative kiss, the triumphs and heartaches we'd weathered together, and the unwavering support that carried us through even the darkest moments.

"Though the road ahead may be uncertain," Principal Miller concluded, "never forget the lessons you've learned, the friendships you've forged, and the love that has sustained you. For you are the future, and the world awaits your brilliance."

As the crowd erupted in applause, I looked at Ethan – my love, my confidant, my rock – and knew that whatever came next, we would face it together, hand in hand. For amidst the chaos of life, one thing was certain: our love was a force to be reckoned with, an unwavering beacon that would guide us through the unknown and into the bright promise of tomorrow.

The valedictorian, a bespectacled girl with a confident stride, took the stage. A hush fell over the crowd as she cleared her throat and began her speech with an unwavering voice that belied her years.

"Good evening, fellow graduates, families, friends, and faculty," she said, her eyes scanning the sea of faces before her. "I stand before you today not only as a representative of our class but also as a testament to the power of perseverance, hard work, and love."

Ethan's fingers intertwined with mine, his sweaty palm a reminder of the nerves we both felt beneath the surface. I squeezed his hand in reassurance, my heart swelling with pride at how far we'd come – both together and separately.

"Each of us has faced challenges," the valedictorian continued, "and each of us has triumphed in our own unique way. Our journey has been one of growth, self-discovery, and resilience."

As she spoke, images of Ethan on the football field flashed through my mind – the frantic energy of the games, the roaring cheers of the crowd, the fierce determination that burned in his eyes as he led his team to victory, time and again.

"Through adversity, we have emerged stronger," she said, her gaze settling on me for a moment. "We have found solace in our passions, whether they be athletics, academics, or the arts."

Her words brought forth memories of my own journey – the countless hours spent honing my craft, the quiet satisfaction of capturing a fleeting emotion on canvas, the thrill of watching my art come alive before my very eyes.

"Today, we stand at a crossroads," the valedictorian declared, her tone shifting to one of hopeful anticipation. "A world of limitless possibilities stretches out before us, ripe for the taking."

"Jordan Torres," the announcer called, and I released Ethan's hand, my heart pounding in my chest as I stepped forward.

"Go get 'em, babe," Ethan whispered, his eyes shining with pride. The weight of the diploma in my hand felt like a promise – a tangible symbol of all that I hoped to achieve and the unbreakable bond that had carried me this far.

"Thank you," I murmured, my voice barely audible over the thunderous applause. As I walked back to my seat, my eyes locked on Ethan's, our shared joy reflected in each other's radiant smiles.

"Ethan Parker," the announcer said, and my heart swelled as Ethan strode confidently across the stage, his broad shoulders squared and his head held high.

"Congratulations, Mr. Parker," the principal said, shaking his hand firmly. "You've earned this."

"Thank you, ma'am," he replied, his voice strong and steady. As he accepted his diploma, I knew without a doubt that this was only the beginning – for both of us.

Together, we had weathered the storms of life, and together, we would continue to forge our path – side by side, hand in hand, our love a beacon that would guide us through the unknown and into the bright promise of tomorrow.

The applause rang through the auditorium like a triumphant symphony, our fellow classmates rising as one, a sea of caps and gowns. I stood alongside Ethan, clapping energetically, as we shared a glance that seemed to say it all – we'd done it.

"Can you believe this moment is finally here?" I asked.

"It's surreal," Ethan replied. His warm brown eyes met mine, reflecting the intensity of emotion that swirled within us both.

"Congratulations!" A familiar face appeared before us, and I felt my cheeks heat as I recognized Alex.

"Thanks, Alex!" Ethan responded, his smile broadening. "You two should talk." He said quietly, releasing my hand and stepping over to another group of friends.

Alex smiled and step forward. "Jordan, congrats on graduation." He said sheepishly.

I smiled, "Thanks Alex. You too."

"Are you excited for the next step? Are you going to CalArts?" He asked quietly.

"I am," I replied, a smile tugging at the corners of my lips. "It's been a long road to get here."

Alex nodded, his eyes twinkling with understanding. "That's awesome. I am going to RISD," he said.. "And you're right, it hasn't been easy, but we did it. We made it."

I looked around at the excited students and their proud families – all of us celebrating this momentous achievement and looking forward to brighter days ahead. "We sure did," I agreed.

"How about you and Ethan? What are your plans?" Alex asked, his tone suddenly more serious.

My heart warmed at the mention of Ethan's name, and I couldn't help but smile again as I thought about him. "We're going to stay together," I said firmly. "We plan to take our relationship further and really start our lives together."

Alex gave me an approving nod before continuing. "That's great news," he said quietly. "I'm really happy for you both."

I felt my cheeks flush with emotion, and I gave him a grateful smile in return. "Thanks. Take care of yourself Alex," I murmured, my voice barely audible over the conversations that echoed around us.

Alex smiled, nodded, and turned and walked away.

Ethan stepped up behind me then, pressing a gentle kiss onto my temple.

"Let's find our families," I suggested, and Ethan nodded in agreement. Together, we wove through the crowd, our hands intertwined, feeling as though we were floating on air. The scent of fresh-cut flowers filled my nostrils, and the raucous laughter of our classmates created a backdrop to this moment that would forever be etched in my memory.

"Jordan! Ethan!" Our mothers waved to us from across the room, their eyes shining with pride. As we approached them, they enveloped us in warm embraces, the love that radiated from them palpable.

"Mom, I couldn't have done it without you," I whispered into her ear, and I could feel the dampness of her tears against my cheek.

"Neither could I," Ethan agreed, his voice cracking slightly. "Thank you both."

"Look at our boys, all grown up," my mom said with a wistful sigh, wiping away her tears.

"Let's take some pictures," Ethan's mom suggested, and we all dutifully posed for the camera, capturing the essence of this milestone.

"Hey, Jordan," Ethan said softly as we broke away from our families for a moment. "I just want you to know that I'm proud of us – both of us."

"Me too," I murmured, my heart swelling with love and gratitude. "We've come so far, Ethan."

"Whatever comes next, we'll face it together, right?" he asked, his eyes searching mine, seeking reassurance.

"Absolutely," I replied without hesitation, squeezing his hand tightly, feeling the weight of all we had endured and the unwavering bond that had brought us to this point. "Together, we can do anything."

The sun dipped low in the sky, casting its warm golden rays over the sea of graduates gathered in the courtyard. The joyous cacophony that filled the air moments ago had faded into a hum as families began to disperse. I glanced at Ethan, his eyes shimmering with unspoken emotion, and knew we needed a moment alone.

"Let's find somewhere quiet," I suggested, my hand finding his as our fingers intertwined. We slipped away from the crowd, seeking refuge beneath a familiar oak tree where we'd spent countless hours daydreaming together.

"Hard to believe it's all over," Ethan sighed, his strong shoulders slumping slightly as he gazed out at the now-empty ceremony grounds.

"Time flies, huh?" I added, feeling a pang of nostalgia for the years that had shaped us.

"Remember when we first met?" Ethan asked, his lips curving into a wistful smile. "I never imagined we'd end up here."

"Me neither," I admitted, recalling the beautiful boy who had first captured my heart at summer camp. "But I'm grateful for every step of the journey."

"Your support has meant everything to me, Jordan," Ethan confessed, his voice cracking with vulnerability. "I couldn't have made it through the past few years without you by my side."

"Same goes for you, Ethan," I replied, my eyes brimming with tears. "We've grown so much, not just as individuals but as a couple, too."

"Facing the future doesn't seem so daunting when I know I'll have you with me," Ethan murmured, his fingers brushing mine tenderly as if to reaffirm our connection.

"Whatever comes next, we're in it together," I promised, my heart swelling with a fierce determination to see us through whatever challenges life had in store.

"Deal," Ethan agreed, sealing our pact with a soft, lingering kiss that seemed to carry the weight of our collective dreams and aspirations.

Hand in hand, we stood up and walked towards the fading sun, ready to embrace the unknown. The world stretched out before us like a blank canvas, inviting us to paint our own unique masterpiece, united by love and bound by the unbreakable bond forged through adversity. No matter where our paths led, I knew we'd always find our way back to each other, for we were more than just high school sweethearts – we were soulmates, destined to leave our mark on each other and the world beyond.

Don't miss out!

Visit the website below and you can sign up to receive emails whenever Morgan Nash publishes a new book. There's no charge and no obligation.

https://books2read.com/r/B-A-UNJZ-TBERC

BOOKS 2 READ

Connecting independent readers to independent writers.

Did you love *Beyond the Field*? Then you should read *Splendor*[1] by Morgan Nash!

[2]

Hey there, fellow geeks and game enthusiasts! I'm Seb, your friendly neighborhood nerd, and I'm here to spill the dice (pun intended) on "Splendor."

Imagine this: I've just landed in Elk City, Oklahoma, ready to kick off my senior year at Elk City High. Exciting, right? Well, it would be if it weren't for one tiny problem—Brad Thompson, the school's jock extraordinaire and master of all things bully-related.

But fear not, my friends, because amidst the chaos of high school, I've found my sanctuary: board games. And guess what's front and center? Splendor, the game of gem trading and strategy that makes my geeky heart sing.

---

1. https://books2read.com/u/3yQBEV

2. https://books2read.com/u/3yQBEV

Now, onto the main event, or should I say, the other main event? Dylan Lewis, Elk City's very own enigmatic bad boy, with tattoos and a motorcycle that could rival Batman's. Underneath that gruff exterior lies a complicated soul.

Our paths cross in the most unexpected ways, and it's like trying to fit a d20 into a Tetris block. Our connection is undeniable, but Dylan's got a reputation to uphold.

"Splendor" is like the quest I never knew I was on. It's not just about board games; it's about finding strength, friendship, and, maybe, a little something more.

So, gear up, fellow nerds, because this story takes you on a journey through my senior year, where I navigate high school, find my inner hero, and just maybe roll the dice of love.

Also by Morgan Nash

Ada
Inside the Huddle
Beyond the Field

Elk City
Splendor

About the Author

Morgan Nash, a supply chain executive and author, was born and raised from the state of Oklahoma. Growing up surrounded by the rich landscapes and warm community of the Sooner State, Morgan developed a deep appreciation for storytelling and a passion for exploring the human experience. Now based in Nashville, Tennessee, he continues to infuse his writing with the warmth and authenticity he absorbed during his formative years.

In addition to his literary pursuits, Morgan finds solace in running, a hobby that allows him to connect with nature and clear his mind. As an avid reader, Morgan delves into a wide range of genres, continually expanding his horizons and learning from the works of other talented authors.

Morgan shares his home in Nashville with two cherished French Bulldogs, who bring joy and companionship to his everyday life. These loyal furry friends offer unwavering support, often curling up beside him as he immerses himself in the creative process. Their presence adds a touch of playfulness and love to his writing routine.